By Cecy Robson

The Shattered Past Series

Once Perfect

Once Loved

Once Pure

The O'Brien Family Novels

Once Kissed

Let Me

Crave Me (coming soon)

Feel Me (coming soon)

The Carolina Beach Novels

Inseverable (coming soon)

Eternal (coming soon)

Infinite (coming soon)

The Weird Girls

A Curse Awakened (novella)

The Weird Girls (novella)

Sealed with a Curse

A Cursed Embrace

Of Flame and Promise

A Cursed Moon (novella)

Cursed by Destiny

A Cursed Bloodline

A Curse Unbroken

Of Flame and Light (coming soon)

Let Me

An O'Brien Family Novel

Cecy Robson

DEDICATION

To Jamie and Nic for always believing in me.

ACKNOWLEDGMENTS

There are many people to thank, including as always my wonderful agent and dear friend, Nicole Resciniti, and my best friend and husband, Jamie. Thank you for putting up with all the crazy and often hilarious. What would I do without you?

To my babies, thank you for your smiles, but most of all for your love and patience. Mommy loves you.

To my fellow authors, Kate SeRine and Amanda Flower, who always have kind words, and even kinder souls, thank you. I treasure our friendship now and always.

To the bloggers and the fans who have stood by me, you're the reason I bleed my soul into every story. Thank you for your loyalty and your wonderful shout-outs. You'll never know the extent of my gratitude.

To those who can relate to Finn or Sol, don't be afraid to find your happiness. You need and deserve it. Take the first steps toward healing and enjoy life to the fullest.

For more information, contact RAINN, the Rape, Abuse, and Incest National Network (www.rainn.org).
Or
SAMHSA (Substance Abuse and Mental Health Services Administration)
http://www.samhsa.gov/find-help/national-helpline

CHAPTER 1

Finn

I see the strike coming at me a split second before it connects with my skull. My head snaps back from the force, the crowds' hollers resonating like a muffled cry in the distance. It was a good punch—lightning quick with enough impact to knock most guys on their asses. But I'm not most guys.

You hit me, I'm only going to hit you harder.

My right hand shoots up, blocking and smacking away the kick gunning for my ribs. I pivot out of the way, again, and again, and again, avoiding Easton's arms and legs as they come at me. He's fast, strong, with a six inch reach advantage. But he's too eager to take me out and not pacing himself like he should. Already he's breathing hard and it's just the start of the second round.

I take my time to figure him out, planning each move, searching for that opening I need. Do I take a few bashes because of it? Sure. It's part of the job. But believe it or not, it's part of the job I look forward to.

Those punches and kicks remind me that I still *feel*, that I'm still human. And that for now, I'm still alive.

"Oh!" some drunk behind me yells when my uppercut finds Easton's chin.

He staggers back, swiping the blood oozing from his lip, yet he keeps his grin. He's trying to make like it was a lucky shot. That it won't happen again.

Like me, Easton needs to win this match. And if he does, he'll move up to the top ten, making him a contender for the UFC Lightweight title.

Talent aside, the guy's a raging asshole, and so are the idiots in his training camp. They've been trash-talking since the moment I agreed to this match. I didn't really care and laughed most of it off until they got personal and took it a step too far.

Again he nails me in the head. It's not as hard as it was last time which tells me he's getting tired. Does it hurt? I guess.

But let's say I'm a guy who's used to pain.

Easton grins. He thinks I'm afraid of him. He thinks he has me where he wants me. But fear is an emotion I don't allow myself to entertain. Fear gets you hurt and rips you apart till you think there's nothing left.

I dodge out of reach. He scowls and takes another swing. This one gets close enough to my jaw to create a breeze that whips across my skin.

"Finn," my brother Killian barks from the side. "Take him out *now*."

He's worried about me. So is my family. But now's not the time to think about them. I keep my hands up as I edge away, letting Easton think I'm backing down, that I'm tired and need to catch my breath.

I sidestep when he lunges forward, avoiding his next swing and use the momentum to drop my head and nail him in the temple with a roundhouse kick.

Like I said, Easton's fast.

Too bad for him I'm a little bit faster.

The kick is my signature move, as natural for me as the next breath. He goes down like I planned. But in the Octagon you don't stop just because your opponent collapses like timber. You charge forward. You show him what you're made of. And you prove just how tough you really are.

That muffled screaming, isn't so muffled anymore. The crowd loses their shit as I pounce, my blows nailing Easton in the face until the ref's arms hook beneath mine as he hauls me off. I back away, my fists up because I already know I won.

I should do a back flip or some crazy shit to incite the crowd. This is it. My time has come to own it. But the good things aren't as great as they can be. Not with the memories that haunt me. And not with the anger they stir.

Killian rushes in as the medic wipes down my face. I'm bleeding from the punch Easton caught me with at the beginning of the round. I didn't think it was that bad, but the way the ringside medic is pressing the towel against my head clues me in the gash isn't closing like it should.

"I'm going to have to stitch you up, Fury," he mumbles.

"I figured," I tell him.

Kill pats my back. "Good job," he says.

Maybe he believes it, but I don't miss the concern in his voice. He thinks I took too many unnecessary hits. I can't really argue, seeing how it's true.

He doesn't understand that I don't feel those strikes the way I should. Hell, I don't think I've felt anything the way I should in a long time. Not like I used to. I try to tell myself that maybe that' a good thing. That numbness is better than pain. But I'm not so convinced anymore, and neither is my family. I try to shrug it off like I'm fine. Except given the way they've been eyeing me, I'm not fooling anyone.

I'm scaring everyone around me. And it sucks. Not only because I don't want them scared, but mostly because I don't know how to stop it.

"The referee has called a stop to this match at two-minutes and forty-nine seconds into the second round," the announcer begins. "The winner by TKO, Finn 'The Fury' O'Brien."

The crowd screams and pumps their fists in the air when my hand is raised. I take the few seconds I need to thank my sponsors, my camp, and my brother, because that's what I'm supposed to do despite the fog clouding my senses. I wish that disconnect had something to do with all the hits I took, but deep down I know that it doesn't.

I'm back in the locker room before I know it getting stitched up, too many people talking at once. God, I barely hear their questions or my responses. But they're there and somehow I make it through.

"I'm worried about you, Finnie," Kill says when everyone piles out.

"Don't. I'm not drinking tonight. I'm headed home," I assure him.

"That's not what I mean," he says. He's sitting in a fold out chair, his arms resting against his muscular legs. "I think you need to talk to someone."

I stretch out my arms. By now they're so tight, they pull against the bones. "I am. I'm talking to you."

I don't have to see him to know he's shaking his head, or that he's looking sad, disappointed, and maybe something else, too. "I'm not who you should be speaking to," he says. "Not for what's going on in your head."

"You're enough," I say, even though I know it's no longer true.

"Finn," he begins.

I don't wait for him to finish, leaving the changing area and heading toward the showers. "Go find Sofia and Wren," I call over my shoulder as I strip out my shirt. "See if they're up for some dinner."

I don't remember peeling the rest of my clothes off. That numbness I've been feeling too much lately claiming me like a mist until it fully engulfs me. Fuck. It's like I've stopped living even though for the most part I think I'm still alive.

I lean against the tile with my arms spread, allowing the water to beat against my back. It's too hot. I should turn it down, but I don't bother. Eventually, like everything else, the sensation fades.

I'm not sure how long I'm in that position. A few seconds? A few minutes? But then Easton and his trainer Yefim are suddenly there. "You got lucky, O'Brien," Yefim calls out, taunting me with his thick eastern European accent.

Shit. Like all the trash talk before the fight wasn't enough.

"Did you hear me, you pussy?" he fires back when I don't answer. "Did you hear me, you goddamn coward?"

Coward? Fuck you. It's what I think, but not what I say, focusing instead on the streams of water that gather along my feet before they swirl into the drain.

It doesn't help. The rage that's building, the one I only manage to barely keep in? It stirs in my gut like a heavy pot filled with hate, sin, and all the curses my Ma would still beat my ass for saying.

"What're you doing?" Yefim asks.

His voice is closer, he's drawing near. I doesn't matter that I'm standing here naked. He wants to be next to me. I shudder, that feeling I keep buried drilling its way up.

"I know about you," Yefim says, not bothering to keep his voice low. "But everyone knows, don't they? Even if you don't want them to."

My body shakes a little more, but it's not from the cooling water. It's from his words and all that anger they trigger. *Don't do it. Don't go there.*

"You like to keep it a secret. Don't you, pussy?"

Yefim laughs when I keep my trap shut. He thinks I'm backing down, just like Easton did before his face met the mat. "He's crying," he calls out to Easton. "What? Not so tough now?"

That's where he's dead wrong. Every muscle I've conditioned serves a purpose—to take down those who fuck with me. And right now, Yefim is seriously fucking with me.

"You like to pretend that it's girls you like, don't you?" he says. "But that's not true, is it? Oh, no, that's not true at all . ."

I raise my chin, knowing that someone's not leaving without bleeding, and I've bled enough tonight.

Yefim kicks at my calf. "What? Nothing to say? Can't speak without your boyfriend here?"

"Boyfriend?" Easton asks, laughing. "No fucking way."

"Yes. Way," Yefim insists. "Didn't you know this little pussy takes it up the ass—"

I punch him so hard, I feel his teeth crack against my knuckles. For someone with decades of boxing experience he never saw me coming. But I see Easton flying at me out of the corner of my eye. I toss him over my shoulder, slamming him hard onto the ceramic tile floor. Like in the octagon, I throw myself on top of him, my fists colliding against his skin.

Voices rush forward, telling me to stop. A woman screams,

but I don't stop fighting off the bodies trying to grab me, breaking through the arms wrenching me back. I need to hit him—I need to feel my fists meeting his face—I need to feel *something*.

God damn it. I need to feel alive.

I don't want the pain.

I don't want the terror.

But once more, it's all I feel.

CHAPTER 2

Sol

"How did you do this weekend?" I ask.

Loretta nods her head, like I'm still talking, but I know she's thinking through how best to answer. "Not great."

I adjust my position on the couch we're sitting on, trying to give the very false impression that I'm cool, confident, and refined, even though I'm anything but.

On paper, my achievements appear impressive. Come May, I'll have my master's degree in psychology. And once this internship finishes, I'll have the clinical hours I need to continue working toward my doctorate. But I've learned quickly that the transition from the classroom to the counseling arena is hard!

I thought for sure I'd say all the right things, turn my clients around, and make everyone I encountered see the light. So far I haven't. Not even a little bit. What I've learned in the lecture halls sounded great in theory. Yet I can't be sure I'm applying those theories correctly. Who am I kidding? I don't know what the hell I'm doing. I'm just praying no one dies on my watch because of something I say or do—or worst, *don't* say or *don't* do.

I'm at a loss around Loretta. She's beautiful . . . as in otherworldly beautiful. Seriously, if she suddenly sprouted wings and pelted me with pixie dust, it wouldn't shock me. The problem is, she doesn't see it, and that makes me sad.

Loretta is sweet, and a genuinely good person. She has great things going for her, yet I don't envy her life and fear for her future.

For years she's been battling bulimia. She hates her appearance and doesn't think she's smart. She doesn't believe there's anything worthwhile about her. When she looks in the mirror, she doesn't see the stunning girl I do, the one who has me brushing my hair and checking to make sure I don't have food stuck in my teeth before we meet.

On my best day, I couldn't match her on her worst. But despite my many imperfections, I like me. I only wish I could get her to like her.

Since I'm in Dr. Mason Shavis's office, my direct supervisor during my internship, I tap into his inner awesomeness and feign that relaxed demeanor he always seems to have. "What wasn't so great about it?" I ask.

"I came in second runner up in my pageant," she admits.

"Second runner up for Miss Lehigh Valley? Loretta, that's amazing!"

She shakes her slowly head, as if it's the most horrible news in the world, probably because for her, it is. "Not when the judge told me afterward that I would have won had I scored higher in the bathing suit competition. He told me he deducted points based on the pounds he thought I needed to lose."

"He said that?" I ask.

"Yes."

"What an asshole," I say before I can stop myself.

Cool, confident, and refined. Oh, yes. That's me.

"Sorry," I offer when her eyes pop out of her head.

"It's okay," she says slowly, like she can't believe that out of all the peer counselors, I'm the one she's stuck talking to.

Loretta was raised a little differently than me. Hmm. Maybe a lot differently. When she was attending prep school, I was sitting in the principal's office answering to Sister Marguerite for punching Carolina Gonzales in the nose. In my defense, I was seven, she was ten, and she started it.

Loretta glances down at her hands, shutting down. But I

can't let her. She's better than this. "You're awesome," I tell her.

"Excuse me?"

"You're awesome," I repeat. "People are going to say anything and everything to put you down, especially because of the business you're a part of. You have to decide if you're going to believe them or believe in yourself." I lean a little closer when she simply blinks back at me, gathering my courage. "You came in second out of how many other young women, twenty? Take a step back, look at the others you beat, and be proud of it because you are fabulous, and talented, and kind. And because you are, you have to make a choice whether to embrace how well you did to advance further, or allow someone who makes a career of eyeing women and ripping them apart hold you back."

The corners of her mouth curve into that "almost smile" she only allows herself. "Easier said than done."

"You're right," I agree. "So what do you think we can do to get you to start believing it?"

What I say to Loretta isn't textbook counseling. But maybe Loretta needs more than the theories I've been taught. Like me, she's only twenty-four. And when you're twenty-four, you're at that weird stage in your life where you've taken a giant leap into adulthood, but are still hanging tight to all the craziness and insecurities of your youth. You don't need a bunch of facts spewed verbatim. You want to feel like someone is listening, believe that you still matter, and that the great things in life have only just begun. I believe it, mostly because with everything going on in my life, I have to.

When I walk Loretta out about thirty minutes later, she's holding her head a little higher. It's not a lot. But it's a start, making me think there's hope, for both of us.

"Has Miss Hemsworth yelled at you today?" she whispers when we're almost to the lobby.

"No," I say, laughing. "But the day is still young."

Miss Hemsworth is our lovely receptionist. When I say lovely, I actually mean evil. The woman has hated me since the first time we met.

The heavy door to the lobby opens with a loud smack, drawing attention to those waiting to be seen. The counseling center is private and held in high regard. The majority of our clients come from money, but a few of our therapists work pro bono, counseling those from working class backgrounds similar to mine. Some are like Loretta, suffering from eating disorders and mild anxiety issues. But the majority are severely damaged individuals with suicidal tendencies. I catch sight of one of our more heartbreaking cases sitting in the corner beside his father. Poor kid, he can't be more than fifteen. And there he waits with his wrists bandaged down to his elbows.

I want to walk over and give him and his dad a hug. Both look like they could use one. Those people on the street who offer free hugs to strangers? I'm one of them. I always have been.

Today though, I refrain, staying focused on Loretta. "Good job," I tell her, knowing how hard she's trying. "I'll see you next week."

"Sol?"

I turn my head. I know that voice. Loretta doesn't bother with a goodbye, leaving me instead with a "Mm, yummy" when she sees who called to me.

"Yummy". Yes, that about sums up Finn.

Finn O'Brien, *damn*. You know those cute guys . . . those really hot kind of cute guys? Finn blows them away. I'm not typically attracted to redheads, but I make the exception for Finn. Oh, and Jamie from *Outlander*.

Finn has the whole bad boy thing going on, tats crawling along his muscular arms, hair buzzed on the sides and short on top. A modern Mohawk, it think that's what it's called. Oh, and don't get me started on that dimple on his right cheek that appears when he grins, just like he's doing now.

"Hi, Finn," I say. His brother is with him, the one that looks the most like him. He's older by a few years, handsome, polished and perfect. Well, if you like that sort of thing. Me? Did I mention how sexy Finn is?

His light blue eyes sparkle as I pass Zorina, the poor girl

trapped in her own world following a brutal assault on the train. She pretends to play instruments that aren't there, reality slipping so far from her grasp, it's almost out of her reach.

I tilt my head in the direction of Finn's brother because by now it's obvious I'm gawking at Finn. "You're Seamus, right?" I ask.

"No, I'm Declan," he answers in a deep voice.

Oh, right. The district attorney. "Sorry. I know that Finn has a few brothers," I offer. I should be impressed seeing how Declan has made quite a name for himself in the political arena, and I am. But Finn is who lures my attention and keeps it, despite my best efforts to appear more relaxed. "What are you doing here?" I ask.

He shrugs. "Waiting for you."

Declan sighs, moving away from us and reaching for his phone. I grin even though I'm sure Finn is feeding me a line. The last time I saw him was at my Cousin Sofia's wedding. I'd brought my friend Alex as my date and Finn, well, he showed up with some girl with big breasts and very little clothes. And funny enough, I still had a hard time keeping my eyes off him.

"Really?" I ask.

"Yeah. Really," he answers, leaning back on his heels and making a show of checking me out. "Don't forget, you still owe me a kiss."

I avert my gaze because he's right. I do. But I'll admit I'm surprised he remembers. After all, I'm not the only woman who's ever noticed him. In fact, ever since his career in MMA took off *every* woman I know has noticed Finn. "Is that so?"

"Been waiting on it for the last few years."

I adjust the folder I'm holding against my chest as I give his words some thought. "Hmmm," I muse. "The way I hear it, you've had plenty of company to occupy your time." I'm not making this up. He gets around.

"So is that a 'no'?" Finn asks, keeping his smile and that dimple firmly in place.

My smile dwindles. If we were anywhere else: a coffee shop, a bookstore, even *church*, I'd talk to him a little longer.

But we're here: A place where those who hurt seek help, and those who hurt for others like me, try to make things better.

"It's a bad time for me, Finn," I confess, but I don't tell him why. "And if you're here, it's probably a bad time for you, too."

"But maybe we can make it a good time for both of us," he says, losing his smile in a way that breaks my heart.

I glance down. "I wish it was true."

"Miss *Marieles*!" the lovely Miss Hemsworth yells at me from behind her desk.

Okay. Here we go.

"This is your internship, not a social hour," she squawks.

"One moment please, Miss Hemsworth," I sing.

"Internship?" Finn asks me.

I don't mean to blush, but the fact that Finn sounds impressed has me doing just that. "I'm graduating with my master's degree in May. I'm interning here as part of my final requirements—"

"Miss *Marieles*!" Miss Hemsworth snaps yet again.

I glance over my shoulder and smile. "I'm coming, Miss Hemsworth. Sorry," I whisper, leaning in close. "She hasn't been the same since the last of her flying monkeys flew out of her ass."

I turn as Finn busts out laughing. I want to wish him well and tell him that I hope he's okay. But I don't want to upset or embarrass him. He's probably already going through enough.

My charting awaits, and I don't have much time before I meet with my next client. But as I make my way back to the office, I pause beside Zorina, the little musician lost in her own world. Her elbows are up and out as she plays her make-believe cello.

I place my hand carefully against her shoulder, hoping to reach her if only for a moment. "Hey, sweetie. I know you love your pretty music, but we're here in the office now. Can we talk about what you're hearing inside?"

She slowly lowers her hands and nods. I'm not sure if it's my voice that brings her back to reality, or my touch. I'm just glad she hears me and that she's still with us to some extent.

Her mother glances at me, offering me a sweet smile. "Thanks, Sol," she says.

"You're welcome," I answer. Although I sat in on her daughter's initial assessment, I'm surprised and maybe a little honored that she remembered my name.

I hurry back to the door leading to the rear offices, hoping Miss Hemsworth doesn't give me a hard time and lets me in. Thankfully, she does, despite the scowl that warns me she'd like nothing more than for God to strike me dead.

As I reach for the door, I steal a glance Finn's way. As easily as that he catches my stare and holds me in place. He looks . . . amazing, like always. I want to stay longer, but I meant what I said, neither of us are in a good place.

If I have any doubt, they're quickly squashed by the text I receive on my way back to Mason's office.

You need to come home. Your mother isn't well.

CHAPTER 3

Sol

Your mother isn't well. That's a hell of an understatement.

My mother wasn't "well" when I was a child, became "sick" when I was a teen, and now . . . I'm not sure how she is. I only know I have to make her better. Somehow, I *have* to.

Mason, being the awesome supervisor that he is allows me to leave, assuring me that I can make up my hours later this week.

I promised to return this evening, but as I pull into my little neighborhood and focus onto our street, I'm not sure I'll be able to keep my promise. Not with how all the elderly neighbors are standing around, gossiping about what "poor Flor" did now, and how "poor Flor" is holding up.

She's not holding up. That's the issue. But as much as they seem to fuss when my mother has an episode, I'm starting to think they're actually entertained by her erratic actions.

I live on a cross street in Philly's Fishtown district in a neighborhood packed with well-kept row houses that were erected in the 1960s, long before I was born. My street isn't fabulous, and it's not in the "nice" part of town. No lawyers or doctors reside anywhere close to here, and their children would never be allowed to visit. But to me it's always been home.

Those so-called higher ups of society don't see past the cracked sidewalks that line the street to the well-swept concrete steps. They skim over the metal railings coated with years of paint and only see the tiny porches. They don't hear the conversations that take place around those little stoops: those that involve the Phil's, the Eagles, and the best way to fry an *empanada*, nor do they see the happy faces of the neighborhood kids when they play stickball in the street. They don't recognize the sense of family and community where residents distinguish their dwellings by painting their doors in alternating shades of black, red, and even green.

But me, I see it, and I feel it every time I come home.

I pull into the spot closest to my house, struggling to keep my chin up, even though I feel more like cowering. Does my mother embarrass me? If I'm being honest, yes, and I absolutely hate myself for feeling this way.

I want to have that mother my friends do. The one I can gush all over Facebook about on Mother's Day. The type of mother I can thank for giving me advice, taking me to lunch, and sharing her wisdom with me. I don't have that kind of mother. But my God, I really want to.

My mother doesn't give me advice. She gives advice to people who aren't there. She rarely talks to me, but when she does, she calls me "Laurita" her dead sister. When she smiles, it's because she sees something that only exists in her mind.

I handle it. All of it. And for the most part I think I do an okay job. But when she weeps . . . I feel those tears down to my soul.

My breath is visible as I hurry along. I step around a patch of ice, careful not to sink my new boots in the piles of snow pushed to the side. When I was little, I thought my mother was fun. She would play dress-up with me and pretend she was a famous actress or singer. But when I became a teen, she would still dress up, except instead of pretending, she believed she was that starlet, that person the whole world over adored.

She was the "eccentric" one for a long while. And for a time, we just accepted her as being quirky. It wasn't until she attempted suicide that we realized just how sick she really is.

No. My mother isn't well, and my heart breaks because of

it.

I smile politely when I see Señora Estefan rush toward me. She was on "Flor watch" today, a job she takes seriously.

"Ay, *niña*," she says, her hands falling to her sides when she sees me. "I'm sorry to text you, I know you're working. But I couldn't reach your Papi."

"It's okay," I say, even though it's likely not. "Where is she?"

She purses her lips, making a face that tells me that whatever she has to show me isn't good. "She's in Mr. Toleman's backyard."

My eyes widen briefly. "How did she get into his backyard?" I ask, allowing her to lead me forward.

"She knocked on his door, asking if she could pick mangoes from his tree." Her eyes cut my way. "You know he doesn't have a mango tree, right?"

It's all I can do to keep my shoulders from slumping. "*Sí, Señora*. I know."

"Well," she continues. "Since she was out on her own, he realized you and your father weren't home so he invited her in until he could track me down. One thing led to another, and, well, you'll see."

Oh, no.

The crowd gathered near Mr. Toleman's house part as I approach. It's not a large group, only about seven of our elderly neighbors, but it's a lot of people when you're feeling self-conscious and a lot of eyes to have on you even during the best of times. And trust me, these aren't the best of times.

I know they're older and this is as exciting as their day gets for them, but I wish it didn't have to come at my mother's expense.

"Good morning," I say, trying to keep my voice steady and hang on to what remains of my polite smile.

"*Hola, mija*," "Hi, Sol," "Good morning", they all say at once.

These are people who've known me all my life. People who bought candy bars and lemonade from me, and whose doors I'd knock on every Halloween. These were the neighbors who attended my *quinceañera,* friends who clapped for me when I stepped out of my house wearing my cap and gown, and who waved to me when I left for college. They're people who care about me and who I care about in return.

Maybe that's why it hurts to see them now, and for them to see my mother the way she is. I avoid their stares, however well-intended and however judgmental, and race up the steps when Mr. Toleman opens his front door.

"Hello, Mr. Toleman." I put on a brave face because I can around him. This is the same man who high-fived me every time I made honor roll.

"Hi, Sol," he says. He frowns at the people gathered at the bottom of his stoop. "Ya should be ashamed of yourselves. Get on outta here. Can't you see this is a family matter?"

"It involves the neighborhood," Señora Montes fires back.

"No, it involves Sol's mama," he points out.

His tone is firm, but I think it's his words that cause the crowd to disperse. It's all I can do not to hug him.

"Thank you for looking after my mother," I say when he shuts the door behind me and Señora Estefan.

He nods, arthritis causing a limp to his step as he moves down the dark hall. Like the other homes on the street, there's a living room to the left and a staircase that leads up to three bedrooms and a bathroom on the right. We pass a half bath, but as we reach the tiny kitchen, he pauses to glance over his shoulder. "She didn't seem right when she came to my door. I was afraid to let her leave."

"Okay," I say like I understand, even though by now I'm out of my mind with worry.

He steps aside and opens the door to his small yard. For all I was prepared to see, I wasn't prepared to see this.

My mother, that sweet woman who used to take such pride in her appearance—who would painstakingly iron our clothes so we wouldn't look messy, is sitting in the middle of Mr. Toleman's yard naked, her legs tucked beneath her as she prays.

If Mr. Toleman wasn't the man he is, he could have hurt her. He could have taken advantage of her. Jesus, anyone could have harmed her.

My eyes sting, but I refuse to break down. "Where are her clothes?" I ask, well aware of the horrible tremble to my voice.

"She buried them in the snow. I tried to keep her covered with these blankets," he says, pointing to the pile strewn across the ground. But she keeps ripping them off." He pauses, as if afraid to say what he says next. "Sol, from what I can figure, your mama thinks she's at a funeral."

A gust of wind sweeps along the row of connecting yards. It's fucking January and my mother is kneeling naked against the frozen earth. Her lips are blue—*blue*. If it weren't for Mr. Toleman trying to keep her warm, she'd already have hypothermia.

"Please call an ambulance," I say, hurrying to gather the blankets.

No sooner do I cover her than she yanks the blankets from her body. I'm vaguely aware of Mr. Toleman limping into is kitchen and Señora Estefan huddling into her gray wool coat beside me. Right now my attention is on my mother as I wrestle with how best to reach her.

"Mami? Mami, can you hear me?" I ask.

She doesn't answer, not that I really expected her to, not given her fragile state. I take a few breaths, trying to keep calm. Mr. Toleman and Señora Estefan are old school. They don't like to cause a fuss, and prefer to keep family matters quiet. They mean well and, I don't know, maybe called me first thinking I could control or somehow fix her. They don't understand that what she needs is medical treatment, and a daughter who can get her act together enough to help her.

My mother is on anti-psychotic meds that my father and I force her to take. I'm serious, we literally have to open her mouth and pour them down her throat. She hates them because they dull her senses, putting her in a fog and making her feel "dopey."

If she's acting this way, she's had some kind of breakdown, the meds aren't working, or she's figured out a way to get them out of her system. I'm leaning toward the latter, but that won't help her now. Again, I wrap the blankets around her shoulders, and again she pulls them off.

I kneel in front of her. "Mami?" I say. "Mami, it's me. Sol."

Her lips move fast, muttering the Lord's Prayer, her eyes rammed tight enough to deepen every wrinkle along her beautiful face.

"Mami?" I say again. "Mami, please open your eyes. I need to see your pretty eyes, okay?"

Like I did with Zorina, the young woman at the counseling center who played the invisible cello, I gently touch my mother's shoulder. "Mami?"

Tears drip down her face, "You weren't supposed to die, Laurita," she tells me in Spanish. "You weren't supposed to leave me."

I bow my head, briefly. She thinks I'm her sister, the one who killed herself. "It's me, Sol. Your daughter. Please open your eyes."

I'm sure she won't when she resumes he prayer, but then something shifts in her tight expression. Very slowly she opens her eyes. "*Oi!*" she says when she sees me.

Terror quickly replaces her sadness, and I realize we're both in trouble. I speak fast, doing my best to keep my voice soft. "It's okay. I'm not going to hurt you."

"You're dead," she tells me.

Señora Estefan hitches her breath. Good for her, I can't even breathe. "Mami," I say. "Laurita died a long time ago. I'm Sol, you're little girl."

Her stare grows cold. "You're a liar. I don't have a child."

Her words shouldn't hurt me. After all, they're coming from a woman who's very sick. I know this, but that doesn't stop my pain. "Mami, I'm Sol. You're daughter."

As I watch, my mother's expression crumbles. "You're dead," she says again.

She lifts her fists, bringing them down like hammers against my shoulders. The movement is so fast, I barely catch it. Agony shoots across my chest as I go down with my mother on top of me. Her fingers grip the lapels of my red coat, using them to shake me hard. "Why did you leave me, Laurita? Why did you leave me?" she screams.

I clutch her arms, digging my nails into her skin. "Mami, stop. Mami, listen to me—you have to listen to me."

I'm not sure if she hears me, not above Señora Estefan's screams, not over Mr. Toleman's frantic yells, and not with the encroaching sirens blasting down the row of homes.

My mother isn't well. My mother is very sick. But I *have* to make her better.

CHAPTER 4

Finn

My legs burn as I reach my last of six miles. I slow to a swift walk, using the last two blocks to cool down. My reward for getting up at five to run? A four egg white omelet with cheese and spinach at Suvio's Diner. It doesn't sound like much, but when you're cutting weight and you feel like shit, you take what you can get.

The cowbell above the door rings when I shove it open. That thing has hung there for as long as I can remember. It wouldn't be Suvio's without that familiar clang.

"Hey, Finnie," Suvio calls from the back. "You want the usual, champ?"

I grin. It also wouldn't be the same without the Philly hospitality, the kind that comes from people who've known you forever. "Yeah, Suv. Thanks."

"Have a seat. I'll be right with you," he says.

I'm about to slide into a spot at the front counter when I notice Sol sitting in the booth in the back. The diner is a local favorite so I'm somewhat surprised I haven't seen her here before. Then again, she's been in school, trying to make something of herself. Can't say I'm not glad to see her, though.

Sunlight trickles in from the window, lighting the strands of her hair brushing against her cheeks and her large gray-blue eyes. She smiles when she notices me standing there, adding an extra glimmer to her pretty stare. For a second, I think she's going to wave me over, but then she glances back down to whatever she's typing on her iPad. She probably doesn't want to assume I'll sit with her. And maybe she's a little shy about asking.

Good thing for both of us, the last thing I am is shy.

I march forward. She's wearing a lavender sweater and a pink scarf. The colors soften her further, not that she needs it. Sol has that whole angelic face thing going on, with an underlying sensuality that no heterosexual man in his right mind could resist.

When I saw her the other day, despite all that she was friendly and sweet, she didn't exactly melt against me. I thought maybe she was seeing someone. When I asked Sofia about it, she told me Sol doesn't date much which shocks me. Someone like Sol can have her pick of guys, so I'm not quite sure she hasn't done more picking. More than once I've had guys mention how hot they think she is, not that I liked them noticing.

"Hey," I say, sliding into the seat across from her. "Mind if I join you?"

She laughs a little, flipping her iPad closed and placing it into her big purse. "Looks like you already have."

She adjusts the scarf she's wearing, the fringed ends brushing just above her breasts. Ordinarily, my attention would fixate to her curves a little longer, but instead it returns to her smile. Like at the clinic, it lacks that extreme gleam I used to always see. It doesn't seem right for her to be without it, so I decide it's my duty to draw a little sunshine back into that smile. What can I say, just call me a hero.

I motion her way. "I take it you're a morning person? Up to conquer the day and all that shit."

"Not even a little bit," she answers as I reach for the edges of my sweatshirt and pull. "I just had some work to catch up on."

Her voice cuts off when I partially remove my T-shirt in the process of yanking off my sweatshirt. It's not intentional, but I'll admit, I like the results. I grin when I catch Sol jerking her focus from the muscles lining my chest and forcing it back onto my face.

I tug my tight T-shirt back in place slowly. "Like what you see?" I ask, adding a wink.

This time she laughs for real, despite how her face turns pink. "You're . . ."

"Hot?" I offer.

She laughs again. "I was going to say—"

"Alpha male sexy with Greek god-like charm?" I ask, cutting her off again.

She grins, but doesn't exactly deny it. "Did you spontaneously pick out all those adjectives? Or do you keep them handy to impress the ladies?"

I think my quickness surprised her, but I can't say she's completely off. "Some reporter wrote it about Gerard Butler," I admit. "But I thought it was fitting enough."

This time she covers her mouth to hold back her laughter. "You're something else," she says, dropping her hand away.

"I've been called worse," I admit. "Thanks, Suv," I add when he drops off a giant glass of water and my omelet. "You want something?" I ask Sol.

"Thank you, but I'm good with just coffee."

I nod and dig into my food. I'm not as hungry as I appear, but I don't want to overdo it with Sol. That doesn't mean I don't like how her smile seems to linger and how it keeps finding its way into her pretty eyes.

"What about you?" I ask.

She tilts her head. "What do you mean?"

"If you were to describe yourself, how would it be?"

She crinkles her nose. "Why do you want to know?"

I shrug, trying to keep my voice easy. "Maybe cause I want to know you." I'll admit, for all I'm messing with her that much is true. We've crossed paths a handful of times, at a couple of weddings and a few parties. But I still don't know Sol as more than as that sweet, sexy woman who hooks me with her smile.

She nibbles on her bottom lip, like she's trying to keep herself quiet. When her attention shifts to the window where a group of kids are heading off to school, I don't think she's going to answer. But then she does, or at least tries to.

"I don't know," she says. "Studious maybe?"

I stop mid-chew, swallowing hard so I can speak. "Studious?" I repeat. At her nod I say. "Is that the best you can do?"

She smirks. "I know it's not the same as having Greek god-like charm, but we all can't be Thor."

"Thor?" I ask.

I'm trying to stir that cute blush again, and while her cheeks go slightly pink, this time she doesn't turn away. "You know Thor, the guy with the really big hammer?" She shrugs. "You have to respect the hammer."

"Damn, there's so much I can say to that." I hold out my hand. "But I won't because I'm a classy guy."

"Classy, alpha, *and* charming?" she rests her cheek on her hand. "Tell me more."

The way the side of her face falls perfectly against her hand coupled with the way she waits patiently to hear what I have to say, momentarily holds me in place. A lot of women I've dated strike poses to look good and show off their assets. I'm not talking about when they're standing for pictures—I mean in general, for attention, so I'll buy them a drink, and yeah, to get me to take them home and fuck them. I've walked in on a few practicing their stances, adjusting their expressions and curves just so in front of a mirror. It's fake, well-rehearsed, and effective. But the way Sol is sitting in front of me doesn't appear anything close to phony. She looks good—damn good—don't get me wrong. Yet it's like she genuinely wants to hear what I have to say and this is simply who she is.

It shouldn't give me pause like it does. Sol's just—I don't know—*real* I guess. Maybe that's why she's been so hard to forget, despite our mostly brief interactions throughout the years.

I push my empty plate aside, crossing my arms in front of me and leaning in close. "What do you want to know?"

She gives it some thought. "What do you think your best

feature is?"

"Besides these muscles you can't stop looking at?" I ask, stretching. When that blush finds its way back into that face, and it looks like it's taking all she has to keep her eyes off my body, I'll admit it's my turn to smirk. I wasn't positive she was attracted to me. Not like I am to her. Now that I know she is, I want to play and tease her a little more. But I hold back, though it takes some effort. "I have to say my jaw," I answer.

"Your *jaw*?" Again it's like she's fighting to keep from looking elsewhere.

"Yup. I can take a hit, and it's never been broken."

"Well, thank God for that," she says cringing. She scans my face. "What about your nose?"

"That's been busted three times."

Her mouth pops open. "Seriously?"

"Hell, yeah," I tell her. "Want to feel?" I ask, leaning in.

I don't think she's going to touch me, but then she reaches out, grazing my skin so lightly, I barely feel it. When most girls touch me, they really touch me, making it clear they want to do a lot more. With Sol, it's different, more like she's afraid to cause me pain. Weird, especially since she knows I bust people up for a living.

She finds the spot where my nose curves just slightly, her features revealing sadness I don't expect. "Wow," she says. "I'm sorry."

"It's all good. Part of the job, you know?"

She nods like she understands, but it doesn't erase that hint of sadness I catch. I watch her hand as she pulls it away and carefully places it on the table. Yeah. Sol's different. But I'm starting to think she's different in more ways than I originally thought. "What about you?" I ask.

"I can honestly say my nose has never been broken," she answers.

I chuckle, knowing that now she's the one trying to lure my grin. "You know what I mean. What's your best feature?"

"My brain," she says. She points to her skull when my stare lowers to her perky round breasts. "This one right here."

"Sorry," I offer, not really meaning it. "Didn't mean to get distracted by your . . ."

"Personality?" she teases, "Sparkling wit, dazzling sense of humor?"

All right, two can play it that way. I lift my arm, bending it enough to bulge the muscles along my bicep and pecs as I pass my hand through my hair.

Sol's gaze drags along my shoulder, chest, arm, all the way up to the broody stare I'm pegging her with before she catches herself. "Looks like we're even," I say when her lips part.

She covers her face with her hand and shakes her head. "You are seriously unbelievable."

"You forgot hot," I remind her. I shift my position so I'm as close as can be with this damn table between us. "So, when are we going out?"

So much for not over doing it.

She lifts her face, raising her brows. "Going out?" she asks.

I glance around like I'm confused. "Yeah. We can't exactly make out here . . . unless you really want to."

"What happened to being classy?" she asks, giggling.

"This place is classy." I motion to the mini juke box perched at the end of the table. "Where else can you hear the Rolling Stones for fifty cents?"

"Good point." It's what she says, but then lifts her coat from where it's lying beside her.

"Where you going?" I ask. "I thought we were having fun."

She pauses in the middle of buttoning her wool coat. "Finn, I did have a good time—and please know I appreciate you keeping me company. This . . ." She purses her lips, cutting herself off. "I'm sorry. I have lot going on in my life right now. I'll see you around, okay?"

"That's it? You serious?" I ask, standing when she does.

Her smile softens, but when she looks at me, her gaze doesn't pass along my form, doesn't stop to take in my muscles, doesn't invite me closer. She simply stares at me, as if trying to gather her words. "You're really sweet," she finally says. "But this is a bad time for me to get to know more of that sweetness."

I frown when she slips a twenty out of her purse and places it on the table. Considering she only had coffee, that's one hell of a tip. "You're not paying for me," I say. "I got this."

She places her hand on my wrist when I reach for my wallet, the same way she touched my nose, barely grazing my skin, but having one hell of an effect. "Don't," she says. "It's my way of thanking you."

I cock my head. "For what? Keeping you company?"

"No," she explains quietly. "For giving me a smile I didn't know I had in me."

It's what she says. But as I watch her walk away, I realize she did the same damn thing for me.

CHAPTER 5

Finn

I reach into the back of Killian's F-150 for a giant tray packed with what smells like stuffed peppers, but Sofia's clasp to my arm holds me in place. "How are you doing?" she asks. "You were really quiet on the way over here."

She waited for Killian to head into her brother's house with another tray of food before asking. I haven't talked to Kill about all the shit going on in my head lately, not like I used to. He's noticed and probably told Sofia I've been pulling away. But I can't seem to talk to anyone anymore, not about anything real. It's probably one of the reasons I've been getting worse, but I don't want to admit as much.

"Good," I answer. Just tired. How you doing?"

"You know what I mean," she says quietly.

I don't want to worry her, or him, or hell, anyone. But somehow I always manage to screw that up. "I'm in counseling," I answer like a dumbass, like she doesn't already know.

Her long springy curls brush against her shoulder as she tilts her head. "Do you think it's helping?"

Nope. I think it's horseshit. "Sure."

"Finn, I'm serious."

"Me, too." I say. I don't add that as motivated as I was to get help, I totally shut down the moment I meet with my therapist. It's not that Mason isn't nice. He is. The court appointed psychiatrist even hand selected him thinking we'd be a good fit. But we're not. Totally not.

Nothing personal, but the guy wears loafers—with tassels! And the first time I saw him, I swear to Christ he was in a sweater vest. He can't be more than in his late thirties. What is he doing in a damn sweater vest?

Let me play out our first session: Mason sat in front of me, crossed his leg, and waited for me to speak. When a few moments passed and I didn't say shit he said, "So, Finn. The way you're looking at me makes me think you don't like me."

He wasn't angry, just sort of smiled politely all the while calling me out. "I don't know you," I'd admitted. "Can't say I do or don't yet."

"Fair enough," he replied. "So let's work on getting to know each other . . ."

Yeah. So far it hasn't happened. Not the first time. Or the second. Not even this last time. I mostly talked sports, and he lets me. Get this, he likes chess and tennis.

Me and him, we just ain't connecting.

"I want you to be okay," Sofia says. She hooks her thin arms around mine and glances up at me. "We're all worried about you, Finn."

I nod like I'm listening, and I am. What she doesn't know is I'm worried about me, too. Lately, I can't get past what happened to me. It's messing me up five ways from Sunday.

For a second, neither of us moves or speaks. It feels good to feel close to someone like this—I don't mean in the sexual sense. God knows I get my share of tail. But as close as am to her and my family, we don't really touch each other. Probably because I don't let anyone touch me. Not since . . .

Kill's heavy feet crunching against the snow gives me an excuse to glance up. I smirk when his stare bounces between me and Sofia. If I wasn't his brother, he probably wouldn't like me so close to his girl. But Sofia has always been just that: Kill's girl, even when they were too young to know what love really is.

"Sorry," I tell him. "I told her to quit fondling my ass, but she can't seem to help herself."

The stare he pegs me with would have sent anyone else running. Me, I just laugh.

"You're lucky I trust her," he warns.

"Don't you trust me?" I ask, my grin widening.

"Not even a little bit," he says.

"Behave, Finn," Sofia says. She pats my hand and reaches for the last tray of food, a fresh blush coating her cheeks. It doesn't take much for her to blush, something Kill can't seem to get enough of.

He grins as he approaches her. "I got it, princess," he tells her, lifting the tray away from her with one hand. He places his free arm around her waist, stopping to kiss her before leading her forward.

I tuck my tray of food and slam the rear doors of his truck shut. "So what were you saying, Sofia? Something about my irresistible ass."

"You're pissing me off, Finn," Kill says.

It's what he claims, but even with his back to me I know by now he's laughing.

I follow them down the stone path that leads to Teo and Evie's, Sofia's brother and sister-in-law. Teo has killed it in the automotive repair industry, but he's never forgotten his friends. Every now and then, they have a bunch of people over for dinner. Tonight is one of those nights, I'm only hoping Sol will show.

Sol . . . yeah. I haven't been able to shake this sexy woman with the even sexier smile from my mind—not since seeing her at the clinic, and especially not after flirting with her at the diner. When I'm attracted to a woman and start talking to her, it doesn't take long for her to warm up to me, and it sure as anything doesn't take long for us to end up in bed. That's not the case with Sol, and in a way it's new territory.

Women like me. I know how to make them laugh and feel good. Call it a gift. The part where I end up pissing them off, call that a need to move on. I don't let women get too close, but that goes for everyone I know. I've had a few relationships here and there between hot make-out sessions and one night stands, but nothing that's ever really meant anything and that's how I like it. My brothers were pretty much the same way. But they had "daddy" issues. Me. I wish our cheating and absent father was all the shit I had to deal with.

"Hey," Teo says, bending forward to kiss his sister. His baby girl, Lynnie is pressed against him, taking everything in. "How's it going, Finn?" he asks.

I shake his hand. "Aside from prying your sister off me in the driveway? Pretty damn good, man," I tell him.

"Sure you were," Teo says with a smirk, laughing when Kill mutters, "Christ."

I kick the snow off my boots and step inside. "Where's your pretty wife?" I ask. *And your hot cousin?*

"Kitchen," he answers as we make our way inside. He puts Lynnie down in the foyer. The little blondie grabs on to her father's finger and shuffles forward.

"She's walking already?" Kill asks him.

"Yeah. It's the only way to keep up with her big brother," he answers.

Teo's house is a huge classic colonial with beautiful wood floors and plaster walls. The kind of house that tells people you made it big with a hell of a lot of work. Lynnie lets go of Teo the minute she catches sight of her mama in the kitchen, her chubby little legs rushing her forward.

"Hi," Evie sings, scooping her up, even though she has their son Mattie perched on her opposite hip.

"Ev. What are you doing?" Teo says, charging forward.

We place the food on the counter, but my attention stays on Teo, knowing something's up.

Both kids leap into his arms the minute he reaches for them. Lynnie's giddy, and kicking out her legs as if she wasn't just with him. Mattie clutches his neck like he's been gone forever.

"Babe," Evie protests. "They always want you. Give me a moment to have some Mommy time."

"You can have Mommy time on the floor. They're too heavy for you now that—" The way he cuts himself off causes an immediate silence.

"Now that what?" Kill asks, grinning.

Teo smirks at Evie's blush, his big muscles bulging as he hangs tight to his kids. "Evie's pregnant again."

The kitchen erupts in cheers, and while I join them in the congratulations, my attention doesn't stay on Teo and Evie. It trails to Sol who's standing in place with two giant bottles of soda in her arms. The way she doesn't appear shocked by the baby news, I figured she'd heard earlier. But even though she's smiling in Teo and Evie's direction, her focus skips to me and stays there.

Cool.

She walks forward. I take a step back, way back, hoping she'll follow. And she does, the hem of her thick white sweater skimming along her curves and brushing against the waist of her dark jeans. Damn, this woman's fine.

"What are you doing here?" she asks when she reaches me, her bubbly voice soft compared to the loud chatter behind her.

I heard Teo and Evie were having a party. I got myself invited hoping you'd be here because I think you're fucking beautiful and I like your smile. That's the whole truth, but I don't share all of it. "I was hoping to see you, again," I admit.

Sol was that one woman I managed to charm, but never had that chance to kiss. Call her a challenge, or call her something else. Either way, considering how her plump lips draw my focus, I still want that kiss.

She laughs, strands of her hair that escaped her ponytail skimming over her cheeks. But it's not the blond highlights that make her eyes sparkle, it's her. All her.

"Finn, this isn't a good idea," she begins.

"Why not? There's food and everything."

She averts her gaze to the side, trying to hide her smile, but doing a shitty job. "You know what I mean," she says.

"You think I'm hitting on you—that I'm looking to hook up or cash in on that kiss that you still owe me?"

Her face jerks back to face me. "You're not?"

"Of course I am. I'm just letting you know you're right."

She tosses her head back laughing, exposing a lovely neck I wouldn't mind nibbling on. She knocks me playfully in the shoulder. "Come on, help me carry some of these things downstairs."

My eyes hone in on her ass as she walks ahead of me and toward a closed door. "Is that a no to the kiss?"

She pauses in the middle of picking up the bottles of soda she set down on the marble counter, glancing at me in that sad way of hers. "Trust me when I say there are plenty of other women who'd like all these kisses you're offering."

"That's true," I agree, lifting the bottles from her hand and making her giggle.

Kill glances at me as she lifts a tray of food from the counter. The way he eyes me tells he's figured out why I wanted to tag along. I'm not sure how he feels about that, seeing how Sol and his wife are cousins. But I can probably guess he's not too excited.

My family thinks I'm a ticking time bomb. As much as I know they're right, and as much as I want to spare them when I blow— it pisses me off that this is what I've become. Despite the hard muscles and fighting skills I possess, there are times I feel so God damn *weak*—times where I lay in bed hoping the next breath I take won't come.

Do I want to kill myself? Sometimes. But given I was raised strict Catholic—despite the fact I'm one shitty Catholic—the belief I'll burn in hell for eternity is ingrained in me, halting me in place before I take that next step—onto that path where I actually think about how and when. Maybe that's a good thing. But there are those moments where I wish I could just die—in a car wreck, a freak incident, even in a fight. Not a fight in the octagon, more like a fight in a bar. Me against some guy packing—who loses what remains of his shit and pulls the trigger.

Does it sound crazy? It does. But it spares me from being the one whose hand is on the gun, and maybe gives me a chance to find the peace I need and crave.

Life . . . is too damn sad sometimes, too exhausting, too *hard*.

"This smells so good," Sol says, her high-heeled boots forcing her to take the wood steps slow.

"They're stuffed peppers, I think," I say, trying to put my head back in the moment so my words don't sound so distant. "Sofia made a lot of food."

Sol bounces across the finished basement. "I'm not surprised. She's so Latina that way, wanting to feed everyone and make sure no one goes hungry."

The more she speaks, the more she pulls me back to the moment, reminding me that I came here to see her, not wallow in all my crazy.

I glance around the large open area, admiring everything from the dark wood floors to the perfectly stained beams across the ceiling. My brothers helped Teo build and design this whole place. I came in to help with cabinets way back when they first started, but back then it was a work in progress and looked nothing like this.

A bar with a built in sink takes up the entire back wall, a door leading to a spare bedroom with a full bath set just behind it. On the opposite side is a media room—full screen and step up seating like you'd find in theatre—only with full reclining leather seats.

"Talk about the ultimate man cave," I mumble, taking in the pool table, dart board, and pinball machine complete with flashing lights to my right.

"No kidding." She sets the tray over a wire stand and starts the flame beneath, then fusses with the food already placed along the long table.

I want to edge closer to those sweet curves, but I force myself forward and across the room to the bar area. I place the bottles of soda in the stainless steel refrigerator, ignoring the tall longnecks calling my name.

Man, I could go for a beer, yet I resist—not because I wouldn't mind a good buzz. Hell, I look forward to that buzz—but because I feel Sol watching me. And because I know she's watching, I stretch as I straighten, flexing my muscles.

I mostly do it for a laugh since she probably can't see much through my long-sleeved T-shirt. So when I turn to flash her a cocky grin—to let her know I'm well aware she's checking me out—that grin widens at the sight of her slacking jaw.

"Full of yourself much?" she asks, averting her gaze. She plays with her hair like she's trying to fix her ponytail, but all it does is cause the band holding it in place to snap. Her hair falls around her thin shoulders in wild messy clumps, making her already pretty face turn all kinds of sexy.

"Nah, just seeing if you'll notice." I march across the room for a better look, chuckling when I see her rushing to tame it. "Nice," I say, hooking a strand around my finger and giving it a playful tug.

She sidesteps away from me, becoming more flustered. "Am I making you nervous?" I ask, my deep voice lowering.

"No," she says, her tone a little higher. "I'm not, you know, easily intimidated or anything."

I step in front of her and cross my arms. "Good to know," I rumble.

She bites down on her bottom lip. If she's trying to halt that bashful grin she doesn't quite manage. But then she makes like it's not there, motioning to the rear deck. "It's hot in here," she says.

"Yeah, it is," I say, inching just a little closer.

Her demeanor relaxes when she sighs. I think I've annoyed her, but then she nudges me affectionately in the arm. "You know what I mean." She motions to the outside patio. "I need some air. If Evie needs me for anything, will you tell her I'm out there?"

She doesn't wait for me to answer, reaching for a coat folded over a bar stool and hurrying outside. Something is off with her. Just like it was at the diner. Yeah, I got her to smile and laugh a little. But the sadness—the one I'm not used to seeing is still there.

I watch her as she closes the door behind her. She expects me to stay inside, and maybe I should and give her space. A couple of my brothers are here with their women, my sister, too, and whatever idiot she decided to bring. But for all my family is tight, today the only person I want to hang with is Sol.

I give her some time, just enough to be social with the other guests. But when everyone heads downstairs to get some food, I find my coat and snag a plate to fill.

She laughs when I plop down in front of the outside fireplace beside her. "Nice set up," I say, leaning back against the couch and offering a plate topped with appetizers.

"Thank you," she says, reaching for what looks like a Cuban pastry.

She smiles before taking a bite. But like my grins, it seems forced. We share the appetizers. Neither of us say much, and at first I don't mind. It's nice out here, quiet and peaceful, a stretch of lawn packed with snow extending out to the trees lining the back. But as the sun sets in the horizon, and the only light that remains is from the fire, the silence becomes too much, especially with how distant Sol seems.

"I didn't see your folks. Are they coming later?" I ask.

The way her shoulders tense, I know I hit a nerve I maybe should have avoided. "They're not coming," she says, her voice tightening. "They're not available."

"Sorry," I say.

"Thank you," she says, swallowing hard.

The way she looks at me—*damn*—it's like I can feel her misery pooling in light eyes. I'm no genius. But I don't need to be one to guess her mother's probably not doing well again. Anyone living anywhere close to Fish town has heard of her mom. Whatever happened must have been pretty shitty. So I don't push it. Instead I lean back, pretending like it doesn't matter because in a way it doesn't. It doesn't change my opinion of Sol, if anything, all it does is make me want to lift her mood.

I watch as she turns back to her food, appearing to force the last bite down. I pop the last mini quiche in my mouth, taking my time to finish it. But when she wipes her mouth, I think maybe it's time to make her feel better. Most guys, would probably ask her about her internship to distract her or talk about something general like movies or some shit. But most guys aren't me.

"So," I say "Kick anyone in the balls lately?"

She lowers her napkin away from her mouth, turning slowly toward me. Ah, there's that smile I like.

"Of all the things you could've brought up," she says.

I toss the empty plate on the table. "It's a compliment. That was one mighty fine kick."

Sol and I always knew of each other, but ran with different crowds. From time to time, I'd run into her at a party. But either she had a date, or I had some girl on my arm— the exception being one night a few years back.

Me and my crew had landed at a party she and her friends were at. Some idiots were giving her shit about her mom, calling her crazy and telling her she'd end up the same way. I stepped in—not just because I kind of knew her—but because here were these assholes picking on someone weaker than them.

"I thought you were this poor a defenseless woman," I confess. "Nothing like watching a dude collapse, clutching tight to his nuts prove me wrong."

She clutches her belly, laughing, but by now I'm laughing to. Except the more we look at each other, the more our humor fades and something shifts between us.

"I never thanked you for helping me that night," she says, her voice gentle and so low I barely hear it.

"It's not too late," I offer, holding out my hands.

"I'm *serious*," she says.

"I am, too," I admit.

Her smile lights up the dimness, even though by now I'm walking that fine line between arrogant and endearing. "You barely knew me," she says. "But you still took on what? Three guys to protect me?"

"More like three pussies," I tell her, unable to pry my attention off her face. I'd stepped in to lead her away and keep her safe. But not before I told those dickheads to fuck off. The guys didn't know I was a fighter. They only knew my friends weren't close and that I was wrecked. One of the bigger ones started shit and tried to grab Sol. Wrecked or not, I made them pay.

"I didn't like them messing with you," I say, my voice

hinting at growl the more I remember.

"I know," she says. "It was really gallant of you."

"Gallant?" I ask. "That's a word you don't hear every day."

"Think of it as another handy adjective you can add to your repertoire." She winks. "It will impress the ladies."

I'm being a cocky prick, in my speech and tone. But I do mean what I say. "What if you're the one I'm trying to impress?" I ask.

Her expression softens. "You already have," she answers quietly.

"Oh, yeah? When?"

I expect her to tell me something related to fighting, seeing my rep and accomplishments in MMA are the only thing people really admire me for. But that's not what she says.

She leans back against the couch, watching me carefully. "That night you helped me. You were brave and kind and exactly who I needed."

I don't move. Her words—the way she means them—shit. Just like that she holds me in place. It's like every muscle in my face tenses. I'm not sure what I look like then. Stunned maybe? Whatever I give away—or maybe don't—causes her to shift her attention toward the fireplace.

Like me, she's probably remembering that night, how I walked her and her friends out to their car afterward, and how I reached for her and tried to kiss her.

I edge closer, enough so my leg touches hers. "You told me I was 'cute', remember? But you wouldn't let me kiss you. Said you would when I was sober."

She meets my face. The way the flames dance across her delicate features and cast light against her hair cause my chest to tighten. Fuck. What the hell is she doing to me?

"You were drunk," she says, her voice barely above a whisper. "I didn't want to take advantage of you."

"I'm not drunk now," I remind her, my voice deepening. "Still think I'm cute?"

She doesn't move, her large eyes fixing on mine.

Before I can figure out a reason why I shouldn't, I lean in

and kiss her.

CHAPTER 6

Sol

My eyes close as Finn's mouth captures mine. I don't expect him to have soft lips, not given how tough I know he is. Yet he does. They brush against mine, sweeping, teasing, playing. But as the heat between us surges, and before the kiss can really begin, it ends.

He pulls away, his eyes searching mine. He's not smiling. He's not joking. He simply stares at me like he's not sure what just happened. "That's still not the kiss you owe me," he says, cementing me in place.

"It's not?" I ask, kicking myself for not coming up with something better. In my defense, those are some damn fine lips.

He grins in that way that's so Finn: playful yet totally sexy. "No. The kiss you owe me is way hotter than that," he says with a wink.

"Finn . . . I can't," I say, shaking my head and wishing I could say different. God, he's so cute. Why does he have to be so cute! I haven't had sex in a year, and decent sex in even longer. But this is possibly the worst time to allow anyone into my life.

"You want me, don't you?"

I do a double-take. "What?" I ask, thinking it's totally unfair he can read my mind.

He puts his hand on my knee. "It's why you came out here,

isn't it? You needed to cool off your scorching womanly parts before you embarrassed yourself and straddled me in front of your family."

I bust out laughing, because around him I can't seem to help it. "Oh, my God. Could you be any cockier?"

"Is that a challenge?" he asks, leaning in.

I press my hand against his chest, trying not to think too much about the hard muscles beneath my touch and how his description of my needy girl parts were spot on. "Finn, I told you. I'm going through a lot right now."

"Okay," he says, edging slightly away.

He backs off. It's what I asked for, but I can't suppress the twinge of disappointment it causes. Since starting my master's program, I haven't had many opportunities to meet men, especially men who spark my interest like Finn. And even though it's more than obvious I like him. I *can't* like him. Not now.

"Is it Sofia?" he asks after a moment.

"What?" I question, brushing my hair away from my eyes.

"I know you love her, but it's okay to be struggling with the fact that she's married and you're practically an old maid."

Seeing how we're the same age and he damn well knows it, once more I grin. "If I'm an old maid, what does that make you?"

"Sadly a hot stud too many women want to drag to bed." He adjusts his position, placing his ankle over his knee. "You should feel sorry for me."

"Oh, I do feel sorry for you." I tap his arm. "There, there, you poor sexy and studly man."

"So now I'm sexy?" he asks. "Not just cute?"

I return my attention back toward the crackling flames, well aware of my widening grin, and damn it, how good it feels to smile and mean it.

"So do you want to get married?"

"Like, ever?" I clarify. At his nod, I crinkle my nose. "I don't know. I've never been serious about anyone to consider it. Mostly, though, I'm too young to care."

"Do you mean that?" he asks, flashing me that dimple.

"Of course I do," I tell him. I tilt my head when he laughs. "Why don't you believe me?"

"It's just weird you've never thought about it," he says.

"Why?" I press.

"Come on, Sol. Don't pretend like there aren't those crazy bitches out there who want to get married the moment they're legal and end up with some asshole who treats them like shit—or worse, steals their cars and go on a cross-country murdering spree."

"Could happen," he adds, when I simply look at him.

I shouldn't egg Finn on, but it feels good to feel good. "As much as all those murderous rampaging potential grooms in your mind sound appealing, no, I'm not in a rush to get married."

"Good to know," he says, his hand finding my knee.

"Um. What are you doing?" I ask, gaping at the size of his hand and trying my best to ignore the tingles his touch stirs.

"Just trying to keep warm. You know, body heat and all that good stuff."

"Did you not hear what I just said?" I ask. "I have too much going on in my life."

"Oh, yeah. Totally heard you," he says, grinning widely. "But it's winter. It's either put my hand here or someplace else." He lifts his brows, his irises shimmering with heat that's not coming from the hearth. "The choice is yours, beautiful."

Beautiful? The combination of his words, that deep voice, and the panty-melting look he's pegging me with . . . Lord, help me. Finn knows exactly how to make a woman swoon. I sigh. In a perfect world I'd probably let him do more than touch my knee. But my world is far from perfect and my guess is that his is, too.

So even though I shouldn't, I give his hand a squeeze, offering him and me a little bit of perfect in our less than perfect worlds.

In the silence that follows, night finishes overtaking the sky, until all that's left is a black canvas and hint of stars.

Ironic, considering that's how my life has been since my mother was first diagnosed with schizophrenia: bits of light often dominated by total darkness. She was doing better, still not herself, but okay. I didn't expect her anger or for her to hit me the way that she did, just like I didn't expect her to be committed yet again.

For a long time, I was worried I'd suffer some kind of mental collapse. It's not improbable considering how depressed I was following her suicide attempt a few years prior. It was a time I should have been out of my mind happy. I had just turned fifteen, I was going to prom with my big crush, and I had friends I absolutely adored.

Instead I spent prom night, sobbing in the waiting room, praying my mother would live. Like the other day, she had mistook me for her dead sister, and seeing me in my dress triggered a memory that compelled her to end her life. So when she calls me "Laurita" it's not a good sign. It's that red flag that screams a warning and tells me exactly how bad she is.

I don't admit as much to Finn. Instead I simply relish his company. For the first time since my mother's relapse, I don't feel so alone.

From inside the house Teo rumbles something that makes everyone laugh. I should be in there. After all I'm family. But it feels nice to have some peace given the chaos of this past week. And as much as I shouldn't go there, it's more than a little awesome to be here with Finn.

He's arrogant, bordering on obnoxious, straddling sexy and rugged like they're his bitches. But he has a heart, he proved as much all those years ago when he came to my recue. Remembering that night, how he took my hand and walked me out, makes me smile every time. Every time. He's a nice guy, a genuinely good person. I only wish I could tell him as much.

I zip open my coat because the fire in the hearth is just that hot. But then against my better judgment I reach for his hand, carefully passing my fingertips over his knuckles. "How are you doing?" I ask. "You haven't said much about you."

He flips his hand over, threading our fingers together. Before tonight, he never struck me as the touchy-feely type. I guess I was wrong. "I'm all right," he says after a breath.

I don't think he is. Not if he's seeing Mason. If anything, he's about as good as I am. "You sure?"

He waits to answer. "Life can be a real bitch," he admits.

"Yes, he can," I agree, causing him to laugh.

He quiets after a moment, the way he takes me in making me feel like he's wrestling with what to tell me. "Do you know what happened with me? Why I'm in counseling?" He frowns when I shake my head. "I thought you would, seeing where you work."

His stance is rigid, as if he's expecting me to judge him. But of course I don't. "It's against the law to read files of clients I'm not directly involved with or to even discuss their cases." I brush away my messy hair with my free hand, but it's probably pointless. "Cute" flipped me off the moment my hair band snapped.

"So you don't know anything about me?" he asks. "Nothing at all?"

I think I surprise us both when my thumb strokes the back of his hand. "I'll only ever know what you tell me."

"Okay," he says. "That explains it."

"Explains what?" I ask, crinkling my brow.

Although he's grinning, I don't miss the edge behind his words, and maybe the underlying warning he feels he needs to share. "Why you're sitting here beside me, and not looking for an excuse to get away."

Teo once told me that no matter my smile, my eyes have a way of giving away my sadness. I believed him. I wonder as I stare at Finn—a guy who's so heartbreakingly gorgeous and who possesses a grin capable of halting me in place—if he can see that sadness I know must be there. "Is it that bad?" I ask.

He turns his attention in the direction of the flames. "Yeah. It is," he answers quietly.

"Do you want me to tell you?" he asks after a moment.

"No."

I mean what I say. Most women would push until he spilled something juicy—eager for a shock or thrill. But I don't. A shock or thrill at the expense of someone who's been hurt sucks. If I know anything, it's that.

"No?" he asks, laughing.

I grin because his smile and that dimple make it hard not to. But as my words come, my smile fades. "I don't ever want you to tell me anything you don't want me to know."

"So there'll be a next time in case I want tell you? Another time with you and me like this?" he asks, motioning to our hands.

"Maybe," I say, before thinking things through.

"Yeah?" he asks, his stare darkening in a way that means trouble. "You know," he says at the sight of my lips parting. "There are ways I can keep you warm that have nothing to do with this fire."

"Ah," I respond, as my girl parts tighten with a resounding, "hell, yeah."

I don't know what he sees in my expression, but it cracks him up. He leans in, lifting my chin so his mouth lingers just a few millimeters from his. "You really know how to make a guy feel wanted," he murmurs.

"Do you really think this is a good idea?" I stammer.

"Kissing?" he asks, his mouth so close his warm breath tickles my skin. "Or touching?" he adds, his hand gliding along my thigh.

My body shudders with a burst of mind-numbing desire. Holy Madonna and baby Jesus clinging to her leg. How is it possible for him to get me this worked up with just his words . . . and that deep voice . . . and that face? As it is, my nipples are saluting him like he's their new leader.

"Did you get any snow in your jeans sitting out here?" he asks, his sly grin telling me he's enjoying watching me squirm. "If so, I could help you get it out."

"Finn . . ."

"Normally, I wouldn't offer," he whispers. "But you seem like a nice girl so I thought I'd help you out."

His comment makes me smile, and maybe gives me a little

courage, too. "Is that right?"

"Damn straight," he says. "I meant what I said. That kiss I gave you is just a taste of what's to come."

"What if I don't want another taste?" I ask, obviously lying to both of us.

"Maybe you don't want it now. But you will."

I avert my chin. "You really are something else."

"No. More like just confident, especially after I caught you looking at my ass."

I gasp, insulted, even though I might have stolen a peek or three. "I was actually looking at your dimple. On your face," I clarify.

"Not my ass?" he asks as if shocked. "Most girls stare at my ass. What's wrong with you?"

Again, all I can do is laugh.

"Doesn't matter," he says. "It's only a matter of time."

"Before I stare at your ass? Finn, I'm not like those other women—the ones who fall all over you when you look at them." Who am I kidding? By now it's clear that I am.

Although he's been grinning and laughing right along with me, his demeanor softens then in a way holds me in place and freezes time. "Maybe that's why I like you," he says, no longer joking.

My mouth pops open. He *likes* me? As in, doesn't just want to have sex with me? Okay, that may have made him that much hotter.

Someone flips on the exterior lights, drawing our attention back to the house. The doors leading into the man cave slide open and out runs Mattie across the patio and into the large yard. Evie hurries behind him carrying Lynnie. "Sorry," she says, adjusting her little daughter's hat when she places her down. "They're getting restless in there. Would you mind watching them? I'm hoping if they play in the snow it will tire them out and I'll be able to put them to bed."

I stand, reaching for what has to be the prettiest little girl on the planet. Like Evelyn, she has fair skin and white-blond hair. I think Evie wanted to name her Arabella or something like that. But since Mattie is technically Mateo Jr., Teo insisted his daughter be called Evelyn like her mother—especially once it was clear she was Evie's mini-me. Evie agreed only if her nickname was Lynnie, claiming she wanted to be the only Evie in Teo's life.

"Of course we'll watch them," I say, smiling when Lynnie wraps her little hand around my fingers.

Finn jogs after Mattie as I walk Lynnie out into the yard, taking in the way her little boots press into the snow. Evie smiles softly as she watches her little girl explore. Yet it's the way Finn starts chasing and playing with Mattie that widens her grin.

"Ev, what are you doing, babe?" Teo calls from the doorway. "It's too cold out there for you."

It doesn't matter if she's wearing a coat, or standing near a fire hot enough to melt steel. Teo is just *that* protective of her.

"I'll be right in, love," she calls over her shoulder.

"He adores you," I tell her, smiling.

"The feeling is mutual," she assures me, her delicate features revealing her love for him.

"I know you have a lot going on," she says, watching as Lynnie places snow in my hands. "But I was wondering if you'd be available to watch our babies on Wednesday night. Teo and I were given tickets to a show, and I'd really like to go if we can."

I love her kids so I don't hesitate to answer. "Of course," I tell her.

"Yeah. Count us in," Finn answers.

Evie and I turn his way at the same time. He scoops up Mattie and starts spinning him like an airplane. "She didn't mean you," I point out.

"No, I didn't," Evie agrees. But then something changes in her expression as she continues to watch Finn interact with her son. When her attention cuts back to me, I realize I missed something she seemed to pick up on. "But I think Finn might be able to help you."

Based on her tone, she doesn't just mean with her kids.

CHAPTER 7

Sol

"I don't like this," Teo says. He turns to Evie. "You said she was bringing a friend."

Finn lifts his hand and grins. "I'm a friend."

"Friends are girls," he says without blinking, his attention now fixed on me. "Don't you have any *girl*friends?"

"I do. But they're all pretty busy hitting the bars and being irresponsible," I answer him truthfully.

"Nice," Teo says.

Evie rubs Teo's arm, like he doesn't appear ready to kill me for bringing Finn. "Baby, you promised you'd take me out. When was the last time we were out on a date, with other adults? And with the baby coming, it's going to be even harder."

"Fine," Teo tells Evie, reaching for her hand. He pauses and glances over his shoulder. "Don't let me catch you making out with my cousin on my couch."

Finn holds out his hands. "I'm not making any promises. Your cousin's hot."

"Christ," he mutters as my face burns.

We follow them inside so they could say goodbye to their kids, but it's the way Teo clutches his babies and helps Evie with her coat that makes me gush.

"All the numbers—our cells, the restaurant, and the theatre are written on a pad beside the phone," he tells us. "Our address is on top in case you need to call an ambulance—"

"Where's the earthquake kit in case we need it?" Finn asks.

"In the man cave behind the bar, next to the zombie survival gear," Evie answers.

"No, shit?" Finn says, sounding impressed.

"It's a power outage kit," Teo says, trying to hide his smirk when Evie starts laughing.

"I would have been more impressed if you were prepared for the apocalypse," Finn says. He shrugs. "Just saying."

I pick up Lynnie when she begins to whimper as she watches her mommy and daddy leave. Evelyn pauses, so does Teo. "It's okay," I assure them. "They'll be fine."

"Totally," Finn adds. "I mean, what could happen?"

"This shit's not coming off," Finn says, tossing the washcloth he was using to scrub Lynnie's cheeks on the table.

"Are you sure?" I ask, dumping the piles of cereal Mattie spilled on the floor into the garbage can. I cringe when Finn points to her face. Sure enough, the giant purple whiskers that start at her nose and end at each of her little ears are still there. I don't mean to sound like an idiot—because believe me, I'm upset, but those are very impressive whiskers. "It's like he used a ruler," I say, shaking my head in awe.

"The kid's got skill," Finn says, sounding as impressed as I feel. "Too bad he used permanent marker. Told you it was a bad idea."

"I was trying to give them a project," I insist. "Didn't your mother give you projects to keep you entertained?"

"No. She sat me in front of the T.V. to watch cartoons."

"She sat you in front of the T.V.?" I question. "That's it?"

He points at me. "There were seven of us and I was the last. If we didn't kill each other or break something, it was a good day. I turned out just fine *and* I never drew on some poor unsuspecting kid."

"I'm not judging," I tell him as I return to the utility closet to put away the broom and pan. "I just figured someone as energetic as you would need more stimulation." I freeze when I realize things are quiet, too quiet. "Finn, where's Mattie?"

"Weren't you watching him?" he asks.

"No, I was cleaning up his mess—just like I was cleaning up his toys when you let him draw all over his sister."

He frowns. "I was busy cleaning up all the papers *and* markers he threw on the floor. I didn't know he was using the one marker that escaped his wrath on his sister. She was laughing, and he was, too. I thought —"

The sound of something spilling from the pantry makes us collectively groan. I rush in and find Mattie climbing the wire shelves as he sorts through Evie's version of a cereal aisle. "Mattie, no!"

I snatch him in my arms, but like Finn said, the kid has some mad skills. He snatches another box as I drag him out, spilling more cereal.

"Holy sh—"

My glare cuts Finn off. "You know what I mean," he says. "The kid can make a mess. What's your problem, little man?"

"Maybe he's hungry. Here, switch," I say, passing Mattie to Finn and lifting Lynnie out of his arms. "You feed him while I give her a bath. As soon as we get them in bed, we can work on cleaning this mess."

"You think a bath is going to remove those whiskers? I was going to look in the garage for something that might work."

"In the garage?" I ask, gasping.

"Yeah," he says like I didn't hear him the first time.

"Finn, you're not putting anything from that garage on this baby."

He grins. So does Mattie, and so does Lynnie. Yeah. Because I'm clearly the crazy one.

"You're really testy," Finn says. "Still sexy, but testy all the same."

"Just feed Mattie," I mutter, trying not to let him get to me. Who am I kidding? He already has. My time with Finn over the weekend was the only time I managed a real laugh, and a real smile. Was my sadness still there? Yes, it always lingers close to the surface. But that little bit of happiness . . . let's say I can use more of it.

Dr. Franco, my mother's psychiatrist is concerned by the increase in her episodes. I thought her recent relapse was due to not taking her meds, or her need for a different anti-psychotic. But he's worried it's something more serious. So instead of bringing her home yesterday, I led my father out of the hospital without her, trying to stay strong when he fell apart. "I miss who she was," he told me in Spanish, tears reddening his eyes.

"I do, too, Papi," I told him.

I hurry up the steps, clutching Lynnie close against me even as she tugs on my hair. "Pooh-po," she says, or something like it, pointing to her cheeks. My guess is purple must be her favorite color. Nice to know Mattie took that into consideration before he went to town on her face. My instinct is to text Evie to see if she has any baby oil. But seeing how I don't think anyone but Latinos from the 70's use that anymore, I don't bother. I don't want her worried, and I want her to have a good time. If this is the kind of trouble her kids get into on a daily basis, she's in serious trouble when the next baby comes.

I start to fill the tub. Lynnie is such a wiggle worm, I put her down thinking she'll be fine for just a second. Ha, ha. Silly me. In the time I take to adjust the water, she strips out of her clothes in a way that would shame Magic Mike and rips off her diaper.

"Lynnie," I begin, jumping when she proceeds to pee on the bath mat—two freaking inches away from the tile floor!

"Oh, crap," I squeak, lifting her at arms lengths as I set her down in the tub. I don't know what kind of bladder this kid has, but it tops mine and finishes emptying the moment her little butt hits the water. "Seriously?" I ask her.

And because her tiny self hasn't made enough of a mess, she starts splashing like me and the bathroom are on fire.

I wipe the floor with her abandoned clothes, certain I received the shit end of the kid stick when I hear Finn yell,

"Mattie, no—*no!*" followed with loads of giggling on Mattie's part and a few swears from Finn.

I almost ask if he's okay, but I'm too busy trying to soap Lynnie's cheeks. I drop my hands down as she continues to splash me. I don't know what the hell they put in markers, but whatever it is I can't get it off her.

After a few more passes and a lot more water on the floor, I lift her sudsy body from the tub and simply gape at the cat whiskers Mattie drew across her cheeks.

"You're father's going to kill me," I tell her. "You're mama, too." I think about it. "But if your Aunt Lety was here instead of England, she'd mostly laugh and point."

She squeals, giggling and kicking out her feet. "Well, I'm glad one of us thinks it's funny," I tell her, cuddling her close with the towel.

I put a diaper on her, hoping she'll keep it on while I find her pajamas. The problem is every stupid pair I find is either pink or purple, both of which draw even more attention to her whiskers. I finally give up and shove her in one that matches her cheeks then carry her downstairs.

Only to scream when I see what Finn's feeding Mattie.

He jumps, dropping the peanut butter crackers he and Mattie are sharing. "What?" he asks between chews. "You told me to feed him."

I point rapidly, stumbling over my words. "He's allergic. He's allergic to peanuts!"

Finn's head whips back at him. "Shit. Are you sure?"

"Yes!" I yell, placing Lynnie on the floor and reach for the landline.

Finn snags the bowl of crackers away from Mattie, and the box perched beside him. "Is he going to die?" he asks, his head jerking from me to him.

"I don't know." I'm trying to punch Teo's number, but my hands are shaking so bad I keep hitting the wrong number.

"You don't know?" Finn hollers. "What do you mean you don't know? Holy fuck," he says rushing back to Mattie.

He scoops Mattie out of his booster chair and runs him to the sink. "Mattie, spit it out. Spit it out now—*ouch*. Shit, he bit me!"

I'm barely listening, swearing up a storm when Teo's number goes to voicemail. "Teo. Call me. Call me now."

Finn's at the sink trying to rinse out Mattie's mouth, but mostly smearing the peanut butter all over his face. "Call 9-1-1," he says.

"*Omigod*—did he stop breathing?"

"No, he's laughing—*fuck*—and biting. But this is serious. Ow—*shit*. Ow—Mattie, cut it out!"

I drop the phone in my hand when it rings. "God damn it!" I yell as I answer.

"Problem?" Teo's deep voice rumbles on the other line.

I take a breath, despite that my heart is ready to explode and I'm officially hyperventilating. "Finn gave Mattie peanut butter," I stammer, throwing open the medicine drawer and frantically searching for an epi pen.

"You told me to feed him," Finn fires back.

"I didn't know there would be peanut butter in the house!" I scream.

"Sol, calm down," Teo says. "I can barely understand you. What happened?"

"What happened?" Evie repeats, from the background.

Her voice is panicked. She knows something's wrong. I let out a breath, knowing I have to fix this and save her son. "Mattie ate peanut butter," I repeat, my voice shaking like I'm gargling marbles.

"Yeah . . . he loves that shit," Teo says. "Then what happened?"

I freeze. "He's not allergic?"

"No."

"I thought he was allergic," I say, realizing I'm probably screaming.

"So did we. But the allergist we took him to said he was a false positive or something like that. Mattie eats it all the time."

I slump against the counter, gripping it tight to keep from keeling over.

Finn gapes back at me, his face paling like Mattie's about

to die.

I hold up a hand, but that's all I can do, torn between collapsing and jumping in the air.

"Sol?" Teo says when I don't answer.

My mouth opens and closes several times as I try to form my words. Finn gapes at me, keeping Mattie tucked against him and his fingers out of his reach. "Teo says he's not allergic to peanuts," I manage.

For a moment, Finn simply stares. Mattie squirms, trying to get down. "Is he allergic to human flesh?" Finn asks. "Because he bit the shit out of me."

"The fuck?" Teo asks.

"Mattie bit him when Finn tried to take the peanut butter crackers he ate out of his mouth."

"Can you blame him?" Teo says. "I would, too, if someone rammed their fingers in my mouth." The momentary pause makes me think he's laughing at us. At the very least Teo is smiling his ass off. "You want us to come home?" he asks, this time there is no mistaking the chuckling.

Finn says yes at the same time I say no. Teo laughs, *again*, taking my side. "We'll see you in another couple hours. Oh—I forgot to tell you—keep Mattie away from the magic markers. He likes to draw on his sister."

He hangs up as Finn sets Mattie down. "Just so you know, I'm never having kids. This parenting thing is fucked up."

"Fucked up," Mattie repeats.

Finn points at him. "Watch your mouth," he warns.

CHAPTER 8

Finn

I flop down on the couch, rubbing my eyes and wishing I could have a beer. Or a shot. Or a shot poured into an ice cold beer. But I won't. It's not just because Mason has advised me against drinking, it's because I'm here with the kids. I'll fuck myself up any day of the week, but not when there's someone counting on me to keep them safe. After what happened to me, I can't risk anything happening to anyone else.

Damn it. I rub my eyes harder when flickers of that day start poking their way in my head—those words said, that door slamming shut behind me. Why the hell can't I stop reliving this shit? Is it because of what that idiot Yefim said? Is that all it takes to bring back everything I've worked hard to forget?

I start to rise when Sol drops down beside me, her back smacking hard against the long sectional. She's not too close, but close enough to reduce my surging anxiety. "You finally get Lynnie down?" I ask her.

Her eyes are closed and her lips are opened slightly like she's already asleep, but she manages to nod. "It took five full choruses of *Born this Way* plus popping in a Sesame Street video before she finally dozed off."

"Yeah, I heard you on the monitor," I say, laughing. "Just so you know, Gaga has nothing to worry about."

She throws a pillow at me, but I catch it and place it behind my head. "How'd you do with Mattie?" she asks.

"Fine. *Ferdinand the Bull* put him right to sleep. I guess he's beat from the mess he made and from coloring his sister." I cover my mouth as I yawn. "I have to tell you, I work out at least four hours a day—more if I'm training for a fight. But those kids knocked me on my ass. Did you clean up the bathroom?"

"And the bedroom, and the playroom, and Lynnie's room." She pries an eye open. "Did you clean up all the cereal?"

"Yup. Cleaned up everything, but Mattie's room."

"Why?" she asks, adjusting her position.

"He's almost three. He needs to own some of his shit, you know?"

She laughs a little, but then her smile falters. "That was scary," she says, her eyes opening to look my way. "I almost had a heart attack thinking he was going to react to the peanut butter."

"Yeah. Me, too," I admit. Bleeding fingers and all, I would have never forgiven myself if something had happened to the little guy. "When I think about it, though, it makes sense he's not allergic—knowing how organized Teo is, and how prepared he always seems to be."

She nods. "You're right. But when it happened, I couldn't keep my thoughts straight. I kept thinking he wasn't going to make it."

Again her voice trails. But this time, the way it does, I think it's because she's thinking about something that has nothing to do with Mattie. "You didn't look good," I say, remembering how her skin blanched.

"I wanted him to be okay—and if he wasn't, I wanted to be able to save him."

"You didn't want him to hurt," I say, letting her know I'm listening and hearing beyond what she's telling me.

She swallows with great effort. "No, I didn't," she responds quietly. "Nothing can happen to him."

She says "him", but I can't help thinking she's also talking about her mom. She doesn't say anything more, appearing lost in her thoughts. At first, I don't like it. I want her to keep talking—to keep me from my own damn problems. Yet despite the silence, the memories—those stupid flashes of things I'd stab my own brain to forget—they don't come. Nope. Right now, my mind is all on Sol.

Not that you can blame me.

Most girls I hang with, screw around with, that sort of thing, don't stop yapping—ever. Even when we're in bed they have something to say, even if that something is them screaming for more. This silence between me and Sol, it's nice. For all I like to talk, and for all I want to get to know her, it just feels good.

Sometimes, I swear to Christ, the quiet and all the memories that come during that silence are going to drive me insane. That feeling is such a scary place and makes me feel alone, even when someone is sitting right beside me.

It's not that way with Sol. Maybe because she feels lonely, too. And like me, maybe just as lost.

"Can I ask you something, without it being weird?" she says, spreading her legs across the couch, but bending them so they don't quite reach me.

I straighten her legs so they do touch me, her feet resting on my right leg. "Well, when you preface it like that—"

"Preface?" she asks. Despite the way her arm is draped over her eyes, I still catch sight of her grin.

"Yeah, 'preface'. I know what it means. Believe it or not I'm smarter than I look." I mean it as a joke, because even though I've made some pretty stupid mistakes, and say some really dumbass things, I'm not stupid, and I'm sure as shit not dumb.

Sol doesn't take it as a joke, dropping her arm away. "I know you're smart, Finn. I don't question that for a moment." Her eyes trail over my arms, taking in my tribal tats. "You're just so 'street'. And 'preface' isn't exactly a street word."

"No, it's not." She has a point. I probably wouldn't use that word at the gym. I have a rep to maintain.

My fingers slide over her bare feet as I think back to our kiss. You can say I want more. Hell, you can say I want a lot more. But for now, I'll behave. Maybe.

Her toes wiggle as I skim her instep. She had on socks earlier, but that's before Lynnie soaked the bathroom floor. "So you saying I should stick to using words with four letters?" I murmur, paying close attention the sweeps of her soles.

"Of course not," she says, averting her chin.

She squirms when I pass my thumbs along the ball of her right foot. I grin, knowing I'm killing her in a way that's probably turning her on. "All right then," I tell her. "Like I was saying, when you *preface* a question by asking if it will be weird, than my guess is that it will be. But what the hell? Ask anyway."

"Are you okay?" she asks.

Am I unstable, she probably means. My muscles tense, but I force myself to keep the massage to her feet gentle. She doesn't know anything about me, what I've been through. So I clue her in before I realize how much I'm really telling her. I shrug. "I've been dealing with a lot lately—pissed over shit I should just let go."

"Like what?" she asks.

My fingers release her feet to trail lightly over her ankles. "I haven't always made good decisions," I answer, meeting her face. I'm not proud of what I have to say, but that doesn't mean I'm a pussy about it. "I have a lot of anger. Fighting has always been a good way for me to release some of it out, but lately it hasn't helped as much as it has in the past."

She nods like she seems to understand even though I know she can't. Women like Sol, they don't rage. Sure, they have their freak-outs. But when they drink too much, they usually end up puking or telling the world that they love it. I don't love the world when I drink. I drink because sometimes I hate it and everyone in it to hell and back. The drinking helps me dull that anger. Or at least, that's what I tell myself.

"Thank you," Sol says, putting my head back in the game.

"For what?"

"For trusting me, and telling me what's going on," she explains quietly.

"Is this the part where you slip me a twenty?"

"What?" she asks.

I remind her what she did at the diner. "You paid for my breakfast to thank me for making you smile. Now you're thanking me for giving you my trust." I rub my jaw. "Hmmm. Trust is a big deal. Don't you think it deserves more than a twenty?"

Her shoulders and a couple of other things bounce as she laughs. "Are you trying to tell me you charge for your services?"

"Nah. That would make me a whore. But I can think of other ways you can thank me."

"You're funny," she says, relaxing into the couch.

"No. You think I'm sexy," I remind her, my palm sliding down her calf. "And I think you used the word hot, too, but either works."

"I never said hot," she claims.

"Maybe," I say, tossing her a wink that causes her to wiggle. "That doesn't mean you're not thinking it."

I expect her to either hold onto her smile, or shove me playfully away with her feet. She doesn't do either, she simply looks at me. So I try a little harder.

"You ready to make out?"

Oh, and there's that laugh. "Finn, I told you. This isn't a good time for me."

"All right." I make a show of glancing at an antique wall clock to our right. "How about in another five minutes?"

She covers her mouth with her hand, as if embarrassed because of how much she's laughing or because of what I say. But then she drops her hand away and glances at the baby monitors that show Mattie and Lynnie fast asleep. "Okay," she says.

For a second, she catches me off guard. Eventually I was sure she'd let me kiss her again, but I'll confess, I thought I'd have to try a little harder. Sol is beautiful, and smart, and *man*, seriously smokin'. So I'll take that kiss and maybe a little more.

My hand glides along her leg. "Okay in five minutes. Or okay right now?"

She sits up, her thick hair falling around her face. There's not a lot of light in the family room. Only the side table lamps are on. But I catch enough shimmer in her eyes that tells me she wants me, and maybe likes me more than she's letting on.

"Okay now," she answers.

Well, all right then.

My left arm hooks beneath her knees, my right circles around her waist. She's tiny compared to me, and a hell of a lot lighter. In one smooth motion she's on my lap, her eyes widening with how quick I move, and how easily I take her.

I wasn't trying to show off. My only intent was to hold her closer. But I don't think she expected my speed or my strength. Based on how she stills against me, she's afraid. Shit. That's the last thing I want. She has nothing to fear from me. Now, or ever. So I do my best to prove it.

I lift my free hand, skimming her cheek, my gaze fastening to hers. "Are you scared?" I ask.

The quick rise and fall of her chest assures me she is, and maybe something more. "Yes," she whispers.

I don't expect someone like Sol to admit she's feeling vulnerable. So her confession alone is enough to ease my hold despite my need for her. "Don't be," I tell her, the rasp to my voice gaining an edge.

I lean in slowly, brushing my lips against hers and teasing her with my tongue until she returns my affections. Her arms wrap around my neck, her pouty mouth inviting me deeper.

She feels so good pressed against my body. I slip my tongue in when she pulls me closer. She likes what I'm doing. Sweet. Cause I like it, too.

Her moan is barely audible, but I hear it, and feel it, just like I feel her full, soft breasts slide against my chest.

The heat between us rises, accelerating my pulse and luring the flicks of my tongue in for a deeper taste. My hands drag along her back. This girl can kiss and knows exactly what to do to make me hot.

I clutch her hip, our make-out session becoming more foreplay than the innocent act I intended when I saw how nervous she was. But now things aren't so innocent. Now, I really want to touch her. So instead of keeping my hands where they're safe, I slide one up to knead her breast.

I barely feel its weight when she draws back. She covers my hand with hers to move it down, but I beat her to the punch, knowing I'm way out of her comfort zone.

"Are you in a rush?" she asks, her lids heavy and her breaths quick.

"No. I just wanted to feel close to you," I say, my heartbeat way out of control.

"To feel close to me?" she repeats.

"Yeah," I say, surprised by how much I mean it.

My hand slides along her waist, enough to feel the bare skin her sweater doesn't cover. Am I turned on? Totally. But she wants me to stop so I keep my hands from wandering. "You okay?" I ask.

I try to focus on her, rather than how tight my pants feel. Except that doesn't help, not when I have a woman like Sol this close to me, and not when she gives me another quick kiss. "I'm not ready for this," she says.

"The kissing?"

She shakes her head. "I mean you."

"You've mentioned that," I remind her.

She dips her chin, looking bashful and way too good to resist. "So why did you kiss me?" she asks, staring at me through a layer of the thick lashes.

My voice lowers. I know how to charm, but right then I'm not trying to get in her pants—okay, I am. But that doesn't mean I don't mean what I say. "Because you're really pretty, cause I wanted to, and because you let me."

She tilts her head, as if trying to figure me out. Maybe she thinks I'm blowing smoke, but for once I'm just being me, someone I haven't been in a very long time.

I have to admit, it feels pretty damn awesome.

"I wish you didn't say that," she says, so quietly I almost don't hear her.

"Why?" I ask, my tone deepening further.

"Because it makes me wish you hadn't stopped kissing me."

Fair enough. So I pull her close and kiss her again.

CHAPTER 9

Finn

"It's that one, with the red door," Sol says.

She had to leave her car for some minor repairs at Teo's shop. I'd picked her up in the parking lot at her internship and then took her out for a late dinner. It was nice. Real nice, reinforcing how much I like her.

I pull my F-150 to the curb, on the opposite side of the one way street. I've been through this neighborhood a few times, and in the ones in the surrounding blocks, but I didn't realize exactly where she lived.

"Something wrong?" she asks.

She must have caught the change in my expression. She's like that, able to pick up on even the most subtle changes. But her soft smile tells me she's not offended. "Nah," I say, setting my truck in park. "I just didn't realize this was your neighborhood. You're not far from where I grew up. Maybe a mile and change."

"Is that a bad thing?" she asks.

"Not at all," I tell her. "I have a couple of friends on this block—they can be real dumbasses sometimes—but they're good people." I reach to play with the edges of her soft hair. "But if I knew you lived here, I would have hung out with them more."

She glances down in that shy way of hers. "Who do you know around here?"

It's what she asks, but I think she's trying to talk just to talk, like she's suddenly nervous. She probably thinks I'm going to kiss her again. If so, she's right. Those kisses on Teo's couch the other night were sexy and sweet, just like her. If I'm being truthful, I can't keep her out of my mind.

I didn't let my hands wander again when she pulled away, but I'll admit it was hard. Sol has that typical Latina body: plump breasts, firm round ass and a tiny waist. But in my book "no" never means "maybe" or "keep trying to see how far you can get". It means you're doing more than she wants, and you need to stop. "Trevell McMurphy and Angelo Conti," I finally answer.

She rolls her eyes, but keeps her smile. "You're right. They are dumbasses. Did you hear what Angelo did when he was at Kutztown?"

"Streaked naked through a sorority house?"

"No—I mean, yes, that, too. But there's more."

"Pissed in front of the dean's house?"

She starts laughing. "Yes. I heard that, too. But did you hear how he and his cousin got wasted and broke into a state store?"

I unbuckle my seatbelt and swivel in my seat. "When the hell was that?"

"Last semester of senior year during finals week." She follows suit and removes her seatbelt, turning to face me and getting all into the story. "They claimed they were drunk and stressed from the exams. So they break in through a back window. But an alarm goes off and the police come." She makes the *raw-oo, raw-oo* sound of a siren for effect, making me laugh. "Well, of course, they panic. And panic and dumbasses don't mix well. His cousin grabs a case of Sam Adams, screaming something like, 'if I'm getting caught, I'm getting caught taking beer.'"

I hold out a hand. "Back up a minute. He thinks it's better to get caught with evidence rather than just taking off with the hopes of not getting caught at all? Nice," I say, laughing harder.

"I know, right? Like you said, total dumbasses." She

bounces in her seat. "So the cousin runs off, carrying a case of high-end beer in hand. Angelo grabs a six-pack of Schlitz and another of Iron City and takes off like the building is on fire."

By now I'm laughing so hard my sides are killing me. "What an asshole."

Sol waves an arm out. "And who gets caught?"

"No way. Tell me it wasn't Angelo."

She nods. "His father had to drive up to bail him out. From what I heard he smacked him upside the head on their way out of the precinct, humiliated—not because his drunk son broke into a liquor store—but because of the type of beer he stole. Is it a wonder Angelo is so screwed up?"

I wipe my eyes because yeah, I'm laughing that hard. "Okay. I have a good drunk story for you. You know my brother Seamus?"

"The contractor?"

"No. That's Angus. Seamus is the carpenter. Anyway, since Seamus never went to college, he never experienced what it was like to hit the parties, join a frat, that sort of thing. He was playing around with the idea of going when Curran enrolled and was pretty much shouting to the world how he was having the time of his life. Seamus felt like he was missing out. Curran, being who he is, invites him up during Greek Week or whatever it's called. Big mistake."

She covers her mouth. "On Curran's part or Seamus's?"

"Oh. Seamus's for sure. Curran still thinks the incident is funnier than hell. So Seamus goes up, thinking he'll check out the campus, maybe go to a few parties and have a few laughs, that sort of thing. And at first, it's all good."

"Until it's not?" she offers when I pause to work things through.

"Until it's way not," I say, starting to laugh all over again. "So Curran and Seamus start making their way to all these parties with Curran's frat brothers. One beer leads to another, a few shots, well, you get what I mean. Curran somehow loses Seamus. Can't find him. Doesn't know where he is. He and a few of his frat brothers take off looking for him. His frat brothers locate him first, lying on the front lawn of some sorority house trying to find his girlfriend at the time. FYI, she didn't even go to the school."

"Oh, God," she says.

"It gets better," I tell her, because it does. "The sorority girls know Curran's frat brothers and insist they take him home to his girlfriend because 'the poor guy really misses her' and 'if my boyfriend wanted to see me, I'd want someone to bring him home'. So the frat boys do."

"That was nice of them."

I huff. "No, they just wanted to get some. Anyway, they shove Seamus's drunk ass into the car and drive all the way back to Philly. They more or less toss him on her front yard so they can get back to the hot sorority sisters, never suspecting Seamus would try to make out with his girlfriend's mother, thinking it was her."

Sol's mouth pops open. "Are you serious?"

I laugh again. "Totally. Seamus stumbles toward his girlfriend's front door completely wrecked out of his mind, falling over when Mom opens it. She screams for her daughter. They hook his arms around their shoulders and are dragging him inside, all worried about him, when Seamus pulls the mom to him and he slips her the tongue."

Sol cracks up. "Oh, my God. Did she break up with him?"

I nod. "Yeah. But he and the mom are still going strong."

Her eyes whip open before she realizes I'm messing with her and starts laughing again. "That is unbelievable!"

"I know."

"So what happened?"

"The mom drops him like a pile of wet laundry and the girlfriend kicks him in the face. If that's not bad enough, they call our mother. Seamus was like twenty-one at the time. Ma shows up and drags him out of their house by the hair, screaming at him that he's going to hell."

Sol says something like, "*Madre de Díos*," before dropping her hand from her face and shaking her head. "I can honestly say, that's never happened to me."

"What? Making out with someone's mother?"

"That, too," she says, nodding. "What I mean is, getting so

wasted I'm sprawled out on some lawn or breaking into buildings to steal beer."

I try to sound casual—like I'm not some asshole who's done stupid shit when wasted—even though I have. "You've never been drunk?"

"I have, but I have a sort of a hero complex. When my girlfriends and I went to parties, I'd start to drink, start feeling good, but then I'd see them getting too drunk, guys eyeing them like this is going to help them get laid, or encouraging them to drink more so they can get in their pants." She shudders. "I couldn't allow them to get hurt, you know? Girls, young women, they're such easy targets when they start partying, experimenting with sex, drugs, things they shouldn't and aren't ready for." She smiles thoughtfully. "I couldn't let anything happen to my besties. I had to keep them safe."

"So you'd sober up before anything could happen to you or to them."

She tilts her chin, her stare growing distant as if remembering. "I tried. Ever since I was little, I've tried to keep people from getting hurt."

Her statement gives me one hell of a pause. And even though it sounds stupid, not to mention in-fucking-sane, for a brief second I wonder if I had a friend like Sol, back then when it mattered, back then when I needed someone to tell me I shouldn't follow that man into that house, if I could have been saved.

My anger, along with that deep-rooted resentment stirs. It doesn't feel right. Not around Sol—not when we were laughing as hard as we were seconds ago. Fuck. For someone who prides himself on being able to take on anyone—to protect himself and those he loves, why would I think what I'm thinking now?

Because you're all sorts of screwed up, I remind myself. *Even with this pretty girl sitting beside you.* In truth, what if Sol was with me that day? What could she have done? She would have been a little kid—just like me. Someone he could have hurt, too. Someone he could have raped—

"Hey," she says, leaning in. Her fingers skim along my

temple, where my hair is cut so short it lays flat. "Where'd you go?"

"Nowhere," I answer, lying through my teeth.

She tilts her head. "Okay . . . for a minute there, it looked like you checked out."

I can't argue, seeing how I did. But lying to her feels wrong. So I tell her as much as I can. "What you said made me think. About things that can go wrong when you get wasted."

"Have you done things you regret when you were wasted?" The corners of her mouth lift a little when I don't answer. "I'm not judging you, Finn. I'm only asking. But you don't have to answer if you don't want to."

"All the damn time," I say before she finishes speaking. I could've lied. God knows I do it all the time, pretending everything is fine. But I don't like lying to Sol. Hell, I don't like lying to anyone. But sometimes it's like I have to, or need to—to keep people off my back or to at least help them sleep at night.

"Do you think you should stop? Drinking I mean," she adds.

"I don't know. I like beer. I like the feel of that cold bottle in my hands when I'm talking to people. It helps me relax."

"The alcohol, the buzz, or the way that bottle feels?" she questions.

I slip my arm around her shoulders and think things through. She surprises me by leaning her head against my chest as she waits for me to answer. She feels good against me. Comfortable. Like this is something we've done a hundred times.

"I think it's all of it," I admit. "The bottle itself is cold, soothing. It also gives me something to do with my hands."

"You need to do something with your hands?" she asks. She laughs when I flash her a sly grin. "It wasn't an offer," she says, lightly stroking my pecs.

"I'm not one to keep still," I admit, chuckling. "Even when I'm lying in bed, I'm texting or something. But yeah, I like the buzz, and the booze itself. I'm okay sometimes. But when

I'm not, I'm really not."

"Have you talked about it with Mason?"

"Not really," I confess. Unless you count him recommending I don't drink.

"Why?" she asks.

"It's easier to talk to you about it."

Her cheek falls against my shoulder. "But I'm incapable of helping you, Finn. I want to, but I'm not qualified yet."

"You may not have the degree, or have taken whatever test you need to take, that doesn't mean you're not helping."

She lifts her head. "I'm helping you?" she asks, sounding shocked and maybe a little hopeful.

"Yeah," I answer, my gut twisting a little when I realize exactly how much.

"Good," she says.

By the way she's looking at me, I know she wants me to kiss her again. And the way her heart is pounding against mine, I know it's going to be one damn fine kiss. Well, at least it would have been if it weren't for the scowling face peering at us from the passenger side window. "Sol . . . Is that your dad?"

She turns, jumping when she sees him. "Yes, that's him," she says, her cute face scrunching. "Sorry, I better go before he shoots you between the eyes."

By the way his glare cuts my way, I don't think she's kidding.

She slips out of my truck, shutting the door behind her. I'm supposed to speed away now, seeing how that's what any reasonable, non-wanting-to-die kind of guy does when an angry Latino father catches him trying to make-out with his daughter. So what do I do? Jump out of the truck, of course, and jog around to the other side.

I hop onto the sidewalk as Sol and her *papasito* start speaking rapidly in Spanish. "Hey," I say, causing them both to freeze.

Sol shoots me an apprehensive glance before sighing and turning to face me. Her father faces me, too, albeit in that same looming "What are you doing with my daughter" way he's supposed to.

"Finn," Sol says, pinching the bridge of her nose. "This is my father, Lino Marieles. Papi, this is Finn. Sofia's brother in law."

I hold out my hand. *"Hola, Señor Marieles. Como le va la noche?"*

Having grown up with Sofia and her family across the street from us, I picked up on enough Spanish to ace it in school and usually charm. Yeah . . . my "Hi, Mr. Marieles. How's your night going?" does jack to impress Sol's father.

He scowls at my hand as Sol mutters in Spanish, "Papi, behave."

Not only does he not behave, he crosses his thick arms and resumes his glare. I keep my grin. "He's going to hunt me down and chop me into hamburger with his machete, isn't he?" I ask Sol.

"And make it look like an accident," Lino answers for me.

It's then I lose my smile. Funny thing, Sol just laughs. She strolls up to me, clasping my elbow as she stands on her toes to give me a kiss. "Goodnight, Finn," she says.

It's just an innocent kiss, likely no big deal around most other dads with grown daughters. But this is a very traditional Latino father so I pretty much think I'm about to die.

"Let's go, Papi," she says, hooking his arm with hers when he takes a step toward me.

He surprises me by following, and not dicing me to chunks, muttering something in Spanish about making sure "they never find the body".

Her father just threatened me. I should just get in my truck and haul ass. But I can't. I watch her cross the street, grinning when she tosses me one last smile before slipping inside her house. It's that smile I hang onto. That, and her last kiss.

CHAPTER 10

Sol

I shut the door behind me. Finn can't see me, not anymore. But that doesn't stop my smile. I shrug out of my jacket, a thick one I could probably use to trek through the South Pole. It's not flattering, and it's definitely not cute. But Finn didn't seem to mind it. In fact, he thinks I'm pretty.

"Pretty." It's a sweet little word I haven't heard in a long time, and probably haven't felt in even longer. But I did tonight because *Finn* makes me feel it. The way he looks at me is something I could really get used to. So is the way he holds me.

"Your mother's upstairs," my father says, instantly erasing my smile.

"She's here?" I ask, my hands slipping away from my jacket.

"She was discharged a few hours ago."

"Oh," I respond, well aware of the disappointment lowering my tone. This is supposed to be good news. But I don't take it that way, worried she was discharged prematurely.

"How is she?" I ask.

"Stable," he answers.

He means so drugged she can't hurt us. So numb, there's nothing left of her. God, I *hate* that word.

"Do you think it's a good idea? To get involved with a boy

like that?" he asks.

I turn away from the small closet and face my father. He's leaning against the staircase wearing his uniform of choice: a white collared dress shirt and tan slacks. Sometimes his slacks are brown, olive, or even black. But the shirt is always white, ironed to precision and perfection.

As stupid as it sounds, it's seeing him in that shirt that causes the happiness Finn gave me to fade even further. My father is the foreman at the local canning factory. It doesn't sound like much, but it's a big deal to us. As an immigrant from Cuba, his first job at the factory was as a canner, barely making enough to give us a home, and food on the table. But he worked hard, stayed extra, and proved his worth until he was promoted to line supervisor, and then ultimately to his position now.

He takes his duties and his role seriously, leaving the house freshly groomed, and somehow returning the same way. My mother . . . she was the one who used to iron all his shirts. She was the one who'd kiss him goodbye. She was the one who'd hurry from the kitchen to welcome him home and draw his smile, gushing about her husband, "the big boss".

Yet she no longer does that. She hasn't in years because she can't.

But I really wish she could.

"Sol?" my father says.

I bow my head, not wanting to think about the first time my father had to iron his own shirts. He doesn't know I saw him cry. Yet I did, crying enough for both of us when I ran back to my room. "He's a nice man, Papi," I say.

"He's a fighter."

Which is one of the reasons I like Finn. He's strong. I could use some of his strength . . . especially now. "That doesn't mean he's not nice." I lift my head. "Or that he would hurt me."

"Don't lose sight of what's important," he says. "We're counting on you."

"I know," I respond. I'm counting on me, too.

We both stand there in our chosen spots, neither of us

appearing to want to move. I suppose moving means pushing on, something both of us seem almost too exhausted to do. Or maybe it's because when we do move, it's not to relax, or escape. It's to once more deal with what's happening.

"Where's Mami?" I question, realizing I've waited too long to ask.

"In our room, watching television."

I nod and start for the stairs. "I'm going out," he says. "Just for an hour."

My hand slides along the smooth surface of the banister. "Where are you going?"

"I need some air," he answers.

Again, I nod, because what else can I do? My father has never "needed some air". Even during the worst of times he internalizes his pain and simply deals with the stress. But he hasn't been dealing well lately, not since this last incident with my mother. He's mourning her. Well, at least who she was.

I suppose that makes two of us.

He's through the door before I reach the second level. I want to beg him not to go, not to leave me, knowing I'll be alone as soon as my aunt leaves. Am I afraid she'll hit me? Not really. I'm more afraid that I'll find her in the way I hate most: absent of anything that resembles my mother.

The door to my parents' room is partially open, giving me a view of a television that's almost as old as I am. There's a black and white movie playing, a Mexican classic whose name I should know, but one that escapes me. I remember watching it years ago with my parents when I was a child. But it's late, too late for movies that make me wish for better days.

I open the door slowly, like a little girl unsure she should enter, and hoping for more than I expect to find.

But I find what I expect, and because of it, my heart finishes breaking.

"Hi, Tía," I say, softly.

Apparently, it's too softly. She doesn't hear me, and she doesn't know I'm there.

My aunt was a battered woman. Although she'll deny it, I think one or more of those blows she took damaged her hearing. But it's the emotional toll the abuse took that robbed years from her life. Although only in her fifties, remorse and exhaustion deepen her wrinkles, making her appear more a great grandmother than grandmother.

"Hi, Tía," I say again.

She startles when she sees me, yet manages a small smile, a gesture I don't think her own children see from her much. But my attention doesn't stay on her, it travels to my mother where she's sitting on the bed.

My aunt perched my mom so her back rests against the old headboard fashioned from fake wood, a pillow placed behind her head to keep her comfortable, though I doubt my mother cares. She stares blankly ahead, to the right of the television screen, her short, curly hair standing on its ends. Tía probably tried to wash it, and comb it, too, by the looks of it. She meant well, but all it does is add a crazed look to my mother's appearance.

Not that she needed help with that.

"It's *Cucurrucucú Paloma*," Tía says in Spanish, motioning to the television. "One of her favorites."

I swallow the lump that's building, forcing a smile as Tía rises from the rocking chair to hug me. "Do you want me to stay with you?" she asks. "Or would you prefer time alone with your mother?"

My aunt doesn't drive. She can't leave until my father returns and takes her home. But I'm not blind to what she's asking. As much as it saddens me to find my mother this way, Tía is sad, too, and she's been with her long enough.

"I think I'd like some time alone, Tía," I answer in English.

She nods like she understands and leaves, but not without one last glance at my mother.

I slip out of my boots and slide across the bed. "Hi, Mami," I say. I take her hand, but as it lays flaccid in mine, I very much doubt she feels my touch. "I went on a date tonight with Finn O'Brien," I begin. "Remember the O'Briens—the family who lived across the street from Tía? I've known him in passing for a few years, but I'm getting to know him more now."

I turn to her, not expecting her to respond, but hoping she will anyway. "Sofia married his brother Killian," I remind her. "Finn was at their wedding. He's a really nice guy, but of course, Papi already hates him."

Again, no response.

"He makes me smile," I say, my words forming tears that blur my vision. "And laugh, too. I can't remember laughing this hard in a long time."

I sniff. "I wish you could meet him, Mami, so maybe he can make you laugh, too." The tears fall before I can stop them. But I don't turn away. She can't hear me, or see me cry, and probably doesn't even know that I'm sitting right beside her.

Yet that doesn't stop me from pleading with her. "You have to get better. This way you can meet him, okay? This way you can let me know what you think and assure Papi that he's a nice man."

By now I'm crying, remembering all those times she *could* hear me—all those times I'd beg her to lay in bed with me when she came to say goodnight—so I could talk excessively about my day, my friends, my *dreams*—remembering those times she was still my mother, and I was still her world. Because this woman, who doesn't laugh, who no longer remembers me—who can't even look me in the eye is no longer the mother I remember.

No matter how badly I need her to be.

CHAPTER 11

Finn

"Finnie—*Finn*. God damn it, wake up."

Someone with a death wish is shaking me. If the "Jesus Christ and all the fucking elves—*wake up*" comment didn't make me realize she was my sister, I might have woke up swinging.

"What?" I mutter, rubbing my eyes.

"The counseling center is on the phone, saying you missed your appointment."

"It's not until eleven," I grumble, sitting up.

"Yeah, and it's twelve now, asshole," Wren snaps.

Okay, now I'm awake. "Shit." I open my palm for her to smack the phone in my hand. "Hello?"

"Finn, it's Mason."

"Hey. Sorry—Look, I'm on my way."

"I can't take you now, I'm only calling to see if you're okay."

Or maybe to make sure I'm alive.

"This is court-ordered counseling," he begins, as if I don't already know. "And while you haven't missed an appointment until today, I don't feel we're moving in a positive direction."

"Sorry," I mutter, mostly because I realize the word has become my fucking mantra. "I slept late—weird, I didn't realize how tired I was." That's the truth. I've always had a ton of energy, and my mind is always going a mile a minute,

I'm surprised I've never needed ADD meds. If anything, unless I'm hung-over, I'm usually up by seven at the latest.

"I believe you," he says.

"That I was tired?"

He pauses, and I can almost picture him smiling with those thin lips of his. "That and that it wasn't intentional."

"Good. Cause it wasn't," I say.

"I can tell given the colorful verbiage between you and your mother," he says.

I grin at Wren who's standing in front of me with her arms crossed. "That was my sister," I say, adding to her, "He thought you were Ma."

She doesn't like the compliment and flips me off. I stay focused because Mason believing in me means a lot.

"I want you to be successful, Finn. And I want to help you get to a more positive place. Look, I don't do this often, but I'm willing to stay after hours so your missed session doesn't count against you."

I throw my legs over the side of the bed. "Okay. Thanks. When can I come in?"

"Tonight from six to seven."

"All right, I'll be there."

"Very well. But Finn, as much as I'm willing to stay, I won't wait around if you're late. Am I clear?"

In other words, don't fuck this up. "I'll be there," I assure him.

I place the phone on the side table when he disconnects, dragging my hand through my hair when I realize Wren's still standing there. "What's wrong?" I ask her.

Wren can be a mothering pain in the ass so I expect her to lay into me for missing the appointment. Instead she sits beside me, careful not to get to close. "How you doing?" she asks.

"All right," I tell her slowly, wondering what's up.

"Did you drink last night or take anything?"

I frown. "No, I'm just tired."

Her blue eyes blink back at me and her lips press tight. "Are you sick?" When I shake my head, she simply stays there, watching me.

"You're creeping me out," I tell her, because she is.

She keeps her arms crossed, turning her attention to the MMA poster I have framed on the wall. "I'm not trying to," she says.

Maybe she's not, but when she doesn't leave, and keeps sitting there, I know something isn't right. And I'm not so sure it's solely about me.

My sister's real name is Erin. She earned her nickname because my older brothers initially had trouble pronouncing her name—but it doesn't really fit her. I mean, it does because that's how I've always known her—but it doesn't because she isn't exactly the delicate little bird her nickname suggests.

She's tall for a girl, five-eight, with long lean muscles that can kick some serious ass. I know because growing up I witnessed that ass kicking more times than I can count. Once, when I was on the receiving end—the time I cut a chunk of her straight black hair off. In my defense, we were out of string and I was trying to make a kite. The other times were when she was fighting on the street. In one incident, me and Killian were jumped by a group of assholes on our way back from school. The boys left her alone, but a bigger boy came after me. Wren defended me, even though she was a lot smaller then. I didn't like her much before that moment—didn't like how she bossed me around. But that day she bled to keep me safe, proving she loved me.

I returned the favor by kicking that bastard's ass. He may have been a few years older, but he hurt my sister so I wiped the pavement with him. We've been tight ever since. "Tight" in our own way. We don't share secrets, we don't tell each how much we mean to each other. We're just still willing to bleed for each other, if that makes sense.

I nudge her with my elbow because that much I can do. "What's up?"

"Your life is shit."

I nod. "Thanks. I'm glad we had this talk."

The corners of her mouth curve just a little. "Believe it or not, I'm not done."

I fall back on my bed. "I have no doubt."

She swivels so that her dark hair swoops against her thin shoulders. "The thing is, Finnie, your life doesn't have to be shit. It's only like that because you continue to mess up."

My arm falls over to drape over my eyes. I know what she means. The thing is, it's not as easy as that. "It's one appointment, Wren. Back off, will ya?"

"But that's how everything starts with you—that's what you don't get." She pauses. "Are you listening?"

"Yeah."

She bumps my leg with her knee. "I'm serious, Finn. No more drinking, no getting high."

I drop my arm away. "I haven't been high in years. What?" I ask when all I see on her face is disappointment. "Why don't you believe me?"

"I want to, I do."

"So then why don't you?" I challenge, frowning. "I missed one fucking appointment."

"It's not just that. It's like ever since that day, a part of you has been dying."

My eyes widen. She doesn't need to tell me which day she means. She and Kill were the ones who saw me immediately afterward, the ones who realized what happened. They were the ones who took care of me, and made it as right as they could. We don't talk about "that day" ever. For her to bring it up now . . . it pisses me off. She didn't hurt that day, she didn't beg Norman to stop—

I jerk out of bed, rage searing through my body like it's burning me alive. I don't think of him—or his name. It gives him power over me, just like he had that day.

"Shut the fuck up!" I snap.

You want to know something about me, I don't talk to my sister this way—I don't talk to any woman this way. So I expect her to start screaming at me, start cursing me out. Instead her eyes soften in a way that they do those rare times I've seen her cry, adding to my already mounting fury.

"Finnie," she says, her voice breaking. "I'm sorry—"

I wrench away from her when she tries to squeeze my arm,

my feet stomping toward the bathroom. I'm in my boxers and didn't bother grabbing any clothes. With a crash, I slam the door behind me, hard enough to splinter the wood frame. I whip off my shorts and blast the water, swearing as I jump into the shower and cold water drenches my skin.

I hurry to adjust the temperature, cursing again when I snag the bottle of shampoo and drop it at my feet. I bend down to retrieve it and drop it, again, my hands shaking so badly I can't keep my hold on it. "God *damn* it!"

The water is scalding hot now, and still I shake. Not from cold. Right then I'm all rage. Right then, I'm that scared little kid taken by some evil bastard who's now burning in hell. He's dead. Norman's *dead*. The brain-injured fucker died last summer after battling pneumonia.

His death should have given me peace. It should have—I don't know—made me feel safe, free—*something*. But as crazy as it sounds all I can think is that he got off easy. All those boys he hurt before me, all those lives he destroyed—all the fear he caused, instilled, *scarred* people with, he deserved more.

For years, as sick as it sounds, I fantasized about getting him alone. More than once I envisioned myself pouring gasoline over his body, lighting a match, and watching him burn. Pneumonia? Seriously? Dying the way good, old, decent people do. It's not right, not fair. Not after what he did.

But did I ever get him alone? Did I ever take him out to that imaginary field that only exists in my mind? Did I ever light that match that cooked his body?

I didn't.

But I should have.

I wanted to more than once.

And I would have, had it been Wren he hurt.

I lower myself to the bathtub floor, bending my long legs so they fit. All those years I could have acted, I never came close. Never jumped into my ride to find him. Never tried to figure out a way to actually do it.

Norman Kessler was nothing more than a vegetable after my brother found him and made him pay. For more than a decade, he was under complete care, incapable of walking or feeding himself. He was a drooling, scrawny bastard in adult diapers, who ate his calories through a fucking straw.

Yet I was scared to death of him. Me. The same guy built like a wrecking machine who kicks ass, takes names, and who people fear. Around him I was that same terrified little kid who he hurt.

Like I said. He's the one who got off easy.

Way easier than me.

CHAPTER 12

Sol

I shouldn't be doing this, I think to myself. I think it's my voice of reason speaking. But that other part—the one who likes the way Finn is kissing my neck tells reason to shut up, that we deserve a little fun, and reminds me how sexy his tongue feels dragging along my skin.

Our lips crash against each other, his hips jerking as he fumbles to remove his seatbelt. The moment he's free, he pounces, pressing his body against mine so my back is shoved against the side door. "I have to get inside," I say, between breaths.

"Don't," he murmurs, giving my earlobe a nibble. "Come back to my place. Sleep there. I promise to keep my hands to myself."

I groan, considering he claimed he'd keep his hands to himself the first time we said goodnight—the first time I told him I had to get inside, I'm thinking short of tying him to the bed—which when it comes to Finn sounds very appealing—no way are either of us going to behave if we return to his house.

"Finn," I say when he unsnaps my bra, gasping when he tugs on my nipple.

"Yeah?" he rasps, slipping both hands beneath my shirt to play.

That rasp—the way his tone drops when he's turned on?—

how have I not had sex with him yet?

Don't call me a tramp. Please don't. I've only slept with three men. One was a guy I dated for over a year who broke my heart when he dumped me for someone else. The other two . . . well, they were idiots, too.

Finn isn't an idiot. He's sweet and, and . . . he unsnaps my jeans, slipping his hand in. I jump when he touches me in just the right spot. It's then he pulls away, slumping in his seat and breathing hard. "Too much?" he asks.

It's not. I'm ready to do more. But Sofia is waiting for me. "I have to check on my mother," I say.

My phone rings. I jump again when I see it's Sofia calling. "Hey," I say, trying to pull my shirt down, as if she can see the half-naked position I'm in.

"Hi, Sol. Are you having a good time?"

I glance over at Finn, who apparently can hear her. He laughs when I answer, "Oh, yeah. Totally."

Her small voice gathers an edge of affection. "I'll admit, I adore him," she says.

I try not to laugh when he puffs out his chest, not daring to admit that I feel the same way. A few weeks, that's all it's really been since we started seeing each other—even though I kept telling myself I should keep my distance. But I can't. Not from Finn. And truthfully, I don't want to.

We've gone out a lot; to dinner, a couple of movies, we even hit a few bars with friends. I meant to keep it casual, intended not to get too physical, and promised myself I wouldn't fall for this guy. But then the casual became a little more intense, the small petting sessions turned more passionate, and . . . who am I fooling? I totally stumbled and face-planted over Finn.

It's like I can't breathe until I see him.

We're not inseparable, not with all his training for his upcoming match—and especially not between my internship and my poor mother. But when we see each other, we make it count, and it's like we haven't been apart.

"Sol?" Sofia asks.

But Finn's already back on my side, nibbling on my neck.

"Yes?" I ask, hoping she can't tell how hard I'm fighting back a moan.

Sofia's voice falls to whisper. "My mother just arrived. She says she can spend the night. So if you're not ready to come home, you don't have to."

"What?" I say, glancing at Finn. He lifts his head, frowning. I realize he didn't hear Sofia and thinks something is wrong. Maybe it's the shock my expression carries, and maybe it's also the nervousness I suddenly feel. This is my opportunity to be alone with Finn—intimately alone—not in a car, not on Teo's couch hoping he doesn't suddenly arrive home—and not in the parking lot of his gym, those times I've managed to stop by to say hi.

He sits up, taking my hand in his. For all the touching and kissing we were doing, this gesture seems more personal, and endearing, reminding me of why Finn is so different from all the other guys I've been with. He does things like this—touches me in a way that shows me he cares. "What's wrong?" he mouths.

"Sol?" Sofia asks, again, as I shake my head. "Can you hear me okay?"

"Yes, I can—sorry," I assure her, my body warming as I say what comes next. "If Tía can stay, let her know not to wait up for me." My eyes meet Finn's. "I may not be coming home."

"Oh," she answers. "Um. Well, I didn't mean you should—that you have to . . ."

I can hear her growing flustered, rushing to probably warn me against doing what I plan to do. But my attention stays on Finn.

His eyebrows arch with surprise before lowering, his blue eyes sizzling the way they do when his hands wander.

I press the phone against my chest, trying to block the sound. I'm not sure if it works, Sofia might still be able to hear me. But right now, I don't care. "Is that okay?" I ask. "Can I stay with you tonight?"

He doesn't answer, but that grin and that dimple are answer enough. As I lift the receiver, I realize Sofia is still speaking. "I'll be okay," I assure her, when it's clear how worried she seems. "Don't worry. I'm in good hands."

It's my last remark that will have her beating her head against the nearest wall. But Sofia has always been like that: scared for others. She knows firsthand how cruel life can be. She doesn't want me to know that side of life—and its lack of mercy. But while I haven't experienced what she has, I know that cruelty isn't what I sense in Finn. When I look at him, all I see is that happiness that's long escaped me. So at least for tonight, I'm holding tight to that happiness and not letting him go.

He bends to kiss me. The contact is brief, but he draws it out to let me know how much he wants me. I hold his stare, enough to let him know I want him, too.

With one hell of sizzling grin, he shifts back to his seat, cranking the engine as he yanks his seatbelt back on. He waits for me to click my seatbelt in place before pulling away from the curve.

"Sol," Sofia says, the poor thing still hanging in. "If you need a break from your stress, you're welcome to stay with me and Killian."

I bite down on my bottom lip, trying not to laugh because she's all but begging me not to have sex with Finn. "Sofia, I'll be okay. I promise I will," I assure her.

"Hey, what happened to me being your favorite, Sofe?" Finn calls out as he drives.

At first I'm not sure if Sofia hears him, until she says, "Be careful."

She disconnects then. Although I was initially giggling like a silly kid, her final words kill my giddiness, reducing it to a distant memory. Maybe it was her tone. There was a definite sadness to it, like her heart was breaking. But why would she sound like that? Sofia likes Finn as much as she claims.

"Hey," Finn says, his hand massaging my knee. "I meant what I said, we don't have to do anything. We can stop whenever you want to."

I nod because I don't know exactly how to respond. When he says he'll stop if I tell him to, I believe him. If I didn't, I certainly wouldn't be alone with him. But again, it's been a while since I've had sex.

It's not like I couldn't *have* sex. It was there for the taking if I wanted it bad enough. I live in Philly. An invitation for sex only requires a trip to the nearest bar and a "hello" if I'm being honest. How many times did I hit the clubs with my girlfriends and have guys point-blank ask me, "Do you want to fuck?"

Finn's not asking me—well, not in *that* way. If he was, I'd be running for the hills. But he's definitely ready to do a lot more than touch me. Yet as much as I was, too—Sofia, my darling and loving Sofia—is making me doubt whether I should. Funny, considering she didn't say much. But what she said was enough, and very much sounded like a warning.

Finn slips his hand over mine, drawing my attention to our entwining fingers. My hands are slender, reminiscent of Barbie doll hands compared to Finn's. His are *huge*, his knuckles rough and calloused from hitting too many heavy bags and even more faces.

"Can I ask you something?" I say to him.

"Yeah, sure," he answers

"What's the worst you ever hurt anyone?"

It's not an easy question to ask—and probably too personal, but I can't help wanting to know. For as much pain as he inflicts in the octagon, and for as brutal as he's rumored to be, how can he hold me with such tenderness? It almost seems impossible for someone so vicious to be this gentle.

He takes a breath, using the intersection we reach almost like an excuse to keep his focus on traffic and away from me. "In the octagon?" he asks.

I tilt my head when I realize what he's saying. Finn has a rep for taking on guys outside the cage. From what I hear, he's just as fierce on streets. Yet I can't help thinking those fights are the ones he most likely regrets. I don't want to make him feel bad, that's not my intention. But I do want to know more about this man I adore.

"Yes, in the octagon," I clarify.

He loosens his grip, probably concerned about scaring me.

I give his hand a squeeze, assuring him I don't want him to let me go. He glances at me briefly, meeting my soft smile, yet this time, he doesn't return it.

"You're not going to like what I have to say," he answers quietly, rolling to a stop at a light.

My other hand covers his. "Tell me anyway."

It takes him a long moment to answer, but I stay silent and give him the time he needs. "At my first professional match, I broke my opponent's jaw."

Um. Whoa.

He waits for me to respond. When I don't he adds, "Like me, this guy had fought in a few amateur bouts. His manager or trainer—whoever he was—was moving him up slowly. Like Kill did with me. See, Kill was pushed pretty damn fast. When he lost his mentor, he thought he found a good manager in that asshole Gil. But Gil shoved him into matches Killian wasn't ready for. Some he won, but just barely. Others could have flat out fucked him up for life. So Kill wouldn't allow me to sign up for a fight on two weeks' notice—like he was duped into doing. Before each match, I get a full training camp, and because of it I'm better prepared and able to dominate more fights."

"Okay," I say, trying to understand where he's headed.

"The thing is, this guy wasn't ready like I was. We had about the same amount of experience and were supposedly evenly matched on paper. But when I stepped into the ring with him, I knew he wasn't ready for me."

I edge closer to him, wanting to erase that distance I inadvertently created. "How did you know? Did he look scared?"

"No. He thought he should be there, too. But he wasn't standing like someone prepared to take a blow. His arms were up, ready to strike, but not to protect. It's like all he knew was offense. No defense there whatsoever, even when I charged."

"So what happened?"

"I nailed him with an uppercut and a hard right. My left hand is weaker than my right—still strong, but not as sharp. I felt his jaw pop with the first strike. But after years of training, I didn't just hit him once. It's been ingrained in me that one punch follows the next, and the next after that."

So he inflicted more damage as a result. Shit. That much is clear.

"If he hadn't gone down, I probably would have hit him a few more times—because that's what you do, you keep going until you hear that bell or until the ref hauls you off." He shakes his head. "But even though I've had several fights and knew I should keep swinging, I couldn't. I knew something was wrong."

"Was he okay after?"

Finn's voice lowers in a way that tells me he's remembering. "No. He had to have his jaw wired and he never fought again. I'm assuming he realized he wasn't ready for the UFC and probably never would be."

"Did you ever talk to him about it?" Although, my brain told me to stop speaking, my mouth kept going anyway. "Sorry, that's probably a stupid question."

He pulls into a residential block, parking in front of a classic brick Colonial. "It's not stupid," he tells me.

He releases my hand and cuts the engine, both of us unsnapping our seatbelts in unison. I turn to face him, knowing he's not done speaking. He angles toward me, his arm sliding across my shoulders. "If you break down what I do," he says. "I'm basically paid to beat people up. It's a professional sport—like football—something that sells out big arenas. Except unlike football, there aren't guys running for a touchdown or trying to catch a ball."

"I know," I agree.

He smiles a little, taking a moment to stroke my cheek before continuing. "Every time I step inside that octagon, and the gate slams shut, I know my opponent is there to inflict pain and take me out. I may not like it, but I respect it, because that's the same thing I'm there to do to him. So when I hit that guy, I meant to hurt him, and I did. I earned my first professional knockout, secured my win in under thirty seconds, and propelled myself up the ranks. But Sol, I'm gonna tell you something I only told Kill at the time, I've never felt more like shit."

"Because you hurt him?"

He shakes his head. "No. Because I hurt someone weaker than me."

"Oh," I whisper. Even though this happened years ago, the guilt in his eyes is as palpable as the strength that surrounds him.

"The promoter told me afterward that my opponent had no business breathing the same air as me. He meant it as a compliment, but all I could think about—when people were rushing up to me to pat me on the back—was that I had beat up on someone that in any other situation I probably would have tried to protect."

"You couldn't have held back, though. I mean, for as unprepared as he was to face you, that didn't make him incapable of inflicting serious injury."

"No. But it took the glory out of my first knockout. For a while, I wanted to find the guy to tell him I was sorry. But Kill told me it wasn't a good idea." He shrugs. "He thought it would affect my performance in the octagon."

"Do you think it did? Even without finding him?"

"Oh, hell yeah. I was almost afraid to hurt someone." He huffed. "That changed when my next opponent cracked me hard in the skull."

"Oh! So you lost?"

Finn shakes his head. "Fuck, no. It was exactly what I needed to put me back in the game and come out swinging."

Which is why he's ranked as high as he is. I press a kiss to his lips. "How do you do it?" I ask him softly.

He cocks his chin. "Do what?"

"Hurt someone as badly as you do, but hold me in a way that I might break?"

He stiffens, that shimmer of life returning to his stare. "Because I like you." His rough knuckles pass along my cheek. "And unlike the men I face when I fight, I would never hurt you."

I mean to smile, but I can't then, so caught up by the way he enthralls me with just his voice and that to-die-for face. "I hope not," I whisper. "Because I really like you, too."

He doesn't say anything, not at first, taking in every bit of my visage as if he can't believe I like him as much as I do. He has no idea how much I think of him or how simply picturing his face lifts my spirits.

Finn is the one thing I look forward to, the one person who makes me laugh and shoves all my misery aside. Of course I don't tell him. But I want to . . . just like I want to make love to him all night.

His fingers travel down my throat to the exposed skin my blouse doesn't quite cover. "Do you want to head inside?"

"I really do," I tell him.

"Good," he whispers.

We both slip out at the same time, him reaching for my hand as we step onto the sidewalk together. The house is large, classic old Philly charm and well maintained. "It's pretty," I say, motioning forward.

"It was my Grammie's. She left it to my mother, but Ma had me and Wren move in when she decided to retire in Florida. She knew we'd take care of it." He shrugs. "I guess she was right."

He's making small talk. Finn isn't shy around girls. I've heard enough about him to know that's true. He's trying to give me space, so I don't feel pressured. But as much as I'm still a little nervous, I'm no longer afraid.

When he told how terrible he felt hurting someone weaker than him, it gave me insight to his character, and something more to admire. He's *such* a good guy. My heart literally warms being at his side.

He unlocks the door, and flicks on the light, illuminating the cherry wood floors. He shrugs out of his leather jacket. As I unbutton my coat, I take in the room around me, so captivated by the rich feel of "home", I barely feel him slip the coat from my shoulders.

Comfortable and classic-looking chocolate brown leather couches make up the family room, a dark wood and stone table at its center. To our right, French doors open to a small library, two comfortable and cushy chairs set in front of a brick fireplace, along with an antique secretary's desk near the window.

"You like to read?" I ask, motioning to the shelves that take up every inch of one wall.

He laughs. "I used to, mostly fantasy."

"Fantasy?" I question, stopping to try to make out the hardcover novels in the dimly lit room.

Again he laughs. "Harry Potter, the Dresden files—action-related fantasy. But I haven't picked up a book in forever. When I train as much as I do, I either go out for a bit or come home and crash." He leads me into the kitchen, his fingers playing with my hand as he walks. "Want something to drink?"

"Water would be great," I say, taking in the wood beam ceilings. "I always wanted to live in a house like this," I add, taking in the freshly painted plaster walls.

"Yeah? Why?"

It sounds stupid, but I tell him because it's true. "It feels like a real home."

He nods as if he knows what I mean. "It does," he agrees.

He tosses his keys on the counter as we step into the kitchen. The cabinets are stained sage green and white granite with swirls of silver make up the counters. It shouldn't work, but somehow it does, adding another degree of elegance to an already beautiful home. "Did Sofia help you decorate?"

"Damn right, she did." He hands me a bottle of water from the stainless steel fridge. "Do you think me and Wren would have been able to pick this shit out?" He cracks open a bottle of his own and downs half of it before pointing. "We were going to go with black and white—the counters, cabinets, even the tile. Sofia didn't want us to lose the classic look of the house—or however she put it, and really had to work to convince us. Hell, I'm glad she did. Wren's friend, a realtor, stopped by after we finished. Said something about doubling the value just by preserving its structure—not that we're going to sell—but it's good to know."

Finn leans against the counter, his ripped muscles bulging against his gray T-shirt. Dark jeans cover his strong legs and firm assets. But it's his face and grin that draw me closer . . . and the knowledge that his powerful body will be on top of me all night.

He frowns at my approach, noticing I've only taken a few sips of my water. "Do you want to watch T.V. or something?"

My eyes fix on his. "No."

The purr in my tone suggests I'm done talking. "Well, all right," he says, pushing off the counter.

His arm slips behind my back and his mouth lowers on mind for a kiss. He smiles against my lips before leading me out through the other side of the kitchen, down a small hall and toward the bedroom. I catch a glimpse of a bathroom at the end before we enter a large bedroom.

Dark wood furniture a few shades lighter than the floor make up his room. There's a framed MMA poster signed by Tito Ortiz near a king-sized bed with a leather headboard and a thick white comforter. A triangular rug with a pattern of white, brown, and gold squares lies parallel to the bed. It's a simple, modern décor, but still very much Finn.

He releases my hand by the door, edging back to the bed and lowering into a sitting position. "Hey," he says.

Seeing how much space he's giving me, I'm beginning to wonder if he thinks I'm a virgin. But like I mentioned, I'm not.

I answer by unbuttoning the top of my black blouse and slipping it over my head. Finn's eyes widen when my lacy mauve bra lands on the floor beside the blouse. Despite my petite stature, I'm pretty busty. And while Finn has played with my breasts, he's never actually seen them. Not like this. His reaction stirs my blush, but also an impish grin.

He likes what he sees. Hopefully he'll like the rest even more. I shut the door and lock it, stripping slowly out of the remainder of my clothes as I make my way across his bedroom.

I step between his knees, biting down on my lip as my gaze falls to the large bulge pressing against his jeans. "Hi," I murmur.

His hands glide along my curves and his smoky stare rakes

down my body, taking every inch of me in before returning to my face. "You ready for me?" he asks.

There's no hesitation. I pull his shirt off and toss it aside.

CHAPTER 13

Finn

Holy. Shit.

Sol's breasts skim over my chest when I haul her to me, her nipples stiffening as they graze across my skin. Our kiss is slow at first, but as it builds, so does my erection, pulsing hard against my jeans. I kick off my hiking boots and socks as fast as I can, flipping her onto her back even faster.

She squeals from surprise, but as I rub against her she gasps and arches her back, encouraging me to pull one of her large brown tips into my mouth to suck. A deep moan rips from her chest as she clutches me to her. But when I slip my fingers between her legs, those moans turn to grunts.

My mouth releases her nipple with a pop as I sit up, needing to see her face—needing to know she's okay with what I'm doing. Her eyelids flutter as my fingers circle her, slickening folds. "You like that, baby?" I ask.

She whimpers yet doesn't answer. Not with words. But the way her skin flushes and her hips swirl tell me everything I need to know.

My fingers move faster while my opposite hand sweeps along her belly and around her curves. Her breasts are heavy against my palms. I massage each one, feeling the soft skin bounce as she writhes, her jaw tightening when I tug and nip the centers.

Her legs fall open, giving me room and inviting me to

explore. I take my time, learning what she likes. But it doesn't take long for her to succumb.

She cranes her neck. "I'm going to come," she rasps, her fingernails digging into my comforter.

Those are the words I've been waiting to hear. I slide two fingers in deep and circle, my skin burning as I watch her lose control.

I'm breathing like I've been running for miles, so turned on by how hot I'm making her—how her body trembles beneath *my* touch, *my* control, it's all I can do not to pound into her. But for now, this is all about her, and I'm going to make sure she damn well never forgets me.

"*Finn*," she says, barely getting my name out before her legs kick out, her body bouncing hard against the bed.

I've given plenty of women orgasms, but to see someone like Sol, who's so sweet, so angelic lose it like this—*fuck*—that's all I want to do to her. I want her so bad my erection is killing me right now. But instead I keep going, prolonging the first and inciting another.

I slow my movements, easing her down as the next orgasm fades. Her small body relaxes gradually, her back lowering to the mattress from its high arc. But her breath . . . those are *way* out of control.

Her hair fans out along my bed, her nipples are taut, and her eyes are heavy with lust as she takes me in. I crawl on top of her, tucking my hand behind her back and lifting her to me to kiss.

For all I want to spread her legs open and wrap them around me, my kissing is slow and lazy, like I'm not in a rush, ignoring the dense bulge ready to tear through my jeans, and once more making it all about her. She has regrets, I know she does. I'm not about to be one of them.

Her hands travel across the hard planes of my body as her tongue swirls mine. But when her fingers make quick work of unsnapping my jeans and wrenching them down, I know our time has come.

I pull away, throwing open the drawer to my nightstand and reaching for a condom. I tear the wrapper open with my teeth while I shove out of my boxers. I want to keep touching her, hell, I never want to stop.

Before I can slide the condom in place, Sol's thin arms wrap around my shoulders. I freeze, thinking she's going to tell me she's not ready—that she changed her mind . . . until she falls to her knees and takes me deep into her mouth. I jerk at her first pull, and her second, her lips forming a seal and creating an intense suction. Each pass takes me further in, making me harder and tightening the muscles along my groin.

I only wish I could relax and enjoy it. But I can't.

I never could.

She's not the first girl to do this. I've lost count of how many women have gone down on me. Most of the time, I clamp down and bear it—wait till they get tired or bored so we can get down to business and do what I really want. But with Sol, I can't zone out—not with the passion behind her motions, and not with how her delicate hands pass along the bulging muscles of my thighs to join her mouth to tease and play.

I tear my stare away from where her head moves up and down on my lap. She's going deeper, her hands working me as hard as those lips. I focus on the ceiling, trying to force myself to get through this. I'm a man—God damn it. I'm supposed to want and crave this shit.

The cords of my neck strain as I struggle to put my mind elsewhere. Instead I jerk again, and again. My body shudders as she releases me and scrambles to her feet. "Hey," she says, her hands gliding across my shoulders.

It takes me a moment to meet her face, but when I do, I fucking hate what I see. All the lust I riled is gone from her features, leaving only worry, confusion, and what resembles fear. She's at a loss. But so am I.

"Am I hurting you?" she asks.

I should say yes, to stop her questions and to keep her from doing it again. But I don't want to put my baggage on her.

"No," I gasp, barely able to speak.

"Then what's wrong?" she asks, stroking the side of my face.

I angle my chin away, wondering what's happening. It felt good, damn it. No, s*he* felt good. "I forgot I have to get up early tomorrow," I tell her. "I should take you home."

Her eyes widen as her attention falls back on my lap. I can't blame her. I'm as hard as a chimney—and I should be seeing how hot she made me. But right now, I can't come. No matter what we do, I won't be able to. Not with her knowing there's something wrong with me.

"I . . . I don't understand," she says, pulling her hands away from me. "Did I do something wrong?"

"No," I bite out, unable to look her. I try to put some space between us, swearing when I lift my hips and agony rips through my groin. Son of a bitch, no way can I drive her home like this. "Take my truck."

"What?"

The pain I'm feeling sharpens my tone. "The keys are on the kitchen counter. Take my keys, take my truck. I'll come by for it in the morning."

"I don't understand," she says again.

I don't have to look at her to know she's upset. I hear it in her voice. She wants and deserves an explanation. But I can't explain what I don't understand myself. I open my mouth to try—Christ above, I owe her that. Yet all I do is end up snapping my jaw shut.

"Finn . . . please talk to me," she begs.

"Just go, all right?" I say, trying to keep my voice soft and doing a shitty job. "Call me when you get there so I know you're safe."

I expect her anger, or at the very least some serious name calling. But, this is Sol—the same woman who meets me with a wide smile and who fits too perfectly tucked against my shoulder. So instead of shouting, arguing, or demanding an explanation, things that would make me feel even shittier, she backs away in silence.

Which is way worse than anything she could have said or done.

I don't watch her dress, don't bother sneaking in one last look at her bare skin; don't try to assure her that it's me, not her. Hell, I don't even bother to say goodbye. All I do is stare at the door long after she shuts it, knowing I'm more fucked up than I ever could have imagined.

And I'm only getting worse.

CHAPTER 14

Finn

"How was your weekend?" Mason asks, exactly the way he does every time we meet.

My counselor—the one that court appointed therapist thought would be a great fit for me—sits across from me in tweed (I shit you not) pants. He has his legs crossed as always, causing the tassels on his shiny leather shoes to dangle to the side. The last person besides Mason I saw wearing tassels was a stripper, and hers didn't exactly dangle from her feet.

"All right," I answer, because it's already ten minutes into our session and I haven't said jack.

"Just all right?" he asks.

No. It sucked balls. Sol left, and she won't talk to me. She didn't even text me to say she arrived home safe. Instead I received a text from Sofia saying she'd driven my truck back to her and Kill's place. No, that didn't raise suspicion or anything. No, that didn't cause Kill to rip into me. Oh, wait—it did.

"What happened?" Kill yelled. Wren gave me a lift to his house, and while she guessed something was up, she didn't expect Kill to be so pissed, just like she didn't expect to be shoving her way between us.

Kill doesn't lose his temper often, but when he does he really loses it. "I asked you a God damn question," he hollered when I didn't respond. "What happened between you and Sol?"

"None of your fucking business," I fired back.

My comment only pissed him off further. "She's my wife's cousin, Finnie. Not someone you can whore around with."

"I said, it's none of your *fucking business*," I repeated, shoving my face an inch from his. Sofia's cousin or not, what happened between me and Sol is private. No way am I disrespecting her.

Kill knows I'd never force a woman to do something she wasn't ready for. But I'll admit, it doesn't look good on my end. Sol was upset when she left, Sofia probably saw as much. They don't know what went on between us and I think it scares them, especially given how I've been lately. But no matter how tight me and Kill are, I couldn't exactly tell him she left because I couldn't have sex with her, even though that's exactly what happened.

I couldn't have sex with Sol, I repeat in my head, barely believing it myself. I couldn't have sex with this hot woman who I can't stop thinking about, who gets me so worked up, I want to tear her clothes off with my teeth. *Christ, what's wrong with me?*

"You seem troubled," Mason says, tilting his head to the side as he scrutinizes me. "If there's something you want to discuss, I'd like to help if I can."

"Would you?" I ask in a way that would make most men back away from me.

Mason smiles softly, like I'm not capable of bashing his face in . . . probably because it's true. Despite that I'm royally pissed, like I said, I don't hurt those who are weaker than me.

"I would," he answers.

"I got some head over the weekend," I tell him. There, he wants to know something about me, there it is.

If I'm expecting a big reaction—slacking jaw, widening eyes, even a gasp—it doesn't happen. Don't get me wrong, my response gives him the barest pause, but not much more than that. If anything, he's probably shocked I finally said something worth scribbling in his notes. "Did it feel good?"

he asks.

"What?" I respond like a dumbass.

Okay, maybe I'm the one who ends up being shocked. It's a simple question, one any guy should be able to answer without much thought, and a cocky smile. But it's the way that he asks that throws me off—not like how guys in a locker room would ask—but in the same manner I'd ask if it's going to snow.

"I asked you if it felt good," he repeats. "You've mentioned there are times you feel numb, as if you're disconnected from the world."

I didn't use those exact words, but it's more or less the one thing I've managed to tell him during this whole time we've been meeting. "That's right," I say.

"So did it feel good?" he asks. "Were you able to derive pleasure from it?"

"It felt . . . great," I say, thinking back.

"So you successfully felt something during the act? That numbness you often experience failed to manifest, correct?"

I nod, but again that cocky grin that should form based on the topic doesn't appear. My expression and tone remain tight. With Sol, *damn*, I always feel. That disconnect he mentioned doesn't happen when she's around. I thought it was because she's a woman I'm hot for, but based on what Doc Mason is saying, I can't be positive that's all it is.

"I felt everything," I confess.

"What about the other piece?" At my frown he explains. "You claim it's something that gave you pleasure, but was it a pleasurable experience?"

It's then I realize where he's going, and what he's asking, and I swear it's like a freight train hits me at the same time the light bulb goes off. "No. I wanted it to stop."

He nods as if he'd anticipated my response. "Why do you think that is, Finn?" When I don't answer he asks. "Do you think it was your partner?"

"No, S—"

I cut myself off when I almost say her name, remembering she works here and could get in a shit storm of trouble for messing around with a client. "Sal's awesome," I say. "Among the best people I know."

"Sal?" he asks, like he doesn't believe me.

"Yeah, Sal," I say. "It's short for Sal . . .veeno . . . ah."

"Salveenoa?"

Shit. "It's French," I add, because I haven't lied enough.

"Very well," Mason says, clearly humoring me. "Is Salveenoa a man or a woman?"

"A woman. I'm not into men." I shake out a hand. "No offense."

The corners of his mouth lift. "No offense taken, Finn," he assures me.

He considers me a moment. "So you like Sal, I take it."

"I like her a lot," I say.

"Do you trust her?"

"I guess," I answer. "I mean, we haven't been together long. I'm not exactly giving her my bank account information or anything, but yeah, I trust her."

"Do you trust her not to hurt you physically?"

"Like punch me?" I ask. "She's not the type to take a swing at me just because I annoy her." I huff. "Not like psycho Chelsea, my ex. Shit, she hurled a toaster at me once."

Mason cuts me off by lifting his hand. "We'll get back to Chelsea. When I ask if she'd harm you physically, I mean during the act."

"When she was going down on me?" I ask. At his nod I say, "No, she wouldn't bite me or anything crazy—at least not on purpose. But I do have a big penis so she did accidently scrape me with her teeth."

"That's not what I mean," he clarifies. "Let's talk about what was happening when she was giving you pleasure. Were you able to watch her?"

I freeze because me and Mason here are going someplace I hadn't planned on when I first plopped down on this leather couch. I can say yes, and switch subjects. I can tell him I'm done talking and we would be. But this thing has been eating me alive. So I stop playing and give it to him straight, even though everything male about me calls me a pussy for doing it. "No."

"Did you encourage her movements or motions?"

Again I say, "No."

He nods like we're getting somewhere, even though I'm not exactly sure where the hell we are. "Has it always been this way for you when it comes to oral sex?" he questions.

Damn it, here we go. "In a way, but in another way it was a lot worse this time."

For a few beats we just watch each other, both of us waiting for the other to say more, and me expecting him to tell me I'm screwed in the head for feeling what I'm feeling. Instead he asks, "Tell me, what you usually do during oral sex?"

"When I give it or receive it?" Again it's like we're talking about the stupid weather.

Mason thinks about it. "How about when you give it?"

"It's not something I usually do," I admit.

"Why?" he asks.

I don't know what's up with me. I want to tell him, but it's like I can't answer.

"Is it an act you don't enjoy performing?" he offers.

It's probably TMI, but I tell him anyway. "It's actually something I love doing, but I don't do it often."

"Why?" he questions again.

I give it some thought. Who am I kidding? I give it a lot of thought, recalling that fantasy I had about Sol—the one I rubbed off to after she left—the one where I'm spreading her legs wide and burying my face against her.

I drag my hand through my hair, pulling my head out from between her thighs and back into reality before I pop some serious wood. "The times I've done it, it's always been with a woman I've been with for a while, someone who I know is clean and who isn't going to give me an STI."

"So when you choose to perform, it's with someone you feel safe performing it on."

I should just nod and move on. But if I do, it's like I might miss something I'm failing to see. "It's not only a safety thing. It's more like if I go down on her, then she'll feel like she *has* to go down on me to return the favor."

"So this goes back to your aversion to receiving oral sex."

"I'm not opposed to it," I tell him, frowning. "Like I said, it feels good. It's just . . . Hell, I don't know what I'm trying to say here."

He leans back, giving me time to gather my thoughts to say more. But I can't seem to, and he picks up on it. "From what I'm hearing, Finn, you enjoy the sensation, but you're incapable of enjoying the act."

I nod despite the tension straining the muscles along my neck and shoulders. "Have you ever achieved orgasm from oral sex?" he asks.

"Never," I admit. It's then I say a lot more than I've ever said to anyone. "I can't come like that. It gets me hard, and keeps me hard, but the tension it causes makes it uncomfortable."

"Do you tell your partner as much, or ask her to stop?"

I shake my head, staring at the gray carpet that makes up his large office. "No, I just let her do it."

"Why?" he asks. "If it's something you'd rather not do, why do it at all?"

I lift my head, despite how I want to turn away. "Because I'm supposed to. It's part of foreplay, expected, you know? I'm supposed to want it and enjoy it."

"But you can't," he reiterates.

"No," I admit.

"How do you achieve release?"

I raise my brows. "Is this relevant?"

His expression is relaxed yet somehow serious. "I believe it is."

"By fucking a woman," I tell him point blank.

"When you say 'by fucking a woman' are you doing all the work?" He holds out a hand when I cock my head. "Are you the dominant party, the one who takes control?" he explains.

"It's consensual," I insist. "I've never forced anyone."

He smiles in that metro-sexual way of his. "I'm not accusing you of overpowering someone through sex, Finn. You've never given me any reason to believe it's in your nature. But when you do have sex with a woman, is it in positions where you're on top?"

"No," I say slowly. "I've fucked women standing up, and against the wall, on top of furniture, in the shower—you know, the usual."

I'm not making this up, or trying to impress him. Being a top ranking MMA fighter, women are all over me. He stays calm, recognizing I'm not bragging, his demeanor split between unaffected and concern.

"Take a closer look at these positions," he says. "*You're* the one holding them. *You're* the one imposing your muscle. It's *your* strength and power you're demonstrating."

Again there's that freight train plowing into me. Holy shit. He's right.

"Tell me, Finn," he says. "Have you ever achieved orgasm when the woman has been the one in control, on top of you, masturbating you, anything?"

I don't know how long it takes me to answer, my mind digging through my memories, trying to find one that will disprove his beliefs. But I can't. "No," I answer.

"Then I think we're onto something here," he says.

I think he's right.

"Oral sex is more complex than people realize," he begins. "It's perceived that men who receive it are the ones in control, because it's about them, and how much they're getting out of it. However, most fail to see that it's the person giving it who's actually in control. She's the one capturing that man at his most vulnerable with his most masculine and susceptible organs within her grasp."

"You're saying I don't like to be vulnerable," I bite out.

He doesn't say anything. But he doesn't have to. I already know he's right. "Is that why I don't enjoy it like I should, I'm afraid to be vulnerable?"

"Exposing yourself in such a way—when you feel compelled to stay in control during sex— doesn't permit the pleasure the act can bring or allow the release that can come. But why do you think that is, where does this all stem from?"

As much as he's opened my eyes, this isn't a question I'm

prepared to answer. Not yet.

"So then why was it worse with Sal?"

He doesn't miss how I skipped over his question, but answers me anyway. "Because I think you like her more than you were prepared to, and more than you're allowing yourself to believe." He waits then asks, "Have you ever been in a serious relationship?"

My mind wanders back to "bat-shit crazy Chelsea", "I'm a psycho and I own it Nancy", and "I'm sorry I cheated on you, but you were at the gym and I was horny Lucille". "No. Most of the women I've been with longer than a handful of times end up being crazy, skanks, or both."

"But Salveenoa isn't like that?"

"Who—oh, yeah. No, Sal's not like them."

He smiles. "Then what is she like?"

Beautiful, funny, kind. Yeah, and didn't I fuck that all up. "She's a nice girl," I answer. "Smart and . . . I don't know, she's different is all."

"And you like her." He's not really asking, more like interpreting what I'm trying to play down.

I rub my hands together, thinking about how shitty I've felt since she left. "Yeah, I do."

"Finn," he says, drawing my attention back to his face and away from the floor. "From what you've said, and based on how this experience with Sal has affected you, I think you want to be able to trust her in a way that's different and more personal than the other women you've been intimate with. I think it means more to you, that you enjoy sex with her."

"You're saying I want her to make me come when she's blowing me?" I ask.

"That's one way to put it," he agrees.

"But shouldn't it be easier with her instead of harder—if what you say is true?"

"I don't think so. Correct me if I'm wrong, but those other women you've had somewhat loose relationships with, they weren't women you completely trusted, correct?"

"Oh, hell no," I say, shuddering.

"So during times they performed oral sex, it was easier for

you to detach yourself, to put up with what they were doing—likely by ignoring them. But with Sal, you're already more attached, you already feel more toward her, thus you're going feel more during the act—both the pleasure, and the vulnerability you don't enjoy nor want to feel."

"So how do I fix that?" I ask.

"You tell her," he says like it's that easy.

"If I tell her I don't like head she's going to think there's something wrong with me."

Good ol' Mason doesn't even try to deny it. "Perhaps, seeing how men are expected to enjoy it and long for it as you pointed out. But Finn, relationships—those that are more serious— require risks. You need to ask yourself if this young woman is worth taking the risk . . ."

CHAPTER 15

Sol

Damn it.

I hurry to pick up the contents of my spilled purse from the floor, then shove my iPad it into my already packed bag. Dr. Harte's door always sticks so I have to pull on it when I lock it. I've always managed to hang onto my belongings before. Not today.

I rush down the hall, anxious to leave. Three hours, that's how long it took me to catch up on my reports. If I didn't know Finn was meeting with Mason I'd be Beyoncé strutting my way out the door, happy I finished my work. Instead I'm all but stumbling out of here with what remains of my pride.

After four days, I should feel less humiliated, shouldn't I? That dark cloud with thunder and lightning that followed me all the way back to my place after leaving Finn's house should be gone and nothing, but a distant memory, correct?

No. Not at all. Those stupid bolts still strike. It's not just the embarrassment that's been slapping me around—and believe me, that's bad enough. Finn hurt me, totally and completely crushed me. He was that one ray of light I looked forward to. The one who caused all my silly grins and giggles.

He was also the one who rocked my world. The way he touched me . . . Oh, my God. I lost total control, thrashing with each orgasm he gave me.

I thought he liked me. It's what he claimed. And I believed

him.

Until he kicked me out of his house.

"Call me when you get home," he told me.

No fucking way, I didn't say.

As it was, I cried when I finally collapsed my bed, wondering what I did wrong. It's not like I get naked in front of just anyone. But I did with Finn because I wanted to feel close to him. And he wanted to feel close to me, too.

Or so I thought.

Every time I reason he simply didn't want me, I remember how hard I made him by standing in front of him naked. But then I'm reminded of how *uncomfortable* he seemed when I touched him.

So even though it's been days since that horrible night, I'm still tempted to crawl into the nearest hole and die. But there's no hole, and there's still life, so for now here I am bolting out into the main hall as fast as I can.

I step into the elevator, sighing with relief as I punch the button to the lobby. Yet my relief turns to panic when I hear steps stomping quickly forward and Mason calling, "Hold the door please!"

I can't hit the button to shut the doors fast enough. But Mason must have been a ninja in his former life because he's suddenly there, his hand shooting out, catching the doors before they can finish closing.

Oh, and look . . . Finn is right behind him.

"Hello," Mason says when he sees that it's me.

"Hi," I spit out, averting my attention away from where Finn is standing frozen in front of us.

I edge back and to the corner, my face burning hot enough to set off the nearest smoke detector when Finn slips inside. I almost expect him to stay in the front, or march to the opposite corner—as in keep his distance the hell away from me. Instead he positions himself beside me, his back falling against the wall as he crosses his arms. "Hey," he says.

Mason turns around, smiling politely. "Finn this is my intern Sol—"

His smile abruptly fades, his attention bouncing between

my heated face and Finn's. There are people who can pull off poker faces and then there's us. Finn's normally fair skin is red from his neck to his forehead. Although my skin's olive, my blush is as bright as a woman kicked out of a man's pad after blowing him, because hey, that's exactly what went down.

Mason turns back to the front of the elevator, his head falling forward as he pinches the bridge of his nose. Dear. God. What did Finn tell my boss about me?

"I take it you know each other?" he says, dropping his hand away.

"Um," I say at the same time Finn says, "Ah."

Freaking geniuses, that's what we are.

The five levels we have to travel are the longest of my life. I should tell Mason we've known each other a few years, and that my cousin is married to his brother—something! But by now, it's so obvious we've seen each other naked, it's all I can do not to climb through the vent and make my escape.

The elevator dings open at the bottom and Mason steps out. "Goodbye," he says, going toward the parking lot on the left, while I shoot to the right.

"Sol, wait," Finn calls out.

Of course, I don't. As soon as I'm through the double doors I take off in a sprint.

Finn, the MMA trained badass he is, keeps up in a steady jog. He doesn't say anything, simply running beside me like he has all the time in the world. When it's clear he's not going to allow me to leave, I ground to a stop, whirling to face him.

"Did you tell Mason about us? About what happened Saturday night?"

He shoves his hands into his black biker jacket and glances around. "No?" he offers, like he's not sure what the right answer is.

My stomach skitters down to cower behind my uterus. "Did you tell him what I did to you? About . . ." I can't even get the words out. But as I catch Finn's expression, and all the guilt marching across it, I know I don't have to ask. Everything I wanted to know and didn't want him to say is right there. I clench my fists, trying to beat back the sting his betrayal causes. "I can't believe you'd do that to me."

I try to walk away, but Finn clasps my elbow, holding me in place. "Sol, wait. It's not like that. I didn't tell him it was you. I told him it was someone else."

I glance at the way he's holding me, as if what happened between us didn't happen. But I know better, and because of it, what I have to say causes my voice to tremble. "But he knows it's me," I point out. "I can tell by the way he reacted."

"Don't you mean by the way *we* reacted?" His fingers slide down my arm to link with my hand, the motion so intimate, it's more like he's kissing me than simply stroking my skin.

"It's hard not to react considering what happened." I swallow hard. "I'm not exactly made of stone."

He pulls me toward him, grasping my other hand. "I know you're not, beautiful."

"Don't call me that," I say, averting my gaze.

"Why?" he murmurs. "It's what you are."

I lift my chin, wanting to wrench away and yell at him. After all, he deserves that and possibly a kick to the balls. Not only did he humiliate me in his home, but then he embarrassed me at work. But as my face meets his, I don't see that idiot who told me to go home—the one who made me cry and who spilled the dirty details to my boss. I see Finn, his soft stare meeting mine and that gorgeous face that reveals both his hardness and his innocence.

This sucks. I've spent the last few days trying to convince myself he's not who I need, and not worth my time. But now, the way he takes me in, I'm not so sure. Puppy dog eyes aside, I refuse to swoon. He owes me an apology.

"I'm sorry," he says, his tone something I feel down to my bones.

I bite my lip. Okay . . . he may have apologized, but it's not enough. He owes me an explanation. "Why did you tell Mason about what happened between us?"

Finn tightens his jaw. When it becomes clear he isn't going to answer, I pull away and start walking toward my car. He trails me behind me, matching my slow pace, but keeping quiet.

I unlock my car, sighing when he leans against the rear door and crosses his arms. "I wasn't bragging," he says, staring ahead and onto the main road. "Back there, when I told Mason what happened between us, I didn't tell him what I did to make me look good."

"All right," I say, glancing his way. "Because you didn't."

He winces like I hurt him, but he's not the only one in pain. "I really liked you," I confess, my words heavy with emotion I wish I could hold back. "You didn't have to treat me this way."

He angles his chin to meet me square in the eyes. "I didn't mean to treat you anyway but good," he says.

"I wish I could believe you," I respond, reaching for the car door. "But I can't."

"Wait," he says. He mutters a curse, turning away from me briefly. "Look, what happened between us was messed up."

"Thanks," I mumble.

"Not what you did," he adds quickly. "And not how you did it."

I almost expect that grin when I glance up at him, but it's noticeably absent. Instead shadows darken his face as the sunlight creeps behind the distant buildings and the February chill gathers around us. "There're lots of reasons I'm seeing Mason," he says. "Like I've told you, I have a lot of rage—anger that sets me off that I can't control. But I also have a lot of numbness . . . numbness I don't feel around you."

The rage I did know about, not only because he told me, but primarily because of his chosen career. Boxers, MMA fighters, people who get paid to knock someone out, don't just fight because it's something they're good at. There's always more to it: a history of pain, some past trauma. I don't know much about Finn's childhood. But he's mentioned his absentee father who cheated on his mother, so I know enough to assume it wasn't ideal. Recognizing as much should scare me, yet it never has. That numbness, however, does scare me.

"When you say you feel numb, what do you mean?"

He shrugs, kicking at bits of remaining salt littering the lot. "It's hard explain. I sort of check out. My mind's still there, but my body isn't. It's like if someone were to come up to me and stab me in the gut, I'm not so sure I'd feel it, at least not as much as I should. The initial sharpness of that knife going in might be there, but the twist and burn would likely fade away."

My mouth falls open as the power of his words dig in. Everything he says should have me stepping further away. This is a man who's deeply hurt. So then why is it taking me everything not to throw my arms around him?

He frowns as he looks up to where a crowd of young men have started to gather at the corner, motioning in our direction.

"Check her out," one of the bigger ones says.

"Get in the car," Finn tells me, as the entire group looks our way.

I do as he asks and lock the door, quickly starting the engine. It's not a bad area since we're outside of the city, but teens sometimes do stupid things and it's best not to wait around for them to act on their stupidity.

Finn, being street, doesn't rush to the other side, even after I hurry to unlock the passenger door. He pushes off the car and walks in slow careful strides toward one of the older teens when he leaves the group and treads in our direction. Another young man follows behind him, but the way the remaining few exchange glances, they aren't far behind.

"You have a problem with me?" Finn asks, meeting the leader square in the face.

The command in his voice freezes them in place, but Finn doesn't wait for them to change their minds and continues advancing. The teens know they're in trouble, and begin to back away fast.

It's only then Finn stops. He keeps his eye on the group, returning to my car and slipping inside only after they disappear around the corner.

When you're a city kid, you learn real fast who's just talking to talk and who has the goods to back it up. Thank you baby Jesus in the manger playing with his toes, those kids knew enough to back away.

I shift into gear and drive around the building. "Where are you parked?" I ask, trying to keep my motions steady.

"Next building, rear lot. There wasn't an open spot on this side when I arrived." His body is relaxed, but I know he remains on edge and it's not solely because of those dumb kids.

"You were saying you don't feel numb around me," I remind him, knowing I can't let something so serious go and that we're almost out of time. "Is that a good thing?"

"Very good," he says, placing his hand on my thigh.

The movement is light, innocent, avoiding any intimate parts, yet so sexually charged, it hitches my breath. However, I'm Latina by heritage and Philly by nature. So despite his panty-dropping performance back there, and the way his light strokes make my girl parts zing, I lift his hand and fling it away.

"You don't get to touch me this way," I tell him. "Not after the way you treated me."

"All right," he says.

"All right?" I ask, my brakes squeaking to a stop in front of his truck. "Is that all you have to say?"

And there's that dimple. "I won't touch you if you don't want me to. But that doesn't mean I don't want to." The corner of his mouth tilts. "And maybe kiss you, too."

I set my car in park and sigh. "Finn, what are you trying to do to me?"

"I'm just trying to tell you I like you, Sol."

"Then why did you push me away when I—" I can't even bring myself to say what I did. "I don't like games," I tell him, wanting to sound stronger than I feel.

"So you don't want to hear it's me, not you?" he offers.

If he means to make me smile and ease the tension, he failed. "Only if it really is you," I say, the sadness in my voice so evident, I know I can't mask it.

"It is, baby," he says, leaning in. He lifts his hand to caress my face, but then pulls away as if remembering he's not supposed to touch me. He slumps back in his seat, or at least he tries to, but the muscles along his shoulders remain rigid. "I liked what you were doing, it felt really damn good."

I don't typically talk about sex and foreplay with the men I've had sex and foreplay with. It's something that simply happens, and then becomes this unspoken fact after all is said and done. But as young as we are, we are adults, so it's time to step up and behave like one.

When I speak, I mean to keep my voice firm, but my insecurities from that night spill into it, reducing it to a whisper. "That's not what it seemed like. You kept jumping, like I was hurting you. But when I tried to be less aggressive it didn't seem to help."

Finn threads his hand through his hair, as if in angry or frustrated or maybe both, but again he doesn't say anything. Doesn't he realize what it's taking me to discuss such a personal moment so openly and honestly?

"I need to go home," I start to say, but he cuts me off.

"I liked what you were doing," he repeats. "But I couldn't enjoy it. Not with you."

"What do you mean—" My words cut off and so does my breathing. *Not with me,* his voice repeats in my head. "You're . . . *gay?*"

Of course he's gay. Of course. All the effin' good ones are always gay.

Finn turns his head slowly my way. "Is that what you think?" he asks, surprising me by grinning. "After how I played with you and made you come, you really think I'm gay?"

My face warms, the shimmer in his stare mimicking the one when his fingers disappeared inside me. "You're not?" I ask, or should I say, more like beg him not to be. Because damn it all, as pissed as I am, I still want him.

"No, I'm not gay," he murmurs, his blue irises smoking enough to fog my windows. "If I was, I wouldn't want to go down on you as bad as I do."

My heart stops beating. Stops. Just like that. Until the possibilities of what he says sends it speeding ahead. "Are you bi?" I squeak.

Oh, man, and there's that heat surging between us again, tightening all my important parts. "Not even a little bit," he answers, his voice heavy and low.

Okay. While I admit I now have hope, and am more than a little horny, that doesn't mean I'm any less confused. "Then why did it seem like you needed to get away from me?"

"Because I did," he admits. He rubs his face hard. "Look, this isn't easy for me to talk about, especially with you."

"All right," I begin, only for him to cut me off again.

"But I want to. I want to make it right."

That's what he seems to insist, but he takes his time to explain. "When you had me in your mouth, I felt the heat from your body, your tongue, and how hard you were working me."

Well, we're just putting it all out there, aren't we? My body warms as I remember, causing me to involuntarily shudder with desire. But it's the sadness trailing along his form that clutches me hard and doesn't let go. "That's not a good thing. Is it?" I ask.

As his features tighten further, I realize it's not, but to hear it is something entirely different. "I usually zone out when it happens, but I couldn't zone out with you." He shrugs. "That's why I told Mason. Like I said, I wasn't bragging. I'm just trying to figure this shit out, you feel me?"

Actually, I do. The frustrated almost-girlfriend in me eases away, allowing the grad student forward. It doesn't seem fair that you can't be your own patient, especially when it matters. But while I couldn't be there for me, I can be here for Finn. "Is this a control thing?" I ask. "Something you need to feel when you're intimate with someone?"

"Yeah."

"Every time?" I question.

At his nod, I try not to think what this stems from, but I do. I try not let that awful feeling digging its way into my chest scrape against my heart, but it does. I try to beat back the nausea and fear. Regardless, it all comes. Someone who needs to feel in control all the time is someone who has suffered severe abuse, sometimes physical, but the majority of times—especially given the circumstances—it's sexual.

Cold sweat pours down my spine. Someone hurt Finn. Someone . . . *raped* him.

"Hey," he says, his hands cupping my face. "You okay? You don't look good."

I don't need a mirror to know he's right. But it's my forming tears that clue him in that I know what happened. His hands fall away from me, a look of horror finding its way into his blanching features.

"I'm sorry," I say, my voice cracking.

His chest rises and falls quickly. He knows what I'm saying, it's that obvious. "I'm so sorry," I repeat.

He wrenches away from me, throwing the door open and placing a foot out. "Finn," I say. "Please don't go."

He freezes in place, but he won't look at me, his voice as rough as crumbling granite. "Don't," he says. "Don't you fucking pity me."

"I'm not," I say. "I'm only sorry about what happened."

Now is not the time to ask him for specifics. But it is a time for forgiveness. "Can we start over? You and me, can we try again?"

For a long moment he doesn't respond, but when he does his voice lowers in anger. "You still want me? Even now that you know what happened to me?" He huffs when I don't answer. "Don't pretend like you don't know. I saw the way you looked at me."

"I'm upset, and angry, and disgusted," I admit, not missing how rigid he becomes at my words. "But only because I hate what happened to you, and it breaks my heart that you hurt so much because of it."

I unsnap my seatbelt, edging as close as I can to him. But when I smooth my hand along his back, I realize how much I've missed him.

He bows his head, his hands balling into fists so tight they shake. He's losing control, I know he is. Without meaning to, I've wounded his pride. "Kiss me," I whisper.

He raises his head slightly, the muscles along his spine

feeling more like stone than flesh. "Don't you feel sorry for me," he rasps.

"I don't," I repeat, surprised by how husky my voice becomes as I tell him the truth. "I just really need you to kiss me right now."

I'm not ready for his speed, or how quickly he lunges at me, gluing his body to mine. Those lips . . . those I'm ready for. Just as I'm ready for the way his arms pull me closer.

I didn't fully believe he wanted me as much as he claimed. But as his mouth devours mine, all those insecurities that have kept me up at night disappear, leaving me and Finn, and reminding me how much our bodies crave each other.

His lips and tongue move fast. It should be an awkward kiss based on our position and how aggressively he charges. Yet it's not, the glide of his hands through my hair making it sweet, steamy, romantic, stirring my moans and making him hard.

His erection jabs me in the belly as he yanks my shirt up. My head lolls to the side, sliding against the cool glass of my window as Finn nibbles my throat. I don't want him to stop. But he does.

"We can't stay here," he says, wrenching away from me and falling back into his seat.

Like some reckless teen, I'm about to say no one can see us, point out that this office building emptied out hours ago and that my car and his are the only ones that remain. Instead my inner adult reminds me we're in public—and wasn't I just bitching about being embarrassed?

"All right," I say.

Finn shakes his head as if I missed something he's trying to tell me. "Those kids are too close. It's not a bad area, but it's dark." He looks at me then. "Will you come back with me? To my place?"

I want to answer yes, but I can't. "Not tonight. I have to stay with my mother. She's not—I can't leave her unattended," I add quickly. I glance at the clock on my dash, groaning when I realize what time it is. "I have to get back," I say, my voice growing quiet.

"Okay," he says. "I'll follow you home."

"You don't have to."

"Yeah, I do," he responds in a way that tells me there's no point in arguing. "I need to make sure you stay safe."

"All right."

Finn doesn't say anything more. He simply slips out of my car and shuts the door. I wait for him to crank the engine of his truck before pulling out of the lot. I'm not sure what he's thinking. Nor do I know if I'm making the right choice. What I do know is that as angry and hurt as I was, I can't deny how much Finn means to me.

I pull into my neighborhood twenty minutes later, parking directly in front of my house. Finn parks on the opposite side a few houses down, but by the time I gather my things and reach my stoop, he's already there.

He's not smiling, but neither am I. He shoves his hands into the pockets of his jacket. "I'm opening and closing the gym tomorrow. I'm also training during and in between classes for my upcoming fight." He sighs. "I should be done by ten-thirty. Will you stop by my house for a late dinner?"

"You're making me dinner?"

He frowns. "Hell, no. I'm picking up take-out from that Italian place you like."

I laugh a little, holding onto my smile when I see his. But my smile dwindles as I realize that he's not just inviting me to dinner, or to talk. Oh, no, not by the way he pulls me to him for another long kiss.

He lifts his hand, his thumb stroking my jaw as he loosens his hold. "I want to make things right between us. Will you let me?"

I want to say something poignant to assure him that I'm here for him in whatever way he needs me to be. But those words I so need fail to form in my mind, so instead I borrow them from my heart. "I'll let you do anything," I answer.

He leans back on his heels, realizing what I'm offering. "Good," he tells me.

He bends to give me a quick kiss, watching me as I make my way inside. I hurry to the window to catch one last look at him, but as I spread the curtains and poke my head out, I realize he's already gone.

CHAPTER 16

Finn

I took a quick shower the minute I arrived home the following night, throwing on a pair of basketball shorts and a sleeveless T-shirt in my rush to set the table. Had I known what Sol would wear, I'll admit, I would have tried a little harder.

I give her a kiss before helping her out of her coat. But as she steps away from me, and I take a long hard look at that shapely dark purple sweater dress she's wearing, I'm no longer hungry for food, and want to do a hell of a lot more than kiss her.

She covers her mouth as she laughs, but then drops her hand away and straightens. "I wanted to look good for you," she says.

Say something nice, before you rip that dress off her. "Nice," I say.

Close enough.

I put her coat away and reach for her hand, leading her into the kitchen and to the table. She pauses to take in the glasses of wine, the cloth napkins, and flatware placed between the sealed containers of take-out. Based on how smokin' she looks, thank Christ I didn't set out the sporks and paper napkins they included with the food.

"Classy," she says, motioning to the candle at the center.

"I think it's apple pumpkin," I tell her, grinning when she laughs.

I pull out her chair, taking the seat near her. For all there should be this tension between us, there's not. Once more, it's just me and Sol.

My hand finds her thigh as she pulls off the paper lid from her container of food. "I'm glad you're here, sunshine," I tell her.

"Sunshine?" she asks.

"You're name means 'sun'. If you can think of a better nickname I'm all ears." I shrug. "In addition to lean mean muscles."

I'm thinking I'm coming on too strong. But after that kiss in her car and our talk—I don't know, all this wasn't exactly what I expected. That's not true, it's more like *Sol* wasn't exactly who I expected.

Last night—when she figured out what happened to me, I swear what was left of my pride was kicked out from under me. All I felt was shame and anger. Anger at myself for letting what happened happen—for being such a stupid and trusting kid—but most of all for being so fucking obvious and letting Sol figure me out. I should have felt like less of a man and more like a coward. I should have felt fear—fear that she knew—fear of who she'd tell, fear that I wasn't everything I wanted her to believe that I am, and initially I did.

Then something changed.

She asked me to kiss her, not because she pitied me. No way. Not the way she kissed me back. She was proving she still wanted me, like nothing had changed . . . even though everything had.

So instead of feeling everything I thought I should have felt: humiliation, fury, and even fear, I drove home like this weight I've been carrying for forever had been lifted, and the chains binding me had loosened. Am I still damaged by what happened? Yeah. That shit doesn't just go away with one kiss. But I can't deny that all too real calm that followed.

Since I started liking girls, and they started liking me back, what happened to me always found a way to ruin even the good moments—as if at any given second they would learn what I've always fought to hide.

The good moments with Sol have been just that, *good*. Yet with her, it's like I've had to hold onto my secret even tighter—pretending to be that someone else—the kind of man women think they like or want to be with. That changed with Sol. She knew. She *knew*. There was no denying it—not by the way she seemed to shove the persona I've held up like a shield aside and see down to that wound that's never quite healed, tearing it open and making it bleed.

It should have freaked me out, and maybe pissed me off that she guessed—and in a way it did, given the raw pain that scorched me like fucking fire. But even though my strength and power had been stripped away, she gave it right back to me when she begged me to kiss her.

So is it easy to be with her now, to pass my hand along her thigh like I am? Yeah. It is.

"I'm sorry about how I made you feel the other night," I tell her. For all that I think things are cool between us, this apology is something I still owe her.

She reaches for my hand, covering it with her own. "Don't be. I don't ever want you to regret what happens when we're in bed."

"In bed?" I ask, lifting her hand and kissing it. "As in not sleeping?"

"Definitely not sleeping," she says, her voice gathering a roughness that turns me on. "But definitely touching."

"Touching me where?" I murmur against her knuckles, my stare welding onto hers.

She tilts her head back, laughing and exposing the swells of her breasts. Jesus, she's beautiful. It takes all the restrain I have not to pull her onto my lap and into a straddle. "Finn, you know what I mean."

"Yeah," I agree. "That doesn't mean I don't like hearing you say it."

Her breath catches when I hook my arm around her shoulders and pull her to me for one damn fine kiss.

"Enjoy your dinner," I tell her, pegging her with a look that widens her large eyes. "Have your wine, and I'll show you exactly where to touch me. . . ."

We're all over each other the minute I slam my bedroom door shut behind us, peeling off our clothes and letting them land in messy piles on the floor. But the moment I'm down to my boxer briefs and she's only in a tiny pair of panties and her bra, we stop.

I'm already hard, and breathing as fast as she is. We're holding hands, but not much else. But the way her large brown nipples poke against the lace of her teal bra, I know she's ready for more.

I lead her back to my bed and sit on the edge, positioning her to stand between my legs. My hands release her, skimming her nipples with my knuckles so the hard tips brush over my skin. "My blood tests came back today," I tell her. "It's a procedure thing I have to do before each fight. Just so you know, I'm completely clean."

She shudders, watching me play. "I am, too. I've never had . . ." She groans when I pinch through the lace. "I've never had anything," she bites out.

I curl my arm around her waist, pulling her close and yanking down the cups of her bra so I can circle the points with my tongue. "You on the pill?" I ask between flicks.

She clutches my head, speaking like it's taking everything she has to stay calm. "Yes. I don't want . . ."

Another groan, followed by a whimper when my teeth clamp down. Damn, I want her.

"Let's not use anything, okay?" she begs, her voice trembling.

It's what I want too, which is why I'm asking. I've always used a condom when I've fucked. With Sol it's the last thing I need. I don't want anything coming between us and our bare flesh.

Sol is worked up from me teasing her breasts, breathing like she's in agony. But I know that's not pain she feels. Her thighs bat against my legs as I continue to suck. Yet by now I'm tired of this bra, her panties, everything keeping her naked from me. Maybe she is, too.

She flings off her bra the moment I unhook it, and steps out of her panties and kicks them away when I yank them down. But she's not touching me, she doesn't know what to do. So I lead her down to her knees and tell her.

"Will you go down on me?" I ask. And just like that, I'm that much harder.

Her eyes shimmer in a way that tells me she can't wait to start. And for once, I'm all but begging for it. She edges closer, but it's not until I pull out my stiff length and place it into her wide open mouth that she starts.

My head cranes back and my eyes squeeze shut as the heat from her throat envelops me. At first I tense at the invasion, but then it's like everything changes. I groan when my tip slides deeper. Damn, it feels good, that misplaced shame completely gone. My scars—all that pain—it doesn't matter. With her, and the way she takes me, it's like I'm fucking perfect.

I thread my fingers through her hair, encouraging her to go faster. But as she fastens her lips tighter, my breath releases in a growl and my hands fall away.

She moans against me as she continues to work me, the vibration in her throat tempting my release. I open my eyes and glance down, grinding my jaw hard enough to snap when I lift her hair from her face and her eyes meet mine. My chest rises and falls with each quick breath, I'm ready to finish—so close I'm not sure I can speak. But when I do, I mean what I say, "God damn, you're beautiful."

I scrunch my eyes closed when her head dips further down. I can't hold out much longer, my body ready to give into that release. "Sol . . ." I rasp, forcing my heavy lids open. She lifts her gaze, meeting mine. "My turn."

Before she can ask, I have her in the air. In one smooth move she's on her back, her legs spread, and my face is buried against her. She screams, her body bouncing off the mattress and her fingernails clawing my sheets.

Her legs kick out on either side of me, flailing as she starts to scoot back. "Oh, *God*," she grunts when I suck harder.

I haul her back, flinging one of her legs over my shoulder.

I devour her soft flesh, returning every bit of pleasure she gave me, and maybe more. She squirms, unable to keep still, moaning so loudly I know that she's close. I increase my efforts, adding a little more suction before sliding my fingers inside her.

My tongue eagerly circles and my fingers move fast. She starts swearing, her hips rocking against my hand. I'm making her hot, but as I increase my speed she loses control, calling my name, pleading for me not to stop. When she comes, it's wild, strands of her hair smacking her in the face as she whips her head back and forth.

I lift my chin, easing her down from the rush and lowering her body to the bed. Her eyes fix on mine. "I want you so much," she stammers, barely managing the words.

I crawl up her body my hand smoothing away her hair. "You sure?" I ask, hoping the hell and back she means what she says.

At her nod, I place my thick head between her legs, slicking it against her folds. "Good," I tell her, my eyes closing briefly from the heat and feel of her body. "So fucking good."

I don't slide in as easily as I think I will, her center taught and narrow. But the pressure only makes me want her more. "Damn, you're tight," I whisper against her mouth.

She shifts beneath me, allowing her knees to fall all the way open. "Sorry," she says, like it's a bad thing.

"Don't be," I tell her. "Just tell me if it hurts."

She's not a virgin. I'm pretty sure she's not. But that doesn't mean I can't hurt her, especially since it's obvious I'm a lot bigger than she's used to.

I curl around her, kissing her as I try to make my way in. She moans, deepening our kiss, trying to taste every bit of me. I smile with total sin as I realize what she's doing. "You like how you taste on my lips?" I ask. She answers with a whimper, her stare growing heady. "Then you're really going to like the way I fuck you," I promise.

Her spine bows as I slide the rest of the way, filling her. I take it slow at first, making sure she's not in pain, but once her hips rock beneath mine, there's nothing slow about what I do.

My rhythm is fast, hard, moving her further up the bed as our bodies collide and create the perfect beat. She fastens her ankles around me, encouraging and forcing each thrust. My head lowers to kiss her ear, causing her body to grip mine and clench me further.

The heat between us builds. She's swearing, and hell, so am I, both of us loud as those familiar jolts of electricity shoot across every nerve cell in my body. But it's like I can't stop talking dirty, can't stop telling her how hot she's making me.

She peaks, her body shuddering as I finally release. Son of a bitch. Normally, I last longer. In my condition, and in my youth, I always keep going. But after what she did to me, and how I went down on her, I don't think either of us stood a chance.

I slow my movements, kissing her as I take my time finishing. When I finally stop and pull out, I realize she's trembling like she's scared, and Jesus Christ, doesn't it just tear me in half. "What's wrong?" I ask, reaching to cup her face.

She turns her head in the direction of the wall. "Nothing. It's okay," she says.

I lower my hands from her face, realizing I'm making her uncomfortable by staring at her. If anything that makes me feel more like shit.

"Did I hurt you?" I ask. We went at it pretty hard, but I thought she liked it. Now, I'm not so sure. "Sol, if I hurt you, you need to tell me."

"You didn't hurt me," she says.

It's what she claims, but she won't look at me then. "Baby, tell me what I did wrong."

She returns her focus on me, smiling softly despite that she seems upset. "You didn't hurt me," she says again. "I'm just in a lot of trouble."

My stomach bottoms out. "Did you forget to take your pill?"

She surprises me by laughing. "No, it's not that," she says.

She slides her hands along the tats on my arms, smoothing her palms across my shoulders until her hands link around my neck.

I adjust my weight above her, worried that I'm crushing her. "Then what is it, beautiful?" I ask.

I think it's my "beautiful" comment that softens her eyes further. "I'm in love with you, Finn," she tells me, her voice splintering. "I know that's probably not what you want to hear, but I love you . . ."

CHAPTER 17

Sol

"Cool." That's what Finn said when I told him I loved him. He grinned and said, *"Cool."*

I think it would have bothered another woman, and maybe even pissed her off. But it was such a "Finn" thing to say and do. I'm not sure if he's heard it before, but I didn't ask. If I'm being honest, I was more worried he'd said it to someone else.

Do I wish he felt the same? Of course I do. But when I think back to everything my mom is dealing with, in a way I'm glad he doesn't.

Maybe I'm too screwed up to love.

"How's Mami?" I ask my dad, plugging my other ear to drown out all the noise from the arena. Finn may not love me, but that doesn't stop him from showering me with affection and wanting me with him. So here I am in Atlantic City, at the fight that can move him from his current rank at number seven to the next in line for the belt.

I crank the volume when I can't make out what my father said. "Sorry, Papi. Can you say that again?"

"I said I think the new dosage is starting to work," he repeats. "She was more alert today."

"She was?" My attention veers in the direction of the welterweight and his camp as they pass me. He's gushing blood from a deep cut on his forehead, his nose is visiting his right cheekbone, and there's so much swelling in his face, his eyes are nothing more than slits.

And this poor bastard won!

I force a smile when he waves my way. He's friendly with Finn and we had dinner with him and his girlfriend the other night. I'm not surprised he remembers me, we had a nice time together. I'm just shocked he can *see* me.

"Is she able to hold a conversation with you?" I ask my father. As I wait for his answer, I take a moment to pray up and down that Finn doesn't end up the same way. Jesus, the guy is one giant bruise.

Yet as much as I'm scared for Finn, the fact that my father doesn't respond right away causes that awful sense of dread to dig its way into my stomach and find its way into my voice. "Papi . . . what is it?" I ask.

"It's probably nothing."

I close my eyes, willing myself to stay calm. "If something's wrong with Mami, you need to tell me." As much as I wish I could be spared from what's happening, it's not a luxury my mother can afford.

He waits, as if debating what to tell me, adding to my mounting nervousness. "She talked to me about remodeling the kitchen," he says.

It wasn't what I was expecting to hear. Not so soon after her meds were adjusted. And while to anyone else it might not sound like a big deal, the news is actually *huge*. Fixing the kitchen is one of those things my parents used to discuss before my mother became really sick. It's needed a major remodel for years. But lately my mother hasn't noticed. She hasn't noticed anything—unable to see things that are right in front of her—unable to live in the present or our reality. The fact that she's starting to notice . . . that's a good thing.

"Really?" I ask.

I can hear the hope in my father's tone. "She was talking about new cabinets, and possibly replacing the counter with granite. I'm not sure if it's something we can afford, but if it will help her—if it's something she wants, I'll try to do it for her."

My eyes sting as I smile. That's love for you, doing

something for your partner just to make her happy. I want to believe that she's better and that the mother I remember is coming back to me. So I ask the question perhaps I shouldn't ask, "Do you think she'd know me?"

My voice is so soft I'm not sure he hears me. When he doesn't respond right away, I'm sure that he didn't, or worse yet, that his answer is no.

"I think she might," he says, hope continuing to find its way into his gravely tenor voice. Except he wouldn't be my father without saying what he says next. "Too bad you're with that boy. Otherwise we could find out tonight."

I try not to laugh, but I can't help it. Papi knows Finn's name. His remarks about "that boy" and his threats to hide "that boy's body" aside, I think he likes Finn. Does he like how practically inseparable we've become, or how I'm staying at his place almost every night? Oh, hell no. He's a Latino father who owns six machetes. But despite his traditional beliefs, he wants me happy. And he knows Finn makes me happy.

"Give Mami a kiss for me, and tell her I love her," I whisper.

"I will. Be safe, *mija*," he says.

I disconnect, but I'll admit, I practically jump away from the cinderblock wall when the roar of the crowd belts down the hall as if in collective pain. I push open the door to Finn's private changing area and rush back in. "What happened? I ask.

All of Finn's brothers, and his sister, are gathered around the giant flat-screen fixed to the wall. Except for Killian and Seamus who are helping Finn warm up.

Finn is so focused on staying loose and hitting his targets, he doesn't answer. But as his family pulls away from the screen, he doesn't have to.

There is Conan McDavis, former heavyweight champ, now unconscious individual face-planted on the octagon's floor. Sofia is the first to look away, crossing her arms as her stare bounces to Finn. "He's not getting up," she says quietly.

"He will," Kill says, his voice tight. He's not looking

toward the T.V., and neither is Finn, but they know what happened. The commentators are losing their minds, screaming over the amped up and hollering crowd.

"Holy God," Wren says. Gorgeous looks aside, she's had her share of street fights and has witnessed more MMA matches than I have. But the way she's staring at the screen, it's like she's never seen so much blood.

Like Killian says, Conan the heavy weight fighter who likely just fought his last professional fight does get up . . . albeit wobbly and walking *into* the fence rather than going around it. The ringside medics rush to him, hurrying to pat down what remains of his face.

Curran touches my arm, drawing my attention. As a cop, I know he's seen his share of pummeled up bodies, and dealt with people freaking out. . . pretty similar to what I'm close to doing. I didn't even notice him come to my side, just like I didn't notice my mouth dangling to the floor until I force it closed.

"You all right?" he murmurs, leaning back and crossing his arms over his super-sized chest.

"Fine," I say, or rather squeak. I glance over my shoulder at Finn, who's bouncing around, swinging, elbowing, spinning into his back kicks, like nothing happened. Like that poor sap didn't just suffer major head trauma and is likely screwed up for life.

Curran drags a hand through his buzzed blond hair. "You sure?" he asks. "You don't look too good."

"I'm a little hungry," I answer, lying through my teeth, wondering how the hell I'm going to get through this match.

Wren fumbles through her purse and pulls out a candy bar. "Here, have some sugar," she says.

"Thank you," I tell her, not bothering to argue. I rip into that candy bar like a woman possessed—scratch that—like a cavewoman possessed on an island where her caveman lover is about to be eaten by a dinosaur.

"Don't worry, sunshine," Finn says, adding a wink. "I'll take you to a nice dinner after the match."

I force what I hope is an encouraging smile, returning my

focus to the screen in time to see the winner being interviewed. Good heavens. Even he seems to feel bad about what he did to Conan. He glances over his shoulder as the commentator congratulates him, watching Conan's camp carry his slumped form out of the octagon.

Angus, Finn's oldest brother who's adding more bulk to his belly by ramming another donut in his mouth shakes his head. "If that's not a career ending injury, I don't know what is," he says.

"Angus," Curran warns, his attention cutting my way.

Angus ignores him, scratching his shaggy dark beard. "I mean, at the very least he's going to need new teeth." He shrugs. "He should have retired two years ago. Before his speech got wrecked to shit."

"*Angus*," Curran says again, this time louder.

Angus of course, isn't listening, reaching for another donut. "After that shot to the skull, he'll have to stick to coloring books and Candyland for shits and giggles." He gives it some thought. "Hell, if he can even manage that."

"Angus, shut up already," Wren yells as she watches me sink to the couch. "Finn doesn't need that shit."

I think she means Finn *and* Sol, because her eyes are on me. But I'm not alone in how I feel. Everyone appears ill at ease following what went down these past two match-ups.

"Finn's going to own it," Killian says, his voice gruff as he watches Finn's strikes.

"Yup. I've got it," Finn agrees. He spins around, another perfect roundhouse kick finding Killian's glove. Sofia and Wren sit on either side of me, watching me as I shove the rest of the candy bar in my mouth.

I've been fine. *Totally* and completely fine with Finn being a fighter. In the past, I even caught a few of his fights on T.V. I know he's tough. I'm confident he's skilled. I'm positive he's focused. But I've never actually seen him fight in a real bout, especially not as his girlfriend.

The matches I saw on T.V., were hard to watch because I knew of him and thought that he was a nice guy. Now that I well, *love* him . . . Jesus Christ and three to four disciples, how am I going to get through this?

I turn to Sofia. "How did you do it?" I ask her, keeping my voice low with the hopes Finn doesn't hear me. "All those times you saw Killian fight, and witnessed everything he had to go through to become a champion, how did you get through it?"

Killian retired after he won the super heavyweight title, walking away from a lot of money, and earning a great deal of criticism due to his young age and the expectation to defend his title. I can understand, to some extent, where the condemnation was coming from. Killian could possibly have held the title for years, become more of a legend, and given his legions of fans more of what they wanted. But he had his reasons for leaving the fighting circuit.

The main one being Sofia.

He wanted the quality of life a lot of fighters don't have after years spent in the ring getting punched in the skull and pushing their bodies to their breaking point. And he wanted to share that life with Sofia. As much as she never asked him to walk away, he knew it was something she wanted, and recognized how hard it was for her to watch him get hurt.

I wait for her words of wisdom, or some sort of silver lining. Yet it takes a moment for those words to come.

She rubs her hands as if gathering her thoughts. But then I realize she's not working through what to say, she's remembering what she saw. "It wasn't easy," she admits. "I . . ."

"She almost fainted during one his worst matches," Wren finishes for her. Unlike Sofia who's in a pretty dress, and me who didn't know better and wore a cute top, jeans, and boots, Wren is wearing a form-fitting and very short navy dress that shows off her long legs. "Seriously," she adds. "Sofe turned as white as my ass and we had to catch her before she fell over."

Awesome.

I glance back at Sofia, my eyes rounding. "I wish she was joking," she says. "But I really had a hard time being strong." She takes my hand in hers, motioning to the T.V... "These fights are brutal. Sometimes the referees don't stop them in time, but more often the fighters keep going, their desire to win interfering with their logic to stop."

"Like Conan?" I ask.

She nods. "Every now and then, Killian wrestles with whether to return to the octagon. He's a fighter at heart, and a fighter's mentality is hard to change. But then he'll catch a match like this one, or run into a former fighter with permanent injuries. Those moments remind him that he wants more for him and us."

I squeeze her hand. "I'm glad Killian walked away before he was permanently injured. But Sofia, Finn's not there yet. It'll be years before he even thinks about retiring. All he talks about is his next fight, or the one after that, or how the belt is going to feel when he raises it over his head. He loves what he does. That fighter mentality you mentioned? He's has it, and he's not letting go." I sigh. "I don't want him hurt. But knowing how much MMA means to him, I want to be there to support him."

"So be there," she says. "Just be prepared for him to get hurt." She bows her head. "Not that it helped me."

"I hear you," Wren agrees. "Sometimes, it's all I can do not to look away."

Wren was quiet during our conversation. If you knew anything about Wren it speaks volumes. But she's listening, and she cares. "I'm sure," I say, acknowledging her worry. "I mean, you love him, too."

She grins, her smile reminding me of Finn's. "You sayin' you love my brother?"

I tilt my head. My voice is soft, but I mean what I say. "I really do."

My words and tone give her pause and dull her smile, but not in a bad way. "Good," she says. "I think you're what he needs."

It's not the first time one of his siblings has told me that. From what I've gathered from the recent family functions we've attended, Finn's drinking had been out of control and he was advised to stop. He still drinks when we go out, a couple beers or so, but he's never been out of hand around me. It's likely because we're making up for that high with the ridiculous amount of sex we've been having.

I'm not complaining. Sex with Finn is so personal. I've never experienced the amount of intimacy I feel with anyone else but him. I think, or at least *hope*, he feels it, too. The way we talk afterward, and the way we hold onto each other, it's like we're afraid to let go.

My attention drifts back to where he's warming up, seemingly unaffected by the chaos unleashing in the octagon as the next fight commences. I can't say I'm exactly what Finn needs, nor that I'm the person who has helped him get better. His intense counseling sessions have played a big role. That much he's shared. Yet we both realize he has a long way to go.

Just last week when we went out, some idiot hit on me and refused to back off. I thought Finn was going to break him in half and kick the leftovers aside. I've honestly never seen him so angry. Thankfully his brothers were there to haul him back, giving me time to calm him and convince him to walk away. Not that he was happy about it.

"I don't want anyone touching you," he told me. "I mean it, Sol. No one's going to hurt you, especially around me."

I recognize where his protectiveness stems from, as well as his rage. That doesn't make it any easier to witness.

That rage is so pronounced, I can sense it behind his smiles and soft touches, and I'm not alone. To avoid trouble, Killian arranged for all the fighters training with him and Finn to have a separate changing area. Finn lost his mind on another opponent and his trainer following his last match. Killian was worried what Finn might do if someone was looking for trouble, but also what his fighters might do as well.

Finn is well-liked by a lot of the other professional fighters, especially the ones who've trained alongside him, and who've followed his career. They're just as capable of starting fights in defense of Finn. And an all-out brawl between MMA fighters is the last thing anyone wants backstage.

"Do you think you might pass out?" Wren asks me as I continue to take in Finn.

I consider her comment. Finn is so . . . *mine*. I shake my head. "I'm more worried I might climb into the cage and jump on his opponent's back."

"No, shit," Wren says, sounding impressed. "Hey. Been there too many times."

"I'm going to advise you against that one," Sofia says, laughing softly. Her humor vanishes when she glances up at the screen.

Once more the crowd in the arena is losing their minds, the commentators yelling to be heard. "*Oh!*" Finn's brothers yell at once.

A super heavyweight fighter who Killian faced years ago, is lying motionless on the mat, his jaw dangling off to the side. I rise slowly with Wren, clutching my heart.

"He broke his jaw," Angus says. Out of all the things that occurred in tonight's bloodbath, this is the one he can't seem to watch. He abruptly turns from the screen and marches to the opposite side of the training area, tossing the donut in his hand in the trash.

Everyone is silent. Dead silent. But I can't blame them. I've seen my share of fights and you can consider me a fan even long before I started dating Finn. But I've never seen back to back matches end like this.

I point to the screen when Curran the cop edges my way. "Is this, um, common?" I ask.

I really don't have to ask seeing how wide his eyes are. "Nope. I've never seen so much shit go down in one night." He hurries out the door when someone knocks, shutting it behind him.

"Bad juju," Angus says. "That octagon is cursed or some shit."

"Nice, Angus," Wren says, rolling her eyes.

I start to pace, only to determine I'm better off sitting. But as soon as my butt touches the couch, Curran rushes back in and I'm back on my feet.

"Finn, it's time," he says. He turns my way. "If you're

going to watch, now's the time to take your seats."

Almost silently, and stoically, Finn's brothers and the girls start piling toward the door, stopping only to hug Finn, murmur words of encouragement, and *cross themselves as they step away*! I know they mean well. I was raised Catholic, too, but this whole funeral vibe they have going on is doing little to soothe me.

I walk cautiously to Finn, trying to work up my courage to say something inspirational. But when he grips my hips and yanks me to him, all my words become jumbled beneath that stare I so adore.

"Hey," he says, resting his forehead against mine. "How you doing?"

My arms tighten around him. "I'm scared," I admit.

Like always, he grins. "You worry too much, you know that?"

His easy tone lifts my mood slightly, yet it does nothing to stop the tremble in my voice. "I don't want anything to happen to you, or this face."

He chuckles. "I'm not sure about my face, but I'll be all right. I promise. Just promise you'll be waiting for me when I'm done."

"You know I will," I assure him. "No matter what."

Finn kisses me then. It's not quick, nor is it innocent. It speaks of our time alone in bed, those moments when the world stops spinning with problems and angst and all that matters is our bare bodies merging as one. At first I was shy about his show of affection in front of his family. But as we grew closer it just seemed right, becoming something I expect and desire.

"I love you," I whisper when he pulls away.

"Cool," he tells me once more. But as he continues to hold my gaze and catches sight of my fear, his smile vanishes. He knows I'm terrified. "It's going to be all right," he tells me softly.

He means what he says. Yet as I leave his arms and walk out with his family, I can't be sure it's a promise he'll be able to keep.

CHAPTER 18

Finn

MMA followers in general are loud, fanatical, and so full of energy you can feel it. Tonight is no different. Everyone is pumped and eager for more action and blood, their need for it luring me to the octagon like a predator to its prey.

I'm ready. I'm willing. I've got this.

The moment I yank my T-shirt on, I head for the door. I know Sol's scared, and I hate that she is. But right now the best I can do to assure her is to step into the octagon and get the job done.

I don't get far.

Kill steps in front of me, blocking my way. His expression is hard, bordering on pissed. "Look, Finn. I don't believe the shit Angus says about tonight being cursed."

"Good," I tell him. "Cause I don't either."

He doesn't move, and suddenly Curran is there, too. "What's the problem?" I ask. Jesus, the adrenaline pumping through my bloodstream has me jumping in place. I need to move, not keep still and hear more of Angus's superstitious bullshit.

Kill works his jaw. "I don't want you to put on a show tonight."

"What?" I ask, thinking he's lost his mind.

Here's the thing, MMA isn't staged, it isn't fixed, but the promoters like the drama. It stirs the crowd, gets fans talking, fills seats, and makes everyone more money. Men, they have to show what they're made of, they have to show off their moves, bash skulls, and talk trash. The women, that's a whole different level of drama. They get personal, vindictive, and nasty. But either way you slice it, you're putting on a show.

"It could cost me the title match," I point out.

Sumar Okafe just moved up from ninth to fourth for the lightweight title. When I win tonight, it will take me from seventh to the number one spot based on my opponent's rank. Technically this puts me next in line for the belt. The problem is, Sumar has a big mouth and a bigger attitude.

Following his win last week, Sumar ran out into the audience and called out the champ, the champ's woman, *and* his mother in front of a capacity crowd. Fans and fighters alike lost their shit all over social media, calling Sumar disrespectful, which the asshole is. But because of what he did—and because he stole the champ's belt during the press conference that followed, fans of the champ are demanding he pummel his ass—which means they'll pay big money to see it. If I don't put on a big enough show, asshole or not, Sumar is going to get that title bout before I do.

"I don't care about that right now," Kill says.

My scowl deepens. "As my manager and my brother, you damn well should."

"It's not always about the money, Finnie," he says.

"You're right," I grind out. "It's also about getting what I deserve."

"I'm not saying you don't deserve a shot at the title. God knows you've earned it," he says. "Just keep cool and stick with the plan." He motions out the door, ignoring the reps beating on the door, telling me I'm needed out now. "You hear that crowd. They're nothing more than piranhas, Finn. They've already seen and tasted blood so they want more. Your opponent knows it. So right now, his camp is telling him he needs to make sure that's what he gives them. They're telling him to fuck you up. You need a fast win, in the off chance he gets lucky."

More knocks on the door, more urges for me to get my ass

moving. Kill keeps talking like no one is there. "Just like you want the title shot, he wants it too. Just like Sumar is making noise, he wants to make some of his own."

"Hear him out," Curran says when I start swearing.

"Just finish Boris quick," Kill adds. "No showing off, no waiting for a shot that pisses you off enough to act. Get in, get a knockout or a submission. That's all I ask."

"If I get the win in the first round, it won't be enough of a show for the higher ups," I tell him. "Not with how much the fans on social media are talking up all the shit Sumar's pulled—and not with how they're demanding the champ lay him out."

"No, it won't," Kill agrees, his voice tight. "But it will give you time to prepare so when the time comes, you'll wear that belt, and be in one piece to enjoy it." He shakes his head. "That last fighter, as young as he is, he's done. You hear me? He was so focused on putting on a show, he got sloppy and now he's hurt because of it."

And messed up for life he doesn't say. Like the others before him, and like Conan who probably won't even be able to tie his own damn shoes.

The door swings open, but before one of the producers can rip into me, I bound past them with Kill and Curran at my heels. The cameraman scrambles when he sees me, pushing off the wall and racing to shove his lens in my face. As soon as it connects and the lights flick on, the crowd loses it.

Roars shoot down the hall like a cyclone. They know I'm coming. But they don't know what Kill just said.

I'm not stupid. The last thing I want is to end up like some of those fighters who've spent years taking blows and can't think straight, can't keep their hands from twitching, and who can barely finish their thoughts. All that aside, I'm not going down like a punk. If he wants me to finish fast, I will. But I can't say I'm not going to look good doing it.

The moment I cross into the arena, that's when the crowds' energy strikes me at capacity. It's not the first time I've stepped toward the octagon, but it is like that first time. And I swear to Christ, it's like I'm reborn.

This . . . this is where I belong.

Invincible is what I am at this moment. Alive is how I feel. And strength is all I own. I thought that part of me had died—that this taste had grown old, dulling to that numbness that had become more friend than foe. But now I'm back. I feel it, I breathe it. It's a part of me once more. And it's not simply because of my newfound commitment to training, or how I'm progressing in counseling.

It's because of Sol.

This woman has been the breath I didn't know I needed to take. Yeah, *her*. The one clinging to Wren and Sofia as I pass. But I don't look at her then. I have a job to do, and that includes proving why I deserve to be her man.

I'm checked by the cut man, every inch of me tensing as he swipes petroleum jelly all over my face. It's supposed to help the punches slide off my face, and decrease the cuts I receive. Personally, I think it does jack.

Kill clasps my shoulder, Curran does, too, both assuring me my opponent doesn't stand a chance. I respond with a stiff nod and make my way up the steps and into the octagon.

Game time.

"Ladies and gentlemen . . ." the announcer begins.

I'm not paying attention to my stats or Boris "the Thorn" Thornsby's. I'm looking at him, like he's looking at me, both of us so wired and ready, we can't keep still. His favorite submission is the rear-naked choke, when he doesn't knock his opponent out first. He hits hard, but so do I. And I'm just as good on the ground as I am on my feet. If he gets me down, he'll try for the choke, guaranteed.

But he better watch out for his arms, or I'm popping one loose with an armbar.

I hear, "against Finn the Fury O'Brien" in time to raise my fist. Yet it's Sol's "Get him, baby!" that almost makes me grin. Almost. I'm a fighter now, I'll be her lover *after* I win.

The ref calls us to the center. "You both know the rules," he says. "Give us a good show and a clean fight. You want to touch gloves, do it now."

I lift my hands to tap his gloves. He responds with a

middle finger. Okay, there's my grin. You want to play it that way? Let's go.

We back into our corners. "You ready?" the ref asks Thorn. Thorn nods. "You ready?" he asks me. I lift my hands and tilt my chin. "Fight," he yells.

"Come on, Finn," my camp begins.

"Come on, Fury," some fan yells.

Thorn and me meet in the center. We smack gloves, trying to get a feel for each other's reach. It looks innocent, cute, even. It's not so cute the minute he takes his first swing. I duck under and nail him square in the chest with a front push kick.

It's enough to get his attention, and knock his air out. I rush forward as he stumbles away. He sees me coming and reacts without thinking. His rush to return my strike making him reckless.

He goes for a jab, but tries to fake me out and does a back spinning kick. I dodge that, and his elbow, nailing him hard in the face. "Oh!" yells the crowd.

Pain is my trigger, it always has been. But apparently it's Thorn's, too. He punches me in the jaw. I punch him back and the next thing I know we're going blow for blow. Considering I knocked the air out of him, he should be slower. Yet he's swinging like it never happened.

Hard, that's how we go at it, throwing our weight into every blow. I don't have to look to know the crowd is on their feet. I barely hear their screams, too focused on slamming Thorn with everything I have. But this guy's no pussy.

I catch him just right in the chin, sending him staggering back. I charge, but he kicks me off and tackles me. Now, we're on the ground. I was the better fighter on my feet. Now I have to prove I'm also better on the ground.

Like I guessed, he goes for the choke. I slip out under him before he can move his arm beneath my chin, swinging my legs around and searching for his wrist. I snag it fast, hooking my legs around his arm and pulling hard, feeling that sweet tap on my shoulder when he submits seconds later.

I roll off him to my feet, raising my fists in victory,

electrified by the roar of the crowd. My brothers rush in, losing their minds in a way I feel down to my bones. Jesus, I feel everything now, and it's never felt so damn sweet.

I climb the cage, straddling the bar to scan the crowd and find the rest of my family. But it's Sol's face I lock onto. I toss her a wink and a grin, halting her screams and her jumps up and down. She smiles, gushing with pride as she clutches her hands against her chest.

That's her. That's my girl. That's the woman I fucking love.

CHAPTER 19

Sol

I lean heavily against Finn as we make our way through the hotel lobby and toward the elevators. What a night. It was an awesome fight, and an even better win. My man kicked serious ass, annihilating his opponent with four seconds left in the first round! But it was the way he pulled me out of the crowd on his way back to his changing area that completely stopped my heart.

He kissed me, in front of all those girls elbowing each other to touch him, in front of all those men patting his back wishing they could be him, and in front of the cameras. I blushed, but oh yes, I totally kissed him back.

"You okay with us heading to the room?" he asks.

"I am," I assure him, stroking his waist.

"Yeah? You look like you were having fun dancing. I almost hated pulling you away." His stare drags the length of my body. "Almost."

His appraising look is one I need then. You can call me insecure, but the more I'm around professional fighters, the more I'm aware how much like rock stars they truly are. Women, lots and lots of women, with bigger breasts, better clothes, and more grace to their movements want to have sex with Finn. His Instagram account alone lit up with "Marry Me Fury" requests. And as MMA becomes more popular, supermodels and celebrities are starting to date the most prominent stars.

Have I mentioned Finn is a prominent star?

I voiced my concerns to Sofia when we returned backstage. "You're beautiful, and he's fallen head over heels for you. You have nothing to worry about," said the woman who resembles a supermodel herself.

Sofia glides instead of walks. She fits right in with all the model types because of her beauty and grace, but it's her endearing personality that makes her a favorite among the wives. And then there's me, loud laugh, loud personality, and someone who bounces when she walks.

I'm not trying to put myself down. I like me. I really do. But after seeing what the other women wore, and how hard Finn fought to win, tonight, I wanted to be something more than his cute girlfriend. I wanted to be a woman who could rival, or at least, somewhat fit in with the other ladies who run in the MMA circles.

While he met with the press, Sofia and Wren hurried back to the hotel with me and into one of the trendier boutiques, minutes before it closed. There was nothing to the strapless black cocktail dress I found, but that didn't make it any less lovely. Yet the shoes Wren picked out took it from elegant to downright alluring.

The glittery charcoal heels sparkle even in the tame lobby light. Both were way more than I could afford. But it was important for me to look good on Finn's arm. And after seeing how tempting the other women dressed, my jeans and blouse weren't cutting it.

I meant to put it on a credit card, but Wren beat me to it, paying cash. When I tried to protest, she shook her head. "It's on Finn. He told me to buy you anything you wanted."

The gesture left me speechless. Finn has paid for dinner, movies, that sort of thing. For someone as proud as me though, even that has been hard to accept. But Wren wouldn't take no for an answer, and the boutique owner liked the idea of cash. She encouraged Wren when she dragged me to the fitting room to change into what has to be the most stylish dress I'll ever own.

"Have I told you how sexy you look?" he mutters in my ear as we wait for the elevator.

"No," I murmur. I smile as my arms circle his waist. He didn't tell me, but the way his eyes flew open when he saw me return to the press conference assured me he liked my new clothes.

"Well, you do," he assures me. "What I didn't like was how those assholes were looking at you when you danced."

I tilt my chin so I can see his face. "I didn't notice them. I was too busy watching my hot boyfriend."

A smirk finds its way into his face. "Even with the bruises?"

"Yes," I answer, even though it was hard watching him receive them.

Following a quick shower, and before he met with the press, Finn changed into a dress shirt and slacks. His camp is trying to give him a more professional persona following the incident that landed him in counseling. But even without these fancier clothes Finn is gorgeous.

His hands slip beneath my coat. "Did you have fun?"

"I did," I admit, despite that this lifestyle is very much new to me.

Following dinner with his family, we attended a small after-party thrown at a club by his sponsor Lethal Punch. Rather than cling to Finn the entire time like I wanted to, I danced with his family and his friends' wives. MMA is a business, but also a circus in itself. It was almost midnight when his fight started, and while he won his match incredibly fast, it was almost two in the morning when we finally sat down to eat.

It's nice being in A.C. with Finn and his family like this, regardless of the fast-pace. Or should I say, it's a blessing to feel *normal*, to have fun and pretend like my life isn't as bad as it's been. Yet as much as I'm enjoying our time together, I can't help feeling guilty. For all I want to support Finn, it cost me experiencing my mother's moment of clarity. I only pray she allows me a glimpse of it soon. I want my mother back. Is it too much to ask to see her as she once was, even for a little while?

"You okay, sunshine?" Finn asks as we step into the elevator.

I nod, trying to smile. This is his night, a moment to celebrate his victory and his hard work, not a time for me to dwell on my problems or wonder what awaits me when I return to reality. I push up on my toes and kiss his chin. "Of course. I'm here with you."

It's my last remark that adds to my grin, drawing Finn closer and tempting him to play. His hands trail down to my butt as the doors shut, circling and reminding me that our night is far from over.

"You sure you're okay?" he asks.

He caught enough in my expression to know my mind had wandered elsewhere. But like I mentioned, I won't take anything away from his night. He's earned every bit of good that's happening, and all that's left to come.

My fingers glide along his temple. The multiple bruises swelling his cheekbones and jaw, keep my motions gentle, but the love I feel is completely there. "You weren't supposed to let anything happen to this face," I remind him.

"I told you I wouldn't be able to keep that promise," he says. "But I kept the one that mattered and won the fight."

He did, and he was incredible to watch. Each strike seemed so effortless, despite the power he packed behind every punch. That didn't make watching any easier, but it did add to my awe of him.

"Still like the face?" he asks as my fingers linger over his skin.

"I like everything about you," I confess, the seriousness in my tone dulling his humor. Maybe I said too much. Sometimes I think I do. It's almost as if how I feel is more than he can take, or believe he deserves. Perhaps I shouldn't be so open. But with Finn, my emotions take on a life of their own, despite how I initially tried to keep him at arm's length.

The floor numbers increase as the elevator shoots up. I rest my head against his chest. It sounds so cliché to say, "I've never felt this way before", but I haven't. Finn is everything to me, and my only desire is to be his everything in return.

He cups my backside, pausing when he feels my bare flesh beneath the fabric of my dress. "You're not wearing panties, are you?" he asks, his tone a low growl against my ear.

Although it's a question, it's like he's pleading with me to tell him yes. "It's a thong," I answer quietly.

"The red one with the lace?" he asks.

I may not have bought any new clothes to wear to A.C., but I did splurge a little on lingerie. "You'll find out soon enough," I promise.

"Jesus," he mumbles, gripping me tighter.

His hands travel beneath my skirt, tracing circles from my outer thighs dangerously close to the center. It's then I inch away, my body heating, but not because I'm embarrassed. I want him so much my flesh aches for him.

He follows me into the corner, curling against me. "Just getting you back," he says, his blue eyes flashing in a way that means trouble.

I laugh. Okay. Maybe I deserve that.

We haven't had sex in three days. Three *freaking* days. As superstitious as it sounds, Finn's a big believer in "not messing around before a fight". His words. Not mine. Certainly not mine.

I seriously thought he was joking, or beginning to lose interest, until he brought me down to Atlantic City with him and still wouldn't touch me!

I was kind of a brat about the whole thing, parading in our room naked every chance I had, lounging across the bed or chair in a way that had him cursing or rushing to take a cold shower.

"You haven't been very nice to me," he says against my mouth, thinking back to the way I've teased him.

"Mmm," I agree nodding thoughtfully. "I suppose I have a lot of making up to do."

"Damn straight," he says. Before he can kiss me, the elevator doors ding open.

I don't expect Finn to be romantic, and he doesn't disappoint. He tosses me over his shoulder and smacks my butt, making me laugh. That's totally us, always playing, always laughing. Some may see it as immature, but to me it's sweet and fun, reminding me how young we both are despite the very mature problems we face.

He stomps down the hall, effortlessly carrying me. "You have no class, tough guy," I tell him, still laughing.

"True," he admits. "But you like what I have and are really going to like what I have to show you."

I don't doubt for a moment, and again he doesn't disappoint. He throws the door to our room open, smacking the security lock in place half a second before he crushes me against the wall with his body. His erection punches against my belly. Our kiss is deep, raw, passionate, the exact same way I've wanted him to kiss me all night.

I tug off his jacket and work on the buttons of his dress shirt when his fingers slip beneath my thong and deep inside of me. The motion is so smooth and arousing, I break our kiss, craning my neck and moaning. He curses, his breath coming fast as he nibbles my throat. "You're ready for me, aren't you, beautiful?" he asks.

My whimpering keeps me from answering, and so do the words that come next. "Do you know how bad I've needed to be inside you?"

He doesn't expect me to answer, not with how fast his fingers are circling, but my gasps and my rocking pelvis are enough. He yanks off my coat just as my hands finish shoving down his pants.

I cry out in total bliss as Finn shoves aside my thong and pushes his thick erection between my legs, each press of his hips stretching me slowly until he fills me. He pauses long enough to secure my ankles behind his back and for his heated stare to lock on mine. "Hang on," he says, ramming his hips upward.

My nails dig into his shoulders as he withdraws slowly and thrusts hard, each fierce push increasing in speed and intensity. My back smacks against the wall, the sound adding to the moment, but nowhere as loud as my screams that beg him for more.

The force of his movements come faster. Finn yanks the top of my dress down, his hot mouth finding my nipple and sucking hard. I clutch him against me, my hips struggling to keep up with his increasing rhythm and my body succumbing to his.

It doesn't take me long to peak, nor does it take him long to finish—not after how long it's been since we've made love. That doesn't mean we're done. Oh, no, there's too much time we need to make up for.

He lowers me to the floor, allowing my breasts to slide along his chest. As he watches and finishes stripping out of his clothes, I back away, pulling off my dress, tugging down my tiny hot pink thong, and unsnapping the bra now clinging to my waist. The shoes, those I leave on.

Finn kicks away his briefs, prowling forward and hardening as he makes his way to where I wait by the bed. My nipples are so taught they sting. I can't even think straight, reaching for him and finding his mouth, eager for his kiss and more of his touch.

I nip his chin as my hands lower to rub his length. Never have I had a lover like Finn. It's so *easy* for me to desire him, to want to please him, to let him take me. It's not a chore or something expected. It's something I hunger for, the taste of his skin so delicious against my tongue.

I allow him to lead us, my trust something he seeks and equally turns him on.

He tugs on my bottom lip with his teeth and positions us at the edge of the bed, in front of the mirror anchored above the dresser. I almost expect him to bend me over. Instead he sits, spreading my legs open and pulling me forward so I'm hovered over his lap.

My back is against his chest, giving us a very nice view of our reflection. Without needing to ask, I lower myself down, placing my hands on my knees to keep my balance as he rubs his silky head against my folds.

My body shudders as he guides me down slowly. This position is new to me, the fit tighter. I arch my back, scrunching my face and releasing a moan as he fills me once more.

I open my eyes, releasing a shudder. The tense angle of his jaw demonstrates his need to pump into me. But he doesn't want to hurt me. That doesn't mean I'm not more than ready for us to begin.

My shoulders tremble as I slide against his lap, the ecstasy I feel coiling around my lower half and clenching my muscles. I withdraw, slowly before pushing him back inside me, my leisurely pace causing me to feel every part of him and making me grunt.

As I make another pass, I lift my chin to look at Finn, hoping he likes what I'm doing and pleased at what I find. His expression is one of agonized bliss. "Does it feel good, baby?" he asks.

"Yes," I bite out, my eyelids fluttering when I realize how easily this position reaches my G spot.

Finn's fingers dig into my hips, his chin falling forward to rest on my shoulder. "I was hoping you'd say that," he says, gasping. He lifts his head, pegging our reflections with one hell of a glance. "This is how I want to watch you come."

My body quivers from his words and my need to move faster. I glide forward and back, whimpering with each sweep of my hips.

With a sharp swear, Finn snaps his head back. My head lolls forward as that familiar ache builds with my increasing speed. It feels so good, I have trouble focusing and maintaining my pace. He clasps my hips, keeping us going. My chest heaves in and out, my body shaking as my core grips him tight.

"Touch yourself," he tells me, his raspy tone lowering.

It's something I've never felt comfortable doing before Finn. But he unleashes my feral side, the one that thrives on pleasing him. My hand slips between my legs as his arm curls around my waist. I force myself to augment our speed, clenching my teeth and trying not to full out scream as I writhe against him.

Our eyes appear closed in the mirror, but I know better. We're both watching, we both like what we see, and we're both losing control. Something this hot shouldn't appear so beautiful. Yet the way Finn's hands pass against the swells of my breasts, the curves of my body, and the way they thread through my hair, it is beautiful. He may whisper dirty words, he may groan with how good it feels, but it's the way we come alive that proves we're making and sharing love.

This time when I finish, I can't keep my balance—not in these shoes and certainly not from the force of our passion. I stumble forward, every inch of me hot and electrified.

Finn hooks his arm around me, catching me and keeping us together as he guides me forward. He steadies me against the dresser, pumping fast as I grip the edge. Another orgasm builds inside me, causing me to fall limp against the slick wood as he finishes filling me.

"*Fuck*," he gasps, collapsing almost on top of me.

It's like he can't believe what happened or how hot it was. Not that I blame him. It's like that with Finn, every time is almost like our first time, the need to please each other overwhelming our senses.

I push my crazy hair out of my face, watching as he nuzzles my neck and trails sweet kisses along my heated skin.

"I love you," I want to say. But I don't. I don't want him to think this feeling stems solely from the physical part of our relationship, so I promised myself I wouldn't tell him anymore in bed. That doesn't mean I don't want him to say it.

If it's how he feels.

It takes some time before either of us move, both of us struggling to keep somewhat vertical and catch our breaths. Finally, I shift my hips, resulting in both of us groaning, but smiling a little, too. There's nothing quite like that ache that follows sex with Finn. It gives me chills, reigniting my desire and making me want to beg him for more.

His palms rest on either side of me, his shoulders rising and falling with each profound breath. "Do you have any idea what you do to me?" he asks.

"No," I answer truthfully. But I really want to.

It's true. Finn has completely changed me. Sex was something I used to do because I believed it was a part of a relationship. I never sought it nor enjoyed it as much as I thought I could. Something was always missing. I realize now it's the passion I was for so long denied. That desire to feel wanted, needed, and special, is everything Finn makes me feel, and everything I want to give him in return.

He hugs me against him, clutching me like he'll never let me go. My arms lower to lay over his. No . . . maybe what was missing was Finn, my perfect hero in my very imperfect world.

I give a little wiggle, drawing his attention. He raises his head, meeting my face in the mirror. "We're not done yet, are we?" I ask, my voice so deep, it's barely recognizable.

His eyes sizzle as his hands lift to cup my breasts. "Oh, hell no," he says, angling his chin and kissing me fiercely.

CHAPTER 20

Sol

We were supposed to check out by eleven and head back to Philly by noon. But given how hard his hips slaps against mine, and how I'm gripping the edge of the mattress to keep from falling over the side, I'm reminded why we extended our stay, and why I had to call my father to tell him I wasn't coming home again.

Finn's arm hooks under my mine as we lay on our sides, his hand arching my neck so he can kiss me as he pumps. I want to kiss him. I do. But the position makes it hard and so does the force of my next orgasm.

His fingers tug on my nipples, only to slip down further to tease my throbbing center. I fall onto my stomach with my next release. As he finishes and he slumps on top of me, I know that at least for the moment we're both sated.

I shimmy beneath him, trying to lift my head. "Sorry," he says, rolling off me and collapsing onto his back.

With a whole lot of sleep-deprived effort, I scoot across the bed and closer to him, bending to kiss his lips. "Are you tired?"

"Oh, yeah," he answers.

I trace an invisible line between his pecs. "Are you hungry?"

"That, too," he confesses.

It's what he claims, but he seems so alert. Impressive

considering we've barely slept. I edge a little closer, causing him to lift his arm and tuck me against him.

As I gather the sheets around us, I debate whether I should order us a late lunch or an early dinner, seeing how we missed breakfast entirely. Mostly though, I'm just ready to sleep.

"I want to talk to you about something," he says.

His tone is serious. Yet I find him grinning when I glance up. "What is it?" I ask.

"Move in with me."

I blink a few times, wondering if I misheard. "Did you say—"

"Yeah. I want you to move in with me."

I lift my head, but my expression must be classic because he laughs. "I'm serious," he insists. "I already discussed it with Wren. She's fine with it since she'll still have the entire second floor to herself."

When I don't answer right away, his expression softens. "You weren't expecting this, were you?"

"No, I wasn't," I answer him, quietly.

He strokes my cheek. "You don't seem happy," he points out.

"It's not that I'm not happy you asked," I answer. "I mean, it tells me you're serious about us."

He frowns. "Of course I am. Don't you know what you mean to me?"

If I'm being honest, I don't. At least not completely.

"If it's Wren, we can find someplace else to live. I've banked and made enough fighting to buy another house outright." He scans my face when I don't respond. "I know you love the house, but I can't ask my sister to move out just because I want someone to move in."

"No, that's not what I'm saying," I add quickly.

He shifts us so we're facing each other directly. "Then what is it?"

It's a lot a things. I gather the blankets against my breasts, thinking matters through. "Finn, I love you. I've told you enough times so you know that it's true."

"But I haven't said it back," he says, finishing my

thoughts, but not exactly my words. "It's not really in me. Not something I go around saying."

My stare falls to his chest. His muscles are so pronounced by the way he's tensing his body. But I'm not exactly sure if I'm the sole cause of the tension or if there's more to what he's claiming. "You've never told anyone?"

"Never," he admits.

It makes me feel better to hear he's never said it to anyone, that doesn't mean I still don't wish he'd say it to me. But I won't force him, or back him into a corner to hear him say something he may never be ready to share. "Okay," I say, trying to respect his honesty and where he's coming from.

"Hey," he says. Kissing the tip of my nose. "That doesn't mean I don't feel it."

My breath hitches, yet I'll admit my surprise is brief. Maybe I'm too much of a girl, but if he can't say it, it's hard to believe he can mean it.

"It's not about the sex," he says. "That's not why I'm asking you to move in, if that's what you're thinking. I don't like being without you. Every time you go home to your folks . . ." He shrugs. "I don't know. I just hate it when you're gone."

"I know," I tell him.

"Do you?" he asks, cocking his head. "Cause it's the truth."

I nod, but the motion is so subtle, I'm not sure he notices. "I can tell by the way you hold me, and how you're always careful not to hurt me."

"So then what's bothering you?" He makes a face. "Besides your dad hunting me down and burying me beneath a plantain tree like he told me he would."

"It was a mango tree," I clarify. We're both trying to make light of it, but he's not coaxing that smile he wants from me, and I can't seem to rile it either.

"Babe," he says, rubbing his forehead with mine.

"Finn, I start the path to my doctoral program in the fall. It's a hard course, and the money I've saved will only cover minimal expenses—"

"I'm not asking you to pay rent, utilities, or even groceries. I'm only telling you I want you with me." He adjusts his position. "Kill and Sofia lived together before they were married. Yeah, her mom and Teo didn't like it, but it worked out for them."

"But Sofia wasn't completely dependent on Killian," I remind him. "She worked and earned her own money. Finn, I won't be able to do that."

"I don't care. I'll take care of you."

"I don't want you to take care of me." I don't mean it the way it comes out, and the hurt registering in his face makes me instantly regret what I said. I press my hand against his chest. "You know what I mean, right? All this is too soon and a lot more than I'm ready for."

"I'm not asking you to marry me," he says.

"I know," I respond, my quiet tone reflecting my disappointment. While I'm not ready for marriage, it would mean more if that's what he was asking.

His hand glides along my curve of my waist, his voice lowering from the depth of his emotions. "Me asking you to move in was supposed to be a good thing— Show you that I'm serious about us, and prove you're the only one I want to be with."

"I know," I tell him, unable to meet his eyes. "But I can't."

For a few long minutes, neither of us speaks. Our chests are touching, but he feels so far away. "Finn, don't push me away," I say when he withdraws.

He squares his jaw. "I'm not the one keeping us apart," he answers.

His words just about kill me. My eyes sting, blurring my vision. But as tough as he is, I swear my tears are his kryptonite.

"Sol, don't," he says gathering me to him. "Look . . . I'm not trying to hurt you."

He clutches me as I weep against his chest. I don't mean to get so upset, and it's not something I generally do around him. He's my heaven on earth. But the fact that I am makes me realize exactly how much I've been holding in. "I'm living a fantasy with you," I tell him.

"A sexual one?" he asks.

He's trying to make me laugh, and he does, even as my tears finish falling. I meet his face, my smile soft yet somehow there because of him. "What I mean is, my life with you doesn't feel real sometimes. It's more like a dream, an escape to someplace better. We laugh, have fun, attend events and enjoy each other, you know?"

He nods, like he understands. "Yeah. It's been real good. That's why I'm asking you to live with me. I like what we have and want to keep it going."

"But it's not reality, Finn. At least my reality. It's only a temporary reprieve from my problems."

"You mean your mom," he clarifies.

Catholic guilt is such a bitch. "Yes, my mom. I've ignored her to be with you. It's not right, and I hate myself for subbing out time with her just to be happy."

"You've had it rough. Is it such a bad thing to be happy? To want some joy after all the shit you've been through? I hope not," he murmurs when I don't answer. "Because *that* kind of happy—the kind I don't have to fake is what I feel when I'm with you."

"I feel it, too," I tell him gently.

"Good," he says. He lifts his hand to hold my face, his stare so intense I grow perfectly still. "Because I think we both damn well deserve it."

I push up when his lips sweep over mine. The way he kisses me is so lazy, but so sexy, my body melts against his. He rolls on top of me, positioning his body so he can play with my breasts and so that his growing length can slide and harden against my thigh.

I adjust my legs beneath him, causing his penis to fall between them. He lifts off me, just enough to grin his thanks before diving back and attacking my mouth with increasing fervor. He knows he makes me hot. But at this moment, I want to return some of that heat.

Using slow tilts of my pelvis, I urge him onto his side, continuing to kiss him and allowing him to play. Does he know what he does to me? How drunk I get from the scent of his skin, his taste, his touch . . . how the thought of him when I'm alone is enough to cause my hands to wander?

Again, I rock my lower body, encouraging him onto his back and rolling on top of him. I doubt I'm the first girl to straddle him. But I want to be the one he begs not to stop. My fingernails trail down his skin to his ribs, causing him to jerk. I do it again, knowing I'm tickling him and making it a game.

He jumps again, snagging my wrist. I grin as I tug on his lip and pull away. "You don't play nice," he says, his eyelids heavy.

"No?" I ask, dragging my pelvis over his thick staff.

He growls, drawing out the sound. Between those throaty sounds and the way his erection builds with each pass of my hips, I'm having a hard time keeping quiet and staying focused.

His palms push against my chest, making me think he wants to be the one on top until they squeeze my breasts all the way down to tips. I whimper, involuntarily pressing harder against his thickening staff and adding to my pleasure.

Finn's smile is so full of lust, I almost can't take it. "You like this?" he asks, rolling my nipples and inciting another gasp. "Yeah, you do don't you?"

If he'd like me to answer, I can't. Not with what he's doing to me. I lift up one leg and reach for his erection, watching him as I attempt to join us. His chest expands and contracts with each harsh breath, but I don't stop, slowly easing down until our bodies become one.

I fall forward, wanting desperately to kiss him. His arms wrap around me holding me tight, making it hard to move. I'm expecting him to flip me over and take control. But then his hands smooth down to my ass, encouraging my movements and forcing me to go faster.

My head snaps away from his. I can't keep kissing him, not with how loud I'm being and not when my core tenses around him. I lift off him, alternating between bouncing and rocking my hips, digging my nails into his shoulders. He arches his spine, clamping his jaw and swearing through his teeth.

My body moves faster, agonized bliss tearing through me. I collapse on top of him when I peak, overwhelmed with passion and the spasms claiming my body. But Finn's firm hold and the way he continues to drag my body against his prolongs it, leaving me a trembling mess.

As my orgasm recedes, he lifts my hand, pulling two fingers into his mouth and gliding them in and out. "Touch yourself while you ride me," he rasps, giving them one last flick with his tongue.

"Okay," I obey, my head spinning from how hard I released.

I lean back in a sharp angle, grasping his ankle for support. It's my lover's turn to feel all that pleasure, and I intend to give it to him. My slick fingers lower between my legs. "Is this what you want, baby?" I ask, my words releasing between my heavy pants. "Is this what you like?"

He mutters another curse as he watches, helping me take him hard. His skin reddens with each quick pass and from the frantic movements of my hand. This is supposed to be for him, but as my body tightens I realize how wrong I am.

This is all about us. It always has been. I feel it as I peak and his body bucks beneath me. As I fall back, I think we're done. Yet as good as it felt, I'm miserable it has to end.

We lay in a mess of limbs for what seems like too long. But then Finn stirs beneath me, untangling my legs just to toss them over his shoulders. As he begins to pump, I know we're far from done. I reach for him, whispering words of love and lust, begging him to go harder. He kisses my throat, eagerly complying, his thrusts deep and primal.

Our insatiable appetites remind us both that we're young, and passionate, and desperate for more of each other. And damn it, we need to be.

I meant what I said, my time with him is an escape, a moment for the darkness to skitter away and the light that Finn brings to gather me in its warmth. What I never expected was for all sense of light to abandon me.

Or for the darkness to arrive in one mighty burst.

CHAPTER 21

Finn

Sol stirs when I turn off the highway and onto the ramp. I rub her thigh when she yawns and tries to sit up. "Ouch," she says, rubbing her neck.

Yeah, that position against the window didn't look comfortable. "You okay?" I ask.

She nods, but still squints as she continues to rub. "Just a little sore."

So am I. And it's not from sleeping with my head pressed against the window that's for damn sure.

We didn't get much rest during our time in A.C.. I mean we did, but it was mostly small naps between rounds. I've had lots of good sex and a crazy amount of it. But it's never been with the same woman—not for this long—and it sure as anything hasn't come close to what Sol and I share.

I'm not complaining. I love Sol. I'm guessing what I feel for her plays a huge part in why I can't keep my hands off her.

And I'm not alone.

I think it was about three in the afternoon yesterday when I went to use the bathroom. I was brushing my teeth when Sol walked in. She was groggy, her eyes still partially closed. But as soon she saw me, it's like she was wide awake. She fell to her knees right in front of me, taking me deep. We were both bone tired, hungry, and pretty damn stiff. That didn't stop us from going at it on the bathroom floor.

It's like we both needed it—this time with just me and her. But as my truck draws closer to her neighborhood, it's all I can do not to turn around and drive us back to my house.

Her hand finds mine, holding me gently. I lift it to me and kiss it, meeting her smile when I glance briefly her way. But that sadness that's never far from the surface trickles its way into her voice as she leans her head against my shoulder. "Thank you for taking me with you," she says quietly.

Man, it always kills me to hear her sound so sad, *always*. But today it hits me worse. Maybe because these past few days have reminded me how good we are when we're together. I hate that I'm taking her someplace I'm not going to be. I want to tell her as much, but I don't want to be a douche bag about it. "Thanks for coming. It meant a lot."

She laughs a little. "That's what he said."

Ordinarily I'd laugh right along with her, since that's what we do all the time: laugh, joke, have a good time. But I don't laugh then because no matter how hot the sex is, I never want her to ever think I'm using her. Have I used girls in the past? Sure, just like they've used me.

My brothers and I are well known in Philly. We've all made a name for ourselves to some degree. Curran for being among the city's most revered cops, Declan for being a bad ass D.A., and Killian and me for our performances in the octagon. Our looks have played a part, sure. But it's our name and status that has gotten us the amount of tail we have.

When a couple of my brothers finally found love, I was happy for them. I was. I may have the rep for saying shit I shouldn't and acting like a clown, but I'm not stupid. Tess and Sofia, they're good for Curran and Killian, and bring out the good in them. Being as young as I am, though, I couldn't help thinking how much they were giving up by settling down. I didn't necessarily think they were pussies for it, but I couldn't relate or understand. To me, the world was full of women for the taking.

I never expected one woman to become my world.

So no, I don't laugh with her. Instead I squeeze her hand. "That's not what I saying," I tell her. I release a breath as I pull onto her street. Once more, my time with her has come to an end. She'll have dinner with her family while me and Wren will either order in, or eat at one of our brothers' places. Either way, Sol won't be with me and I totally hate it.

"I know," she answers quietly.

Most of the spots along the one way street are taken, so I have to park almost on the corner. I'm still on her side of the street, but we're about eight houses down. I cut the engine, abruptly shutting off the heat and the radio.

It's only fifteen degrees outside despite the sunshine. Being this close to March, it shouldn't be so damn frigid, but there are years where it's still snowing in April. I should keep the engine running, leave the heat on and keep her with me a little longer. But I've already pressured her enough by telling her I want us to live together. So if she needs a little space from me to think things through—needs to get back and check on her family, I want her to know I understand—that I'll give her the time she needs, despite that it's taking all I have not to pull back onto the street and drive away with her.

"What are you thinking?" she asks.

I don't look at her because I can't. I don't want to meet those large, light eyes right now, the ones who looked so sleepy yet so happy when I took that selfie of us this morning. Man, I can picture that image so well: her tucked against my chest as I held my phone up and away from us. It's my new wallpaper. You can't see much skin, but it's obvious we were naked and in bed. Maybe it's inappropriate, but it's my damn phone and this is how I like us: her close to me—not like she is now, moments from walking away.

"Finn?" she asks.

"You don't want to know what I'm thinking," I tell her.

She waits a beat, her small fingers skimming over my rough knuckles. "Are you mad, I'm not staying with you tonight?"

"I'm not mad that you're not staying with me," I admit. "I never want you to stay if you don't want to. But I am kind of pissed you have to leave."

"It's not that I want to leave you," she says. "I hate us

being apart."

Me too, baby.

For a moment, I just hold her. But when I look at her, even though I'm frustrated, sad, and somewhat angry, I smile. I can't help it. Sol makes me happy. "This is why it's hard to let you go. If you didn't want to be with me, it would be tough to hear and take, but I'd let you walk away because it's what you feel and want to do. But you sitting here, telling me you don't want to be without me, makes everything that much harder."

The way her stare travels along my face, I know she's not only listening to what I say, but sensing how every word carves into my bones like a saw.

"I wish me living with you could be as easy as that," she whispers.

My lips skim over hers. "And I wish you could see it's not as hard as you think."

I'm making her feel worse by saying what I do—and I hate myself for it. I don't want to guilt her into something she's not ready for, no matter how much I wish she was. That doesn't mean I can pretend like I never asked, or deny how I feel.

I'm ready for more. A lot more. Her moving in with me is just the start. "Will you at least think about it?" I ask quietly.

She averts her gaze, but nods. "I'll think about it."

"Yeah?" I ask, not sure she means it.

"Finn, it's not that I don't want to live with you." She leans in close, her pretty stare begging me to believe her. "I want to wake up with you beside me every morning, and your face to be the last one I see at night. But I'm not sure it's the right thing for me and my family. At least not now."

"I get it," I tell her.

"I hope so," she says, her voice laced with so much emotion it tugs at my heart in a way nothing else can. "Because when I tell you I love you, I mean it."

Her face lights up at my grin. This is one of those moments when life seems too perfect to be real.

So when the screaming starts, I'm reminded that nothing is perfect, and that life can be fucking cruel.

CHAPTER 22

Sol

Finn and I both jump, our bodies turning toward the sounds of those screams. It only takes me seconds to see what he sees, but those seconds freeze time and etch in my mind like words chiseled on stone.

Tía stumbles out of my house, barely clutching the metal railing in time to keep from falling. She's the one screaming—the one crying for someone to help her!

The clicking sound of Finn's seatbelt releasing and his door swinging open breaks through my shock. In the moment it takes me to unfasten my seatbelt and leap from his truck, he's already tearing down sidewalk. I'm running full out, skidding over the patches of ice and falling on my knees in front of Señora Segura's house. "*Sol, que pasa?*" she asks.

I can't tell her what's wrong. I don't know myself. All I know is that it's bad.

I ignore the pain of my throbbing knees as I struggle to stand. Finn reaches Tía who's now in hysterics. Between her sobs and her speaking rapidly in Spanish, I'm not sure how much he understands. But he understands enough: that she just arrived, my mother's name, and that she's not moving.

I didn't run far, but my heart is already ramming against my chest and my breath is burning through my lungs.

"Sol?" Señora Segura says, despite recognizing the severity of the situation.

"Call the police," I tell her in Spanish. I lurch forward only to slide yet again, vaguely aware of the growing numbers of neighbors opening their doors and hurrying out of their homes.

I make it to the bottom of my front steps just as Finn reaches the top. "Stay here," he barks before charging inside.

The aggression in his voice halts me in place. Something is very wrong. But as much as I'm afraid to see what it is, I can't do as he asks. I hurry up the concrete steps, stumbling when Tía snags my arm and pulls me back.

"Don't go inside!" she yells at me in Spanish.

I yank free from her grasp only for someone else to grab me. Tía and others gathered holler to those holding me to keep me back. I push up on my feet, slapping away the sea of hands trying to restrain me and sprint inside.

The heels of my boots slam against the wood floors as I reach our small foyer. I slow to a stop when I realize that no one is following me, and that the house is oddly silent.

"Finn?" I cry out.

It's like he's not even here. "*Finn?*"

I start toward the back when he yells from upstairs.

"Sol!"

His voice is pained, appearing to echo from all sides. "I need you to call an ambulance," he says over the rushed sounds of his movements. "Do you hear me? I need you to go to your neighbor's house and call an ambulance."

He doesn't want me upstairs. He's trying to get me to leave. Tears leak from my eyes. This is bad. This is really bad.

I turn to where Tía and a few of the neighbors are huddled at the front door. Mr. and Mrs. Turner are holding Tía up as she sobs. A few of the women are already crying. The men . . . they aren't much better.

"Sol?" Mr. Toleman extends his hand from where he's standing beneath the threshold, his face distraught. "Come on out here, baby," he says. "Come and wait with us outside. The ambulance is already on its way, sweetheart."

I stare at his hand and the lifeline he's offering. He wants to spare me from what's upstairs, from what I might find. I'm already crying. I know I should step outside. But I can't. That's my mother up there.

"*Sol, no vayas, niña,*" Tía wails. "*Por favor no vayas, mija.*"

Don't go, girl, she says. *Please don't go*. But I do. Forcing myself up the battered wood steps until I'm all but running. I slide down the hall, landing on my side, unsure what I slipped on until I see my hands soaked with blood.

For a second, all I can do is stare at the bright red fluid coating my palms. Somehow, I push up on my wobbly legs and stumble forward, halting in place when I reach my parents' room.

Finn is kneeling on the floor beside my mother, both are covered in blood. His jacket is draped over her body and he's pressing towels against her arms. "Sol, get downstairs," he bites out. "Get downstairs *now*."

My body checks out, slumping against the door frame as my mind takes in the room. Obscenities written in Spanish with my mother's blood splatter the walls, while she lies on the floor smiling and repeating the words.

"*Mami,*" I sob. "What did you do? *What did you do?*"

I fall beside her, my screams, my demands that she tell me how she could do this to herself—to my father—to me, drowning out Finn's words and his urges for me to leave.

My mother smiles despite her pallor, staring at the ceiling. I don't hear the police arrive. All I see is her. But they're suddenly there, storming in and surrounding us.

"Curran, get her out of here!" Finn hollers at his brother. "I don't want her to see this!"

My body is lurched backward. I fight to get back as medics speed past me.

"Sol, *Sol,*" Curran says in my ear. "Don't fight me. I need you outside, you hear me? Come outside with me so my boys can help her."

I continue to writhe, trying to fight my way back. But Curran is a big guy and I can't break free from his hold. He carries me down the stairs, away from the horror, and away from my mother. The cluster of neighbors gathered outside part, covering their mouths when they see me.

"Teo, *Teo*," Curran calls when he steps forward. "Take Sol and keep her with you."

Teo has me, but I don't see him. I'm crying so hard all I make out is Curran racing back into the house and the police ordering the growing crowd of neighbors back. Teo is talking to me, and Sofia, too. I think Killian is there, but I'm not sure. I'm crying so hard I'm sick down to my gut, wanting to vomit.

I look up when the crowd gasps. Finn, his light blue shirt soaked through with my mother's blood, robotically walks down the steps; his face ashen. Teo in his shock loosens his hold, allowing me to wriggle free and run to Finn.

Finn gathers me to him, shielding me with his body. "I'm sorry, baby," he says. "Jesus Christ, I'm so sorry . . ."

My hands quiver as I lift the paper cup to my lips. It's tea. Killian was nice enough to buy it for me, but I can't bring myself to sip it and lower it back down to my lap. I'm shaking so badly it can't be normal. That chill, that same one that's claimed me since first seeing my mother, continues to rack my bones despite Finn's strong arms around me.

In the corner, Teo is on the phone with Evie. This is the second time she's called. But like the time before, Teo doesn't have anything new to share.

The cuts to her arms weren't fatal, nor did she sever any major arteries, but she'd lost so much blood. My head pounds as I recall the smears of red splattered all over the walls, the floors, and on our clothes.

Sofia crouches in front of me. "Do you want me to hold it for you?" she asks, motioning to my cup.

I nod because I'm done talking. Thank God the questions from the police were few, and thank God Curran assured me they'd stay that way. Tía called Teo instead of the police. It's just like her not to phone the police directly. Thankfully, Teo reached out to Curran and he took charge, assembling everyone my mother needed.

My mother . . . my mother is a sick woman.

My attention travels to my right, where my poor father sits in a metal chair, his head bowed and his focus on his clasped hands. I think he's praying again, for my mother, for strength, and for heaven knows what else. God knows we need it all.

Finn tucks me against him when I cover my eyes with my hand. He probably thinks I'm going to cry. But even if I wanted to, I'm all out of tears.

No, crying is the last thing I want to do right now. I just can't look at my father then. It's too hard. Not only because he appears so worn, but because he seems so defeated.

When I wasn't looking, my father became an old man, aging as a result of caring for the woman he promised forever. How could he know this woman would change so much, that she'd forget who we were, and that she'd inflict so much damage to herself and those she should most love?

"Sol," Sofia says, quietly. "I know you don't want to take anything, but the doctor on call says he can prescribe something if you need it."

I lower my hand slowly. "I don't want any meds."

"I know you don't, sweetie, and ordinarily I wouldn't push you. But Sol, right now you're not in a good place, and I'm worried."

Sofia doesn't like medication and avoids even ibuprofen at all costs. For her to insist I should take something, proves I look about as good as I feel. "I don't want anything," I repeat, adding to her concern by shuddering.

She watches me, but doesn't say anything else, lifting her chin to face Finn. "How are you doing?"

"Don't worry about me," he says, his hand stroking my arm. "I'm fine."

He doesn't sound fine. He hasn't since he ran into my house. My body tenses when I see how pale he remains. Killian and Teo offered to get him something to eat, but like me, he declined.

"I thought she was okay," Papi says.

We turn his way, but he doesn't look up, choosing instead to talk at the floor. "She seemed in good spirits. Happy. When they called me into work early, I thought it would be a good way to make money—to remodel the kitchen for her. I thought, I thought . . ."

My father breaks down, weeping into his hands. Sofia rushes to his side, hugging him and whispering kind words in Spanish.

"He wasn't gone long when I arrived," Tía adds. "Five, maybe ten minutes."

It's not the first time they've told us as much, but their guilt over what happened causes them to repeat their stories. Mami was fine. Papi left. Tía walked in after paying the cab and found her. Mami wasn't alone long. But it was long enough to carry out her plan, or should I say, the plan the voices came up with.

We glance up when the attending physician walks toward us. Teo stands to greet him, Killian just to his right. But it's my mother's treating psychiatrist that my attention skips to. "Mrs. Marieles is stable," the doctor says. "Physically, she should make a full recovery."

But not mentally, he doesn't add.

"We'll keep her here until we're sure she's safe to transfer."

"Transfer her to a different unit?" Teo questions.

It's what he asks, and what we expected. But the doctor's tone leaves the impression that a different unit won't be enough. He edges away allowing Dr. Franco to step forward. "I need to speak to you privately, Mr. Marieles," he says to my father.

Papi shakes his head. "No. If you have something to say, please tell all of us. We are her family."

"Very well," Dr. Franco says, taking a moment to gather his thoughts. "Flor's mental health has deteriorated significantly. She's not only a danger to herself, but to others. I'm recommending she be admitted to a psychiatric hospital."

The knot twisting my stomach tightens further.

"For how long?" Papi asks, frowning as if he doesn't

understand him.

Dr. Franco meets my father square in the eye. "It may be permanent," he says. "I'm sorry, Mr. Marieles, but your wife may never be well enough to return home . . ."

CHAPTER 23

Finn

I check my phone as I take the elevator down to the lobby, hoping Sol has called. It took a lot to convince her to come down to A.C.. And while she wouldn't drive down with me, claiming she had to visit her mom, she still said she'd head down tonight if she could.

"If" she could. It doesn't sound like much, but it's better than her original "no". It gave me hope, maybe things between us aren't as bad as I think, and maybe we just need time. But I'm not so sure.

I shove my phone in my back pocket. No new messages from her, no texts, not even an email. I cross my arms and lean against the elevator wall, trying not to react when a young couple who can't seem to keep their hands off each other steps on.

These two with how happy they seem, that used to be me and Sol. Things were so good between us until they weren't.

I don't want to think about losing Sol, and I don't want to keep reliving that day we found her mom. But I can't shake the thoughts no matter how hard I try.

Sol was supposed to be here hours ago so we could catch the fights together. Like me and Kill figured, Sumar got the title bout against the champ. He brought the drama and the hype to get fans talking and helped sell out the arena.

The champ beat his ass tonight three minutes into the first

round, proving Sumar wasn't ready to take him on. So who's next in line for the belt? Me, if I can win my fight next month against the number two guy who challenged me.

Kill gave me the news earlier. I should have been out of my mind. It's what I've worked for. But the combination of finding Sol's mother almost dead, and the distance between me and Sol sent me back down that dark path I thought was finally behind me. So instead of losing my shit, it took all I had just to fist bump Kill, the images of Flor's suicide attempt erasing any joy I could feel.

I step out of the elevator. We're at a different hotel than we were in last time. Still, it feels weird being in A.C. without Sol. What's stranger, though, is what's happened to us.

The woman in front of me jumps when her boyfriend or whoever grabs her ass. She shoves him away, laughing. I scoot around them, unable to watch. They remind me too much of what I no longer have.

Damn, wasn't it just a few weeks back that me and my girl were practically inseparable? How the hell did we go from doing everything together to nothing at all? I suppose I could handle our time apart better if this was all about her mom—her needing to deal with what happened, needing to spend more time with her family, and maybe needing therapy of her own. But I can't shake the feeling she's cutting me loose.

Ever since we found her mom, it's like there's this wedge shoved between us, forcing us apart. It doesn't matter that I tried to help or spare Sol from it. The way she's acting toward me, how distant she is, I feel like she blames me for what happened. I've tried talking to her about it, but she's barely speaking to me. And even though what happened occurred in her home, she hasn't spent the night with me since her mother was committed.

I know what she saw messed her up. It messed me up, too. The blood, the violence—I don't know, it tripped me up worse than anything in the octagon ever has. I spoke to Mason about it, and how it's unearthed a shitload of memories I've tried to forget. He prescribed anti-anxiety and anti-depressant medication, a double whammy that hasn't done anything. I made the mistake of telling Sol I was on meds. If I didn't think she could look more upset, she proved me wrong.

I hurry across the lobby, glancing toward the restaurant where I'm supposed to meet Kill and Sofia when my phone rings.

Killian's face flashes across the screen. "Hey, Kill," I say.

"Finn, it's Sofia."

"I'm coming. You already inside?"

"No. I'm so sorry," she whispers. I hear noise in the background, but it's like she's tucked away in some corner or in another room. "We're still at the arena dealing with what happened."

"What do you mean?" I ask, slowing my steps.

"You haven't heard?"

Oh, this can't be good. I stop a few feet from the entrance to the restaurant. "No . . . What happened?"

She pauses. "Ruban tested positive for steroids."

"Are you fucking kidding me?"

"No," she says. "The opposing camp suspected he was doping, and demanded a test following his win. It came back positive. Killian completely lost it on him. Gosh, Finn. Here's a guy with so much natural talent, and someone we've spent months helping, and he does this. Killian is livid and dealing with the press now."

Son of a bitch. We recruited Ruban out of Drexel and have been training him to be the next Bantam weight champion and *this* is what he pulls? "I want him off our team. He had his chance and he blew it."

"Killian says the same thing. I guess you both can meet with him on Monday and give him the news." She sighs. "It's not pretty down here. It might be a while so get something to eat without us."

"All right," I say.

She doesn't disconnect right away and neither do I. "Is something wrong?" she asks.

I don't want to sound like a pussy, but I'm hoping Sofia knows something I don't. "Have you heard from Sol?" I ask.

I can almost picture her knitting her brows. "No. Isn't she there with you?"

"No. She hasn't shown and she hasn't called."

There's some shuffling on the other end before she answers again. "She's not herself, Finn."

"Tell me something I don't know," I mutter. The thing is, I'm not myself either, which is one of the many reasons I need her here with me. As it is, another image of her mother lying on the floor flashes across my mind.

I step away from the clear glass doors leading into the restaurant when the hostess struts forward and opens the one on the right side. She motions me in with a tilt of her head. I lean my back against one of the large pillars, averting my gaze from hers when she smiles.

I caught her eyeing me earlier when I came in following the fights, checking me out like she wanted a bite. But based on that grin she's flashing me, she's wants more than a nibble now.

"You don't sound good, Finn," Sofia says.

My hand drags across my face as yet another image of Sol's mom pops in my head, this one of her laughing as she's carried out on a stretcher and placed in the back of the ambulance.

"Finn?" Sofia says again.

Her voice draws me back to reality. I've been doing that a lot lately—zoning out just like I used to. Only this time the memories I see revolve around Flor . . . and what happened to me when I was a kid. It should scare me, worry me— and it does— but given what's happened, I can't say I'm surprised.

"Finn? Are you okay?" Sofia presses.

"I'm fine," I tell her, because it beats telling her I can't shake the image of her psychotic aunt, or that I keep looking down on my arms expecting them to be covered in blood. I don't want to admit how I still picture the way Sol cried against me—how shitty I felt when I couldn't ease her pain. I also don't tell her how bad the experience fucked me up—how I keep dreaming about it, except that in my dreams, I'm the one lying on that floor.

"I'm fine," I repeat, before I realize I already said it.

"I don't think you are," she says. "Look, maybe I can get away—"

"No. Stay with Kill," I insist. "You said so yourself he's pissed. You're the only one he's going to want to talk to after this whole thing wraps up." And probably the only one who can calm his ass.

"Finn," she starts to say.

"You worry too much," I say, forcing a smile like she can somehow see me. "I'll be fine."

I say it because I need to and disconnect. Too bad I don't believe it. Like I mentioned, every time I close my eyes I relive every detail of the day—the look on Tía's face when she told me what she found, how the floor felt against my feet as I raced into the house, and Sol's screams. Shit, her *screams*. I remember them down to pitch and length. I didn't understand all her words—not with how fast she was speaking in Spanish. But her pain? I felt that loud and clear.

What it comes down to is that as much as it hurt me, it hurt her a thousand times worse. My pain isn't the same. I'm not going to pretend like it is. But the pain I do feel is something I don't need. It claws at my insides, exposing my wounds and spilling my bad memories. All of them. Especially the ones I've spent a lifetime beating down.

Come on, why don't you trust me? the voice of that bastard says. *You're hurting my feelings.*

My thumb passes over the screen of my phone as I ram my eyes closed. "No . . . not now," I mutter.

Come on. Just come in for a little while. I have plenty of toys you can play with . . .

Before I can think, I'm already headed in the direction of the bar. But each step brings another shitty memory: My father yelling at me and my brothers to clean the house as he heads out to see his mistress. My mother crying as she holds me, promising me that I'll be all right. The agony I felt the first time I had my nose broken. And the look on Angus's face when he told me Papa was dead. The memories fade in and out like winds of a wicked storm as I slip onto the stool, but it ends with the one I can't stomach the most. The one of the door slamming shut and trapping me inside that monster's house.

"What are you having?" the bartender asks.

"Beer—non-alcoholic," I add quickly.

I think I'm okay. No booze is a good start. But if so, what am I doing sitting here? And if it's a step forward, why won't these memories stop?

I reach for my phone again, skimming through the pictures. I stop at the first selfie Sol took of us. I tried to be all cocky about it. After all, there I was with this hot young woman pressed against me. But the way she looked into the camera wasn't like she was showing off the famous Philly boy holding her. She was just, I don't know, *happy* to be in *my* arms.

I skim to the next picture. Again, she's beaming. Her arms around my shoulders, her face against mine. Damn, she's beautiful, too beautiful for the likes of a screwed up sap like me.

That doesn't stop me from texting her.

Right now my memories are drowning me in darkness and saturating me with their poison. As stupid as it sounds, only Sol and the memories of us are capable of stopping this shit.

"Sol, I really need you here," I speak into the mic, my voice shaking even though I don't want it to. Another memory flashes across my mind, this one of Killian when he found out what happened to Sofia. Hell, it's like these memories are sucker-punching me, demanding I pay attention.

I glance down at the screen. Of course the voice to text translates her name into "soul". I don't bother fixing it, probably because she found a way into *my* soul.

Shit. Or what's left of it.

I watch the screen, waiting for her to text back, swallowing my pseudo drink down with a lot of effort. I'm still watching my phone, waiting for it to ring when the bartender makes his way back to me. "You want another one?" he asks, motioning to my empty bottle.

It tastes like shit and I feel like shit because I can't drink the "real" kind. And because my girl isn't down here with me or bothering to text back.

"I'll take a Corona," I say, twisting the bottle in my hand.

"You sure?" he asks.

Because only alcoholics trying not to be alcoholics drink that piss water, he doesn't add. "Yeah. I'm sure."

One beer. A real one. What could it hurt?

I lift my phone when it buzzes. I'm relieved when I see it's Sol texting until I read what she has to say.

I'm sorry. But I'm not going to be able to make it.

"Oh my God. That's the Fury—Finn O'Brien," some woman squeals behind me.

I ignore her, and the friend she's with who asks if she's sure it's me.

Because of your mom? I text back.

She waits to respond. *Because of a lot of things*, she finally answers.

I start to text back when she adds, *I don't think I'm the best person for you right now.*

Fuck. Doesn't she know she's the only person I need?

You're wrong, I text back. *Come down to A.C. so I can prove how wrong you are.*

The bartender slides a Corona in front of me. I reach to pull a twenty from my wallet, but the bartender shakes his hand. "It's on the ladies," he says, jerking his chin toward the end of the bar.

I nod my thanks in their direction. Big mistake. The blond and the brunette—both with extra-large fake tits shimmy down. "Hi," the brunette says. "I'm Lindsey, and this is Tiffany."

"Hey," I say. I huff when Sol sends me another text.

I'm sorry. I can't.

My breath spreads across the screen before disappearing. I know she's screwed up from the way we found her mother. Hell, how can she not be? But she has to realize it screwed me up, too.

Her mom may be suffering from mental illness. But right now, so am I. Is that where I'm headed? Part of me knows that it is. This depression shit—that's what it'll do to me in time. These meds I'm on, aren't doing anything—I've been on them what? A couple of weeks? Mason said it would take time for them to kick in, but what am I supposed to do in the meantime? When will they stop me from seeing all the bad stuff I've lived and breathed?

I still wake up hating myself, fucking agonizing over what I've been through. But now, after the incident with her mom, it's like I can't get away from it even long after I'm awake.

It's more than anyone can take. I know it is. There's no relief from it . . . well, almost.

It's only when Sol's with me that I see how good life can be. She doesn't judge, she doesn't stare at me like I let her down—like I can't possibly screw up worse. She just listens, speaking softly like I need her to, and lighting up my world with her smile.

At least she used to. Now she's not even here.

Please, Sol. I need you, baby, I type out.

"Girl problems?" Mindy or whatever the hell her name is asks.

"That's one way to put it," I answer, waiting for Sol's response.

I can't, she texts back. *Finn, I'm not in a good place.*

Neither am I without you, I respond. I don't mean to put my baggage on her. God knows she's going through her own kind of hell. But she and I, together we make sense. We're good as one. But apart, I don't think either of us can make it.

When she doesn't reply to my last text, I toss my phone on the bar and lean against the slippery wood, frustrated and nervous about the next swarm of memories that will come without her here. No sooner do I close my eyes than I see her mother covered in blood, that crazy smile glued to her face as she looks at the ceiling, laughing at shit that wasn't there.

I want to shake my head and admit how messed up that is—and it is. But there's a piece of me wondering if one day someone will find me that way, alone in a row house, happy that I'm dying so I'll finally have some mother-fucking peace. I pinch the bridge of my nose, trying not to curse with frustration since the other part of me doesn't want to hurt my family or Sol—it wants to live and be happy.

I just don't know how.

I down the beer, the liquid cooling my insides, but offering only marginal relief. "Can I ask you something?" the brunette says.

I turn, like the blonde, she seems all excited, even though I've mostly ignored them. "Sure."

"Are you Finn O'Brien?"

"That's me," I say.

Her friend does a little finger wave to the bartender, similar to what Sol did a few weeks back when she wanted me to follow her into my bedroom. The bartender doesn't miss a beat and slams another Corona in front of me.

"Your brother's Killian O'Brien, right?" she asks.

I nod because what else am I going to do?

"I knew it," she says. "Me and Tiff have been following MMA for years—we were like, so thrilled when your brother won the championship." Her smile goes from cheery to playful. "And when you came along. Let's just say we were a little more thrilled."

"Thanks." I throw back the beer. Maybe it's because I've been sober, or maybe it's because I've been cutting weight, but this one has me feeling something. It's not much. But it's there.

She inches over. "Do you mind getting a picture with us?"

"Sure," I mutter.

I slip my arms around them when they ask the bartender to take our picture. He drops a few shots close to the blonde before lifting their phones from the bar. The celebrity thing comes with the MMA status. I see it as part of the job, part of the image. It's all good, and it doesn't mean anything. So when they lean against me and press their palms against my pecs and abs, I let them. Just like I let them kiss my cheeks. But when the blonde flicks my earlobe with her tongue and tries to take a tug with her teeth, I step away.

"Sorry, sweetheart. I have a girlfriend," I tell her.

She glances at her bestie like she's disappointed, like she

expected a lot more. But I mean what I say. My problem is, I'm starting to feel a little too good. I finish my beer as another is placed in front of me along with a shot. There's another shot after that, making the beers that follow easy to take.

I'm not supposed to drink. I'm not supposed to be here. But I want to forget about everything—Sol's mother, all I've seen, and what I'm feeling by not having Sol and her smile here with me.

Except after another few drinks I forget *too* much.

Like why I shouldn't be here at the bar and with these women.

CHAPTER 24

Sol

I crank the heat in my car. God, it's already April, but the nights are still freezing. At a light I call Wren.

"Hello?" she says.

"Wren, it's Sol. I'm down in A.C., but I can't reach Finn, and Sofia and Killian are tied up. Do you know where he is?"

"You're just getting here now?" she asks.

It's almost two in the morning. Like Finn, she probably expected me hours ago. I'm too embarrassed to admit I almost didn't come. To be honest, I didn't have any desire following the week I had.

The only institution my father's insurance would cover was something out of a nightmare. I've spent every day visiting my mother, trying to protect her and shield her in the way I failed to do before she attempted suicide.

If it hadn't been for our extended family rallying and offering to pay for her care at a private facility, that horrible institution is where she'd still be. I couldn't stop crying when Teo gave me the news—so thankful they could help her, but so crushed that this is what's become of her life. She doesn't know me. As much as I need my mother, it's like I'm nothing to her.

"I couldn't leave until late," I say, sparing Wren from the latest drama.

Obviously, she can hear in my voice that there's more to

my story. "You okay?" she asks, that underlying tone of concern softening her speech.

"Not really," I answer.

I'm drained. I'm done. I can't even pretend that I'm okay. It's clear in my tone and in the way I carry myself. Emotionally and physically I'm beyond exhausted. Yet despite my need to sleep, I haven't been able to. Not really. Just like I haven't been able to be there for Finn.

Finn . . . Christ. I can't believe I did this to him. As hard as life has been for him, finding my mother was the last thing he needed. Who am I kidding? *I'm* the last thing he needed. But he's trying. It's only fair that I try, too.

"Sorry," Wren responds. "I'm at the hotel. Come here and we'll figure things out."

"You're at the hotel?" I repeat.

She doesn't miss the surprise in my voice. Wren loves club hopping and partying following the big fights. It's odd for her to already back in her room.

"Yeah. Rough night," she mutters. "How far away are you?"

I glance at the overhanging street signs. "I just turned on Renaissance Way."

"Okay. I'll come down. Just grab your stuff and have the valet park your car. We'll register it under my room and I'll help you find Finn."

"You don't know where he is?" I ask.

If he wasn't with Killian and Sofia, I thought for sure he'd be with Wren. "No. But there are a couple of fighters he's chummy with here, too. He's probably with them."

It's possible. But most fighters party hard following the main event, something Finn's tried to avoid. If he's with them now, it could mean trouble.

I shouldn't go there, but I can't shake the feeling that if he's out partying, I've pushed him to it. My family problems were the last thing he needed in his life.

"Wren, I'm here," I say, when I see the sign to the Water Club. "Could you come down?"

"I'm on my way, girl," she says.

The valet opens the door for me as a big gush of wind slams into me. I huddle into my coat and snag my large purse. A change of underwear and a toothbrush are all I brought with me. I can't stay with Finn like before, my mother needs me. But I also can't ignore him. Not after how good he's been to me and not with how much he still means to me.

After rereading his texts, I realized that in trying to protect him, I was hurting him, deeply. He's already been through so much. I won't allow him to suffer more at my hands.

"Are you a guest of the hotel, miss?" the valet asks.

"Yes, sir," I say.

I hurry into the lobby, seeking warmth and hoping it won't take me long to find Finn. My phone buzzes. I hurry to see who's texting me, hoping it's him, only to see a message from Sofia.

We're on our way back to the hotel. Where are you?

The hotel lobby, I answer. *Wren's coming down for me.*

Where's Finn? She asks.

I don't know, I respond.

He hasn't replied to my last few texts. I know he's mad. I can't blame him and wish I could make things right. But I swear as much as I love him, I can't help feeling like I'm hurting, rather than helping him.

"Sol!" Wren calls out when she sees me.

She's dressed in those Victoria Secret sweatpants she loves and a long-sleeved shirt, leaving me with the impression she's been back to her room a while. But it's the large bruise along her eye and cheek that has me hurrying to her.

"Oh, my God. What happened?" I ask her.

She shrugs. "Went to a bar, got into it with some stupid girl. Her boyfriend nailed me when I knocked her on her ass."

"Wren! Some guy hit you?"

She shrugs again. "Like I said, rough night."

"Were you by yourself, did anyone help?"

She grabs my hand, leading me toward the front desk. "Yes. And yes," she says, before turning her attention to the woman working the desk. "Hey, I need to register a car under room 1129."

"Wren, what aren't you telling me?"

"Only that the bouncers tossed him out," she answers. "They were calling the police, but I didn't want the hassle and left."

The clerk passes me a card to fill out, but all I can do is gape at Wren's bruises. She's a tough girl, and she teaches self-defense. This guy must have been a fighter, or trained, or something. "Your brothers are going to freak out," I say, pointing out the obvious.

"Probably. But most of them aren't here because Finn wasn't fighting. I was bored and needed to blow off some steam. Thought I'd go for a drink. If I knew this would happen I would have stayed in."

She's giving me too many details and explaining *way* too much, like she's been rehearsing what to say. "You weren't with the other fighters?" I press. Whoever hurt her is someone who's used to brawling. Based on the damage, that much is clear.

"No, I told you I was by myself," she says, trying a little too hard to sound casual. She laughs and taps on the card I'm supposed to be filling out. "Come on. It's not like it's the first time I've ever been in a fight. Fill out the card and let's find Finn so I can get back to bed."

"Okay," I tell her, even though it's not.

Something happened she doesn't want me to know. Yet based on how she shuts me out, she's not ready to talk about it. Someone like Wren, you can't push. She pushes back, cementing walls around herself to keep her safe.

I fill in the information and hand it to the person at the desk, mowing over what to do. The moment I'm done, she starts to walk away.

"Wren, wait," I call, hurrying to catch up. When she turns to face me, I can practically feel those walls around her. No, now is definitely not the time to talk about what happened. But I want her to know that I care. "Look, if you ever want to talk . . . I'm here for you, okay?"

Her tough girl persona softens a little as she takes in my wounded demeanor. "Sol, you have enough going on without worrying about my shit. Just be there for yourself and my brother. I can handle the rest on my own."

Based on those bruises and how hurt she seems, I'm not so sure. She puts her arm around me, leading me forward. "There are a few people I can call to see if they've seen Finn," she says, quickly switching the subject. "Let's head back to my room and we'll split up the list."

Her voice trails as her attention cuts toward the bar. "What the fuck?" she snaps, charging forward.

With how pissed she seems, I almost think she spotted the man who attacked her. I come to an abrupt halt when I see what she sees. *Finn* is slumped across the bar, two girls hanging all over him and attempting to drag him away.

I don't remember bolting after Wren. I'm just suddenly there. "Come on, Fury," the blonde to Finn's right giggles, slurring her words. "Let's finish the party back in our room."

She stops laughing at the sight of me and Wren. "Who the hell are you?" Wren snaps.

The brunette pushes her hair away, the humor in her face morphing into annoyance. "One of his dates for the night. Who the hell are you?"

Oh, honey, we're so not the right women to talk to this way. I may be nice. And I may be considered a professional. But right now, I'm the irate Philly girl whose man these skanks are touching.

Wren and I edge closer, but it's Wren who speaks first. "I'm his sister, the same chick who's going to knock you on your ass if you don't get your hands off him." She hooks her thumb my way. "And this is his girlfriend, who trust me, won't be as nice. Get the *fuck* away from him."

They don't budge, but neither do we. Anger like I've never felt burns its way through me. Finn is wrecked out of his mind. These girls know it—in fact, they probably helped get him this way. But it's the underlying guilt—the belief that my problems played a role in his condition—*and* the way the blonde strokes his arm possessively that sharpen my tone. "Touch him again, and I swear to God I'll smash that beer bottle across your damn face."

She freezes, as she should, and drops her hand away. She steps back as I move forward, and so does her friend in time for Sofia and Killian to arrive.

"What the hell is this shit?" Killian snaps.

One of the girls whispers to the other, causing her eyes to widen. They recognize Killian, just like they recognize their fun is over.

Wren shakes Finn's shoulder. "Finnie, Finnie, can you hear me?"

He lifts his head in my direction. "Sol?" he says, stumbling forward. He pulls me to him, kissing me hard. But when I jerk my chin and break our kiss, he practically falls on top of me.

Killian snags him, lifting him off me before I topple over. "He's wasted," Killian mutters, hooking his arm over his shoulder. "Come on. Let's get him upstairs."

I grab his phone from the bar and follow, Sofia and Wren hot on my trail. "He wouldn't have gone with them," Sofia says. "Not willingly."

"Even as drunk as he is no way would he cheat on you," Wren adds.

They're trying to make excuses for him, for why he was with them. They know I'm livid. But I'm not solely pissed about what I saw and who I found him with.

My eyes burn. Yet for now, I refuse to cry

We slip into the elevator, hauling ass before anyone else sees him. "Where's Sol?" Finn mumbles, his head slumped.

"She's here," Sofia says, glancing my way when I don't answer.

He starts to fall forward again when he attempts to walk, but Killian holds onto him. "We can't leave him alone like this," Sofia says quietly.

It's her way of volunteering to stay with him. But that's not her job. For now, it's mine. "I'll take care of him," I say, my focus glued to the door.

"Are you sure?" she asks.

"I'm sure," I say, anger and hurt causing my voice to quiver.

Wren takes one look at my face and backs away. "Shit.

You're not going to kill him in his sleep are you?"

She's joking, even though she knows I'm angry. But I can't laugh then. "I would never hurt him," I answer, that awful tremble in my voice showing how close I am to losing it.

Who am I kidding? I've already hurt Finn in ways I never thought possible.

The elevator door dings open and we step out. Sofia pulls out Finn's wallet and fishes through it. "I have his key," she says.

Killian doesn't respond, his face shadowed with worry. He doesn't say anything until we reach his room and he lowers him to the bed when I pull away the blankets.

"You need us, you call," he says to me. "We're one floor above you."

He marches out, Sofia's hand tight in his. Wren doesn't appear any happier, crossing her arms as she takes in Finn's unmoving form. "You want me to stay?"

I glance at her. In all the fuss, and with all the low lighting, Killian and Sofia didn't see her bruises. But I noticed she kept her unaffected side to them. Yet I can't talk to her about it now, not with the condition Finn is in.

I return my attention to him. "I'll be okay," I answer.

I remove Finn's shoes and socks and cover him with a sheet. But it's not until I fill a pitcher of water and place it and a glass on the bedside table that she speaks again.

"Sol, thanks for being here," she tells me. "Like I said, Finn needs you."

I walk her out and push the security lock in place, but as I return to the bedroom area and take in Finn's draped form I realize she's wrong.

I'm the last thing he needs.

CHAPTER 25

Sol

For a long time all I do is watch Finn sleep. He seems so peaceful. But it kills me to know he had to get wasted to achieve this kind of peace.

I slip out of my coat. I didn't even realize I still had it on, my mind too preoccupied with how I found Finn. I know why he did what he did. "Anesthetizing". It's what one of my former Profs called it, a fancy way to describe drinking or drugging to numb the pain.

God, it hurts knowing I'm the cause of his relapse.

Yet it hurts more knowing what I have to do to help him recover.

I'm not being a martyr. At least, I don't mean to be. But I can't deny the role my family and I played in his downward spiral. We practically shoved him off the wagon. Seriously, how could he possibly stand a chance at sobriety seeing what he saw, and then dealing with me afterward?

My intuition warned me to keep my distance the first time I saw him at the clinic, reminded me that two damaged people shouldn't get involved, shouldn't be together— not when their wounds were still so fresh. I knew this. Every passage I've read about codependency reinforced these facts. And still I let him into my heart.

Yet somehow, all the facts I read weren't always true. We were good together. We laughed, we supported each other, and we loved. We were *so* good together.

Until we weren't.

I lower myself to the edge of the bed. As angry and upset as I am about everything that transpired, my old friend exhaustion creeps in, making it hard to remain standing. I should sleep on the couch, and not be near him. But as much as I know it's time to walk away, the need to feel close, this one last time, lures me.

My fingers smooth his hair. He hates the slight wave to it and usually doesn't allow it to grow long enough for the edges to curl. I don't mind, and like the softness to it. But then I like everything about him, everything that makes him "Finn" . . . even those demons he hides because don't we all have our share?

Yet as much as I've wanted to support and love him, I fed those demons instead of lulling them to sleep.

"I should have stayed away from you," I whisper. "I should have kept my distance and left you alone."

It's my last comment that stirs the misery I've tried to beat back. But when his hand covers mine, and he moves it toward his face, I just about break down.

"Hey, beautiful," he whispers against my palm, his breath soft and warm.

The gesture is my undoing. I miss him and his sweet personality. I miss that tender side he reserves solely for me. I miss how we laughed, and I miss the way we touched. But I've been selfish, keeping him with me and causing him trauma he could have done without.

Shit. It was bad enough that he found my mother the way he did. But then he prolonged the experience by staying to comfort me when I fell into hysterics. Some counselor I am. I couldn't save my mother, and I worsened Finn's depression.

I bend and kiss his cheek, my tears dripping onto the bed. "I'm sorry," I say quietly, because God knows, I truly am.

I wish I could say I don't regret my time with Finn, but I do. If I hadn't come along, he wouldn't be this bad off. Mason would be helping him recover, and he'd be in a better place. "I'm sorry," I say, again.

He mumbles something I can't quite understand. I think he wants water. I start to rise to hand him the glass when his grip tightens over mine. "No," he slurs. "I want you to lay with me."

For all I know, he thinks I'm one of the women who planned to spend the night with him. It should make me angry, but instead it makes me sadder. I lay beside him, my back against his chest. He fastens his arm around my waist as I gather the sheets around us. But when his lips pass along my neck and his hand slips beneath my shirt, I know we're not going to sleep.

I should tell him, no, and leave the bed. Wasted or not, Finn wouldn't force me to have sex with him. Yet as much as I know I shouldn't be with him, I don't stop him, allowing him to roll me onto my back and kiss me.

My arms slide around his neck when he climbs on top of me and starts to rub his groin between my legs. I don't think he can get hard, not with how drunk he remains. But as his erection presses against me, he proves how wrong I really am.

He shouldn't feel this good. But he does. He always has.

I tug off his long-sleeved T-shirt when he strips me out of my top and bra. His movements aren't smooth, not like I'm used to. But that doesn't stop me from craving his touch, nor does it stop my whimpers when he dips his head to suck on my nipples.

He swears with frustration when he tries to yank off his jeans and briefs and they tangle on his ankle. As he struggles to kick them off I realize this is my last chance to stop him—to get out of bed. But as much as he needs me then, I need him just as much.

My kisses, my wandering hands, and the way my hips instinctively mimic his rhythm are what finally incite him to pull off what's left of our clothes. He reaches between us, sliding his thick length inside me, causing us both to moan. His eyes were closed as we teased and played. They aren't once he begins to thrust. They take me in as they have so many times before, lustful yet loving, his hands passing along the swells of my breasts and through my hair.

It doesn't take me long to peak, not with how fast and hard he's ramming his hips. I'm sure he'll take longer in his condition, and he does, repeatedly spiking my desire and making me orgasm. My fingers dig into the muscles on his shoulders as once more my core clenches tight. It's then he finally falls forward, his release hitting him like a primal force.

As he slows his rhythm and finishes filling me, his eyes once again close. It's just as well, I don't want him to see me then—not the way my heart feels like it's breaking. So when he lowers himself to my belly, stopping only to kiss the spot between my breasts, I see it as a gift.

I love Finn. Maybe I always have. That doesn't mean I get to keep him.

I don't remember falling asleep, but when I see the rays of sunlight poking through the drawn curtains, I realize we slept a long time. The phone rings, my muddled mind determining that's what woke me the first time. Finn rolls off me to answer it, but not before muttering a few swears.

"Yeah?" he asks, rubbing his eyes as he shifts to the edge of the bed.

"Good morning, Mr. O'Brien," the woman on the other line merrily answers. "Your checkout time was at eleven, but we haven't heard from you. Will you be extending your stay with us today?"

"What time is it?" he asks, groaning.

"It's twelve-thirty, sir."

He reaches for the glass of water I'd filled for him and takes a sip. "Yeah, we'll stay another night."

No. We won't. I inch off the bed to the opposite side, searching for my discarded clothes.

"Thank you, sir," the woman on the other line says.

Finn disconnects. "She's entirely too peppy to be from Jersey," he mutters. He downs his water and reaches for the pitcher as I wiggle into my panties and put on my bra.

He finishes another glass while I tug on my jeans. "Hey . . . Where are you going?"

I don't have to turn around to know he's frowning. But I don't answer, pulling my shirt over my head as I struggle to gather my thoughts. This is goodbye. I know it is, and hurts so bad, I can't even look at him. The mattress scrunches slightly as he crawls along the bed to my side.

He presses his hand against my back, trying to get me to face him when I sit on the edge to pull on my socks.

"Sol, what are you doing?" he asks.

I don't answer.

"Look, I know I fucked up, and that you're probably pissed at me," he adds.

I shove my foot into one of my boots. "I'm a lot of things right now, Finn," I tell him truthfully, hating how my impending tears start to find their way into my voice.

He throws his legs over the side of the bed, stroking my cheek to draw my attention. I avert my face in the opposite direction and step into my last boot. I can't find the words I need to say, my thoughts so jumbled I can't think straight. I only know I *have* to leave. All I need is my coat, my purse, and I'm gone.

Yet when I charge forward, he rushes past me, blocking my way. "Don't go," he says, his voice hard. He steps in front of me when I try edging around him, his hands clutching mine and keeping me in place. And still I can't bear to look at him.

He squeezes my hands, like he always does when he wants to reassure me, or comfort me, or just show me he's missed me. This time, I don't squeeze back. Instead my hands lie limp in his.

"I wasn't going to fuck those girls, if that's what you're thinking," he says, his voice deepening.

I lift my chin and meet his face. "You could have fooled me."

He releases his hold, frowning as if he's hurt, insulted, and maybe even angry. But whatever he's feeling can't compare to the misery I feel. "Did you know that was me last night?" I ask. He squares his jaw, clenching it tight. "Or did you figure it out when you woke up on top of me this morning?" I cross my arms and shake my head. "I could have been either one of those girls, Finn, or both—"

"That's not true," he snaps, this time yelling. "I was drunk, not fucking insane. Don't you get it? I would never do that to you."

"How do you know?" I ask, my voice growing louder. "You were completely drunk."

Every angle in his face sharpens, but he doesn't deny it. "I still knew I shouldn't leave with them. Just like I knew it was you I was touching—" I drop my arms as he edges closer, his chest pressing against mine as he hovers over me and closes the small space between us. "—Touching you like I've wanted to this whole time we've been apart."

I want to believe him, but now isn't the time. Nor is it the time to hold him like I want to, despite how his body begs for my hands.

Finn's short nails graze along my upper arms. "You've been pushing us apart, Sol," he tells me, his voice quieting. "*You*. That hasn't stopped me from wanting you or staying committed."

My stare trails from his chest to his eyes. "Can I ask you something?" I don't wait for his response. "Why did you get drunk last night?"

His hands drop away, the abrupt disconnect from our bodies almost painful. "I . . . haven't been feeling right lately," he answers.

"Because of what happened with my mother?" Again, I don't wait for him to answer. I already know the truth by the way he turns his head. "You wanted to forget, didn't you? You wanted to stop feeling what you have since you found her."

He whips his head back, his features flashing with surprise. "Come on, Finn. Don't you think I know what finding my mother did to you, what it must have felt like watching her smile like she couldn't wait to die? I know it messed you up. I know it was traumatic. Just like I know it was the last thing you needed to see."

I don't care about my spilling tears, but Finn does. He lifts his hands to cup my cheeks. "Baby," he says.

"I know what that did to you," I repeat. "I know how it sent you tumbling backwards from all your progress in therapy. I know because of how I found you, and how much you must have drank to forget."

My voice is raised, my words and the hurt behind them slicing at my vocal chords. "You're angry because you think I don't trust you. But even though I think you might have left with those women, I couldn't blame you if you had."

"*What?*"

I pull away from him, digging my fingers through my hair. "I did this to you, Finn. You said it yourself, I've been pushing you away."

"You didn't push me into being with them, if that's what you were thinking. I was at the bar, when I shouldn't have been. I didn't have to drink. That was on me, *my* decision, *my* mistake—"

"Because you wanted and needed to forget what you saw," I remind him.

He shuts his mouth. He can't deny it. It's the truth and he knows it. I lift my coat and purse from the floor. "You don't need this," I say. "Any of it. Not with the championship bout so close, and not when you were making so many gains in your recovery."

Again he steps in front of me when I try to walk away, his breaths releasing in quick succession. "What are you saying?"

In the tears that follow his face blurs in front of me. "That you don't need me, Finn."

The silence between us is so pronounced it feels like an invisible weight shoving against my chest. It pushes me further away from him. But he won't let me go. "You're wrong," he says, snagging my arms and yanking me close when I try to leave. "You're all I need."

His arms circle my waist as his lips collide against mine, the force strong enough to bend me backward. "Don't leave me," he rasps between kisses to my neck and mouth. "I need you."

My body betrays me, aching with how it responds to his touch. But Finn's needs—the ones I've neglected for far too long are more important than anything I'm feeling. I wrench away from him, staggering backward and holding tight to my belongings.

"Sol," he says, following me as I step away. "Please, don't do this."

"Finn, I *have* to," I say, choking on my words. "Don't you see? All I've done is hold you back from the good you can have."

"No," he grinds out. "You're the only good left in me." He marches forward, grasping my hips and lowering his face inches from mine. "I love you. Do you hear me? I fucking love you."

I fall apart then, sobbing into my hand. Of all the things he could have said, nothing could have crushed me like this. Pain . . . all I feel is pain.

"Sol . . ." he says. "You told me you love me, are you trying to tell me you don't? Are you trying to say that all this time you've been lying about how you feel?"

I compel myself to look at him. "No. I'll *always* love you, Finn. But right now, you need to love yourself more. Right now, I'm the worst person for you. I don't want to be, but I am."

He throws his hands out. "That's not true!"

I take a step back, motioning to him. "Finn, look at yourself. You're hungover after getting so drunk last night you could barely walk. And why? Because of what you saw, what you experienced, and everything you've endured by being with me."

For a moment he simply stares, but he doesn't argue because he can't. "Let me go," I plead with him. "Give yourself this chance to get well."

"Don't do this," he says. "Sol, don't fucking do this to us!"

My arms ache with the need to hold him—to soothe that bruised expression claiming every inch of his face. But I can't. So despite what *I* want, I give him what he most needs: an opportunity to heal.

My purse slaps against my side as I turn away, hurrying out the door before I change my mind. I'm not what Finn needs to be healthy. That doesn't mean I don't want to be.

The door slams hard behind me as I rush into the hall, a sob breaking through my throat when he calls my name one the last time.

CHAPTER 26

Finn

"Elbow, elbow, push kick. Elbow, elbow, knee. Knee. Rear push kick. Okay, now pushups."

I bark my orders as I perform each task. I'm dragging myself and everyone on my team to the breaking point, and still, I can't feel anything but rage. I hit fifty pushups and leap to my feet. "Roundhouse, roundhouse, roundhouse. Higher. Roundhouse, roundhouse."

My shin repeatedly slams into the Muay Thai bag, each strike as hard as the last. I don't care what's happening. And I don't ease up, ignoring the way my heartbeat pounds like a sledgehammer.

My body is warning me I'm exhausted, and that I need to slow down. That doesn't stop me or scare me from issuing my next set of commands. "Switch, roundhouse, roundhouse . . ."

"That's enough," Killian calls from behind me. "Take three laps, cool down, and stretch."

Our team collectively groans, abandoning the row of bags and starting their half-assed attempts at a jog around the gym floor. Me, I keep going. *Roundhouse, push-kick, jab, jab, spinning elbow, uppercut.*

"Finn, stop," Killian says, lowering his voice.

I ignore him, leaping into my kicks.

"Come on," he says. "Take a break from the bag."

"Gotta make weight," I tell him, switching from legs to

arms.

"You keep this shit up, you're going to come in underweight. Come on, start your cool down."

I shrug. "Okay." I walk away from him and head for the treadmill, cranking it almost as soon as the engine starts. I'm being an asshole to him, and anyone who tells me shit I don't want to hear. The problem is, lately that includes everyone.

That numbness I've felt in the past, hell, I thought that was bad. But all this rage that's been unleashing since Sol walked out on me, it's made me a dangerous man. Knowing how bad I can fuck someone up should scare me, force me into action, *something*. But instead I stopped going to counseling the minute my court mandated time was up and let my anger brew—let it take me, reasoning it's better than feeling nothing.

I don't hear Sofia approach. She appears from one second to the next, leaning against the railing. "Hi, Finn," she says.

I don't answer. "How are you?" she asks.

Again, I don't say anything. Out of everyone who's been trying to talk to me, she's been the one person I haven't laid into. And I want to keep it that way. If I rip into her—someone who's so unbelievably gentle—there's no going back. So I don't answer, my way of clinging to the human still left in me rather than surrendering to the irate beast no one can stand to be around.

"My wife just asked you a question," Killian snaps, coming forward. "Show her some respect and answer."

"Killian, it's okay," she says.

"No, it's not. If he wants to have an attitude with me, that's one thing. But he's not pulling that shit on you."

Son of bitch. I so don't want to deal with this right now. I hop off the treadmill, not bothering to turn it off and storm to my office as I strip out of my shirt.

Heavy footsteps follow behind me, slapping against the mat. "Finn, get back here," Kill snarls through his teeth.

Those sprinting past me slow their steps. I can feel their eyes on us. They're anticipating trouble. Maybe they're even hungry for it. Can't blame them seeing how hard I've been working them.

I keep walking as if I'm not ready to go to blows. Yet I am. Do I like the idea of fighting my brother? No, not really. It makes me sick, if I'm being honest. We only ever came close twice: once, when I was sticking up for Sofia, and again when he reamed into me about Sol. That doesn't mean I'm not willing. That's how messed up I am. So angry, so *furious*, I'm waiting for that swing that gives me an excuse to act.

Sofia urges him back. I don't bother turning around, don't bother caring if he charges. If he wants to go, we'll go.

Maybe it's what I need or . . . Shit. I don't know what I need.

I slam the door to my office and storm to the mini-fridge. I pull out a bottle of water, flinging the cap into the garbage can and cursing because that's all I feel like doing. Just like that, my rage resurfaces and I get another flash from the past. This time it's of Sol as she walked away, not bothering to glance back. But then the image abruptly switches to the night before when I was on top of her. I have to say, it's the latter that hurts me more, no matter how good it felt.

She thought I didn't know who I was making love to, whose body I explored, tasted, wanted. She's wrong. It's like the moment I knew she was there at the bar, I could live again. It wasn't the booze I took that made me forget all the shit running through my brain. It was all her, being there for me, letting me know I still mattered.

Up until she left.

I finish downing the water when the door opens behind me. "*What?*" I snap.

Sofia jumps, her long inky curls bouncing from the force. "Sorry," I say, holding out a hand. "I thought you were Kill."

"It's okay," she says, closing the door behind her.

I bow my head and take a few breaths, working to rein in my anger as she approaches. I didn't mean to scare her, but that's exactly what I did. Christ, maybe I should head out and find some puppies to kick for an encore.

Kill throws the door open, his stare cutting between the two of us. "You all right?" he asks Sofia.

I'm not surprised he heard me yell at her, just like I'm not surprised he came to check on her. But as much of a prick as I've been, it pisses me off that he thinks I'd hurt her.

She walks to him slowly, stroking his arm to snag his attention. "Give us a moment, okay?" His attention flicks back to me. "Please, Killian," she says.

I can tell he doesn't want to, but he does anyway. He bends to kiss her, his way of assuring us both that he'll be close by.

He starts to head back out, but not before shooting me a warning glare. I roll my eyes and toss my empty bottle in the recycling can.

Sofia edges closer, smiling softly like me and Kill weren't both ready to fight. "You didn't answer my question. How are you?" she asks.

I've known her almost my whole life. We grew up across the street from each other and I swear to God, Kill has always loved her. I can't blame him. She's just as kind and pure as she was when we were kids, one of those people who simply cares. Maybe that's why the bullshit wall comes down and I'm able to be honest. "Not good," I admit.

She sits on the edge of my desk, folding her hands in front of her. "We're worried about you, Finn." She sighs when I shut my trap. "Why did you stop going to counseling?"

"I put in my time," I answer.

"Do you think it helped you?" When again I don't respond she adds, "It seemed to. You were a lot better for a while. Better than I've seen you in a long time."

Sofia's skin tone is a little darker than Sol's, and her eyes are light green instead of gray blue. They're first cousins, but they don't look anything alike. Sofia is taller, thin, where Sol's curves fall in all the right places. And where Sofia glides into a room quietly hoping not to call attention to herself, Sol bounces in and waves, hugging anyone who'll let her. They're different in so many ways, but right then, Sofia reminds me so much of my girl—not because what she looks like, like I said they're both really different, but because she's listening.

"It wasn't just the counseling that helped me," I mutter.

She nods like she understands. "I see."

Yeah. She does.

Her attention wanders to her lap, where she's playing with her hands. It's something she does when she's nervous or unsure what to say. She hasn't mentioned Sol these past few weeks, so I have no way of knowing if Sol's mentioned me. I didn't text or call after she left—partly pissed, partly stubborn, but mostly reeling because what she said is true. The incident with her mother did screw me up. That doesn't mean I don't want her with me.

"How is she?" I ask before I can stop myself.

At first, I don't think Sofe's going to tell me. I'm ready to march out and jump back on the treadmill, but the sadness trickling into her features holds me in place. "She's not good, Finn," she answers quietly.

My gut churns. "At all?" I ask.

She shakes her head. "Sol, um, quit her internship."

"What?" That counseling gig meant so much to her, and was credit toward her masters. But then I huff, realizing why she did it. "All right. I get it."

"It wasn't because of you," she adds.

I cock a brow because I don't believe her. One of the reasons I stopped going to counseling was because I couldn't stand the thought of seeing her and not being able to touch her, or be with her like I want to.

"I'm serious," she insists.

"Then where has she been?" I don't mean to sound like I'm challenging her, but that's how it comes out. Like I said, I've been a miserable prick.

"With her mother," she answers, totally shutting me up.

I lean back against the wall and cross my arms. "I thought she was in an institution."

"She was, but now she's in a private facility that allows Sol to visit more frequently. She uses the time to work closely with her mom."

I frown. "Work closely with her how?"

Sofia considers me, like she thinks she's said too much, and for her, I guess she has. "She's trying to get her mother back to a healthier state, a better place of mind."

"Is that even possible?" I hold out a hand because I'm not trying to be negative. But after how I saw her mother—laughing at shit that wasn't there, smiling at the words she wrote with her own damn blood, I don't see someone like that getting better, period.

"I'm going to tell you something you probably don't know," Sofia says, her soft voice lowering as if she's afraid of being heard. "When Flor first tried to kill herself following Sol's fifteenth birthday, everyone credited Sol for helping her recover from her breakdown." She glances down as if embarrassed. "Even me. She'd visit her after school, show her pictures from her childhood, and redirect her the way the therapists and nurses would. I think it kindled that drive in her to be a psychologist."

"Sol's the one who brought Flor back from the edge?" Although I'm asking, I can totally see that, given how she did the same thing for me.

"That's the thing," she says. "I'm no longer sure she did. I think it was more a combination of Sol's vigilant care, the medication my aunt was placed on, and the intense treatment she received. Whatever it was appeared to work, but it was only temporary." She pushes off my desk. "The problem is, Sol really believed she impacted her mother's care and improved her mental health. We believed it, too, encouraging her when maybe we shouldn't have."

"So you don't think she helped her?" I question.

"With how bad Flor is now? No. If she did, it was only temporary. But Sol still thinks she can help her and make her better." She swallows hard, trying to keep her emotions from getting the best of her. "But she's not getting better, Finn. On her best days, she's so doped up she simply sits there."

"And on her worst?" I ask, my voice lowering.

"She calls Sol by her dead sister's name, and at times turns on her." Her eyes well. "Sol needs her mother back. But she's gone, Finn."

"I know," I tell her. I knew that the moment we found her. That doesn't mean it doesn't destroy me to know what my girl is going through.

I don't realize how hard I'm glaring at the floor until Sofia speaks again. "Evie thought you could help each other." She smiles a little when I look at her. "She said you and Sol reminded her of her and Teo. Two broken souls who needed each other to be whole."

My frown deepens. "She said that?" At her nod I ask. "But she barely knows me."

"I know, but I think she recognized your pain. Just like she's recognized Sol's."

"Evie wanted us together?" I repeat.

"That's right," she says, knitting her brow when catches my smirk.

"But you didn't," I remind her.

She half-laughs. "It's not that. You know you've always been my favorite. I just . . . I don't know. I never expected you to get so serious about her, especially so quickly."

"Because of how much I've whored around?" I offer.

I grin at the sight of her blush. Evie may not know me very well, but Sofia has known me well enough. My humor fades. "I didn't whore around with Sol if that's what you're thinking."

"Oh, good—"

"I mean we had lots of sex. Shit," I add, thinking about it. "*A lot* of sex. Couldn't keep our hands off each other, you know what I mean—Kind of like you and Kill. Hey, has that changed for you guys now that you're married? Cause damn, girl, you and he went at it like bears during mating season—

She holds out a hand. "I'm going to stop you right there," she says.

I can't help but chuckle. For someone with olive skin, her face can turn as red as mine. I cross my arms, going back to eyeing the floor. "It wasn't just sex," I tell her.

"I know," she says, quietly moving forward. "You were making love."

I lift my head. "Don't pussy it up for me, Sofe."

She laughs, still blushing. But I mean what I say and tell her as much. "She made everything better," I confess. "I talked, she listened. She was . . . She was always there for me. Despite everything I did, and what I've been through, she liked me."

"No, Finn. She loves you."

She means well, but her words are like a kick to the chest. "I don't know if that's true," I mutter. "If she did, she wouldn't have left."

"It's because she loves you that she did leave, and the reason she's keeping her distance—"

I lift my palm up, stopping her. "Don't. I heard the same thing from her and it doesn't make sense."

"Finn, it may not make sense to you because you want her with you, but you can't blame her for how she feels. Her mother's actions triggered your depression, anxiety, and accelerated your trauma."

"But that's not on Sol."

"Isn't it?"

"No," I snap. "She didn't cause it."

I don't typically talk about my assault. I bury it deep where I think it belongs. Acid burns its way up my gut, warning me I need to shove that shit back down, except Sofia isn't done talking.

"She wasn't the cause of your pain. But her mother was the cause of the trauma that triggered yours." She moves forward to stand in front of me. "Sol has liked you for a while. I'd always catch her eyeing you from afar, at my wedding, at Teo's. She's *always* been attracted to you, Finn."

Yeah. Same here. I just never knew what it would lead to, or that I'd end up loving her like I do. "Why didn't you ever tell me?" I ask.

"Because unlike Evie, I didn't want to encourage you to be together," she admits.

"Because I'm so fucked up?"

"No. It's more like I wasn't sure you were ready for each other."

A few beats pass when there's only silence between us. "I guess you were right," I finally agree.

"I don't know if I was," she confesses, closing the distance between us and wrapping her arms around my waist.

I hug her, too, more for her than me, tucking her head beneath my chin. "I don't know what's going to happen, Finn," she says. "I only know that you're in very dark place, and that it scares me."

I keep her against me, reassuring her with my body even though my mind is telling me she's right. I am in a dark place, and right now, there's no light in sight.

CHAPTER 27

Sol

"Hi, Mami," I say. Like always, she's sitting in the sunroom, looking in the direction of the small lake, though it doesn't appear she can really see it.

"Hello, Sol," the nurse says, adjusting the blanket around her shoulders. "It was a little cold out here so I wanted to keep her warm.

"Thank you," I say, trying to smile. She's an older nurse, from the South, and while it appears she's worked here a while, she's only recently been assigned to my mother's care. I'm embarrassed to say I forgot her name.

"It's Violet," she says, holding onto her smile.

"I'm sorry," I tell her. "Thank you, Violet."

She nods and steps out to give me time with my mother. But like Violet says, it's cold here in the Pocono Mountains. I unbutton my light coat, but leave it on. As I sit beside Mami, I lower my heavy cloth bag to the floor. I found an old album, one stuffed with pictures of me and my cousins when we were children—memories from a time she once cherished.

I'm hoping the pictures will trigger a thought, or at least focus her back into reality . . . if only for a little while.

"Did you just finish lunch?" I ask her in Spanish, working not to lose my smile when she doesn't answer. "I had some leftover paella Tía made. It was good, almost as good as you used to make." I laugh a little. "Remember how you and her used to sit in the kitchen, arguing which country made the best *adobo*? You insisted it was Colombia, but Tía said the best blend came from El Salvador."

"I like *adobo*," she says.

My heart lifts, like it always does when she seems to be listening. Maybe that song I played for her the other day, the one Papi said they played at their wedding, helped her somehow.

"Yes, you do," I answer quietly, worried that if I speak too loudly, I'll somehow spook her back into that place in her head where I don't belong. "It's your favorite seasoning to cook with."

"I like to cook," she says, turning my way.

That flicker of hope surges. "I know. You used to fret over every meal, wanting it to be perfect and hot for Papi when he came home."

She nods, like she's listening. I say a silent prayer of thanks. It's working . . . after all this time I'm finally reaching her!

I lift my hand, covering the one she's resting against the white wicker chair. The wrinkles and veins are so pronounced, yet so familiar. I relish the feel of her warmth.

She looks at the way I hold her, analyzing the gesture as if it's something of significance, and perhaps realizing that I'm more than just the young woman who visits her every day.

But then she returns her attention toward the water. Again, I'm not sure if she's really looking at it, yet I speak as if she does. "The grounds are really pretty here with all these trees," I say, motioning to the blooming pink and lavender dogwoods lining the path to the lake.

She keeps quiet yet that doesn't stop me from saying more. "Do you remember that day you took me and Sofia to that park near Doylestown? It looked a little like this, don't you think?" I edge closer. "But if you don't remember, that's okay. It was a long time ago."

"Javier says Laurita is dead, but I don't believe him."

I grow alarmingly still. "What?"

It's not like I didn't hear her, it's more like I don't want to believe what came out of her mouth. Because if I do, it means that this new medicine, the one that's supposed to keep her from turning into a drooling vegetable and give her more clarity, isn't working.

She looks at me, smiling. "He's just saying that because he's mad and wants to fuck her. Boys like doing that, taking girls into the woods and daring them to show them their titties."

I take a few slow breaths, trying to keep the acid roiling my stomach from building. My mother doesn't swear. Ever. She's the person who washed my mouth out with soap when I said, "damn" back when I was thirteen and she still remembered me.

She lifts my hand, swinging it. "Laurita, Laurita," she sings. "Won't you help me pick the pretty flowers to lay on your grave?"

Her hold on me tightens, shooting pain into my wrist. "Mami, let go of my hand."

"Laurita, let's bury you deep in the earth."

She keeps her smile, tapering her grip hard enough to tremble our hands. It hurts, holy shit it really hurts. "Mami, let go."

She starts speaking fast, random words that don't mean anything. I jerk my head, hoping no one notices. Violet looks over from where she's helping another resident. Without meaning to, I give away that I'm in trouble. She motions to another staff member and hurries to the glass doors leading out to the sunroom.

"Mami, the nurse is coming. Mami, you need to calm down." I pry my hand free as the doors swing open. "Mami, *please*."

"You all right, sugar?" Violet asks.

"Fine."

Of course Violet doesn't believe me, and of course she looks to my mother. "Laurita is dead," she says in English. "We need to take her to the cemetery where she belongs."

This whole time she spoke Spanish. But now, it's as if it's imperative Violet understands her, and that she helps her bury

"Laurita."

"This is Sol, your daughter," Violet says, her voice firm.

Mami turns her head, back to the lake, and back to her world.

"I don't think the antipsychotics are working as well as they could," Violet offers.

"It's too soon to be sure," I respond. "Perhaps a different dose or-or maybe she's restless." I'm not one to stammer, but stammering beats crying which is what I'm ready to do.

Violet nods, yet offers no hope, nothing to kindle that spark I so badly need. "I brought an album with me," I say, motioning to my heavy bag. "Pictures from when I was little. I was hoping to show them to her so . . ."

My voice trails when I realize my mother is crying, tears releasing in tandem along her cheeks. "This might not be a good day for a visit," Violet says.

"But I have to visit," I insist. "It's the only way she'll ever know me."

Violet looks at me, probably in the same way she's looked at other family members who she thinks harbor false expectations. But I'm not one of them. I can't be. I need my mother, and more importantly, I need her to get better.

"I hear what you're saying," Violet says. "And can sympathize with what it means to you."

"Good," I answer, forcing a smile. "Then I'll see you tomorrow."

I lift my bag, swinging it over my shoulder as I walk away. I'm trying not to move too fast or too slow, working to keep my steps natural and pretend like I didn't just receive yet another emotional ass-kicking. Somehow, I manage to hold onto my smile, through the heavy metal door leading out of the locked unit, past the reception area where a few of the staff are gathered, and to the front porch.

I cut a hard left when I see another family walking up the wide wood steps, reaching for my phone and pressing against my ear as if I just received a call. "Hello?" I say, pretending yet again.

Get it together, girl.

I don't want that family, or the one behind them, to see the tears of frustration that want to come. From the outside, this place looks like a beautiful old colonial mansion. Strip away the pretty furniture on the inside, the soft demure colors painted on the walls, and the nurses who dress in pastel scrubs, and this is just another institution where the severely mentally ill spend their days far from those they can hurt, and from those who most need their love.

"I was supposed to fix her," I say without meaning to.

My eyes widen from my momentary lapse of weakness. I can't be weak, my mother needs my strength. I keep my back turned, waiting for the families to pile through the front door. I'm not sure if they heard me, but if they did, I don't want to know.

I glimpse back at my phone. The words that spilled are those I want to confess to Finn. But admitting as much confirms that I didn't accomplish all I set out to do. And that all this time away from him has caused me nothing but torment.

Sofia told me he's hurting, and that sometimes he'll be at a heavyweight bag, pounding it viciously, his stare absent of anything human. "He seems to check out," she said.

I know she means well, her calls are a way of looking out for him. But hearing how he's suffering only reinforces my belief that I'm the cause. I don't think she realizes how badly I miss him, or how I wake dreaming his arms are around me, and that when I think about all the times he made me laugh, all I want to do is cry.

I did this to him, I want to tell her. But I don't. Instead I keep quiet at the mention of his name, even though all I want to do is spill my soul.

The heels of my boots *clip, clop* against the wooden floorboard as I walk to the end of the porch. My hand lowers when I spot the sun porch. It extends out slightly further than the building. My mother's seat lays empty. Violet or perhaps a few of the staff must have coaxed her inside.

Are they drugging her? I wonder.

Is she safe?

Does any part of her remember she once loved me?

"Sol?"

The voice is so familiar, but in my preoccupation with my mother, I don't realize it's Mason speaking until I turn around and see him standing by the entrance. As a renowned psychiatrist, and a well-credentialed one at that, I shouldn't be surprised to find him all the way out here. But I am.

"Hi, Mason—I mean, Dr. Shavis," I say. In the private setting of his office, he was always simply "Mason". But this is a professional setting and I need to address him as such.

He moves forward, his camel wool coat brushing against his legs as he walks. He motions to the phone in my hand. "Am I interrupting your call?"

I quickly pocket my phone. "Um, no, just finished." Jesus, I'm such a horrible liar.

Like always, Mason smiles kindly. It seems like an innocent and genuine reaction, but this is a brilliant man. He knows there's more to my response, and has likely already analyzed and made a diagnosis, tracing my nervousness and awkwardness to my toilet training or that time I face-planted on roller skates.

"Are you interning here?" he asks, tilting his head.

"I'm inquiring."

Okay. Another damn unnecessary lie. Since first meeting Mason, I've picked his brain, observed him during sessions, and followed him around like a giddy little puppy simply ecstatic to be around him and hoping for that proverbial pat on the head. But I never told him anything about me. At least not anything that mattered, especially pertaining to my mother. He may be a professional, but I was trying to be one, too.

"If you need a recommendation, I could give you one," he says, surprising me by taking a seat on the porch swing. He doesn't seem to be in a rush to leave, not by the way he stares out to the lawn covered with lingering patches of frost.

I sit beside him. "You'd do that?" I ask. "Despite that I left earlier than expected."

He gives my comment some thought. "You mean following the weeks you worked, putting in double the hours your degree required, assisting the staff with extra projects, connecting with your clients and supporting them through their issues, and reorganizing our library so we can actually use it." He nods, thoughtfully. "Yes, I believe I have cause to recommend your services."

My gaze falls to my hands. My right throbs from the way my mother gripped it, and it appears slightly swollen, yet that's not why I keep my head lowered. I miss my work at the center. It's where I was learning to be a real therapist and where I was helping instead of hurting. God, all I've ever wanted to do is help.

"Loretta misses you," he says. "As does Zorina, her mother, and the other clients you deeply affected. Loretta especially seems at a loss. She told me no one has ever understood her like you."

"They miss me?" I ask. "All of them?" I don't mean to sound so pathetically grateful, but right then, I truly am. "What about Miss Hemsworth? Does she miss me, too?"

Mason presses his lips in a thin line, but I notice the smile lingering behind it. "It's okay," I say, grinning. "I know the woman hates me."

"She hates all of us, Sol," he admits.

I laugh a little, and he does, too. "So what brings you here?" he asks as our humor fades.

This is my moment to remind him that I'm here inquiring about my make-believe internship even though we both know it's a bold face lie. *Or* I can tell him I'm here to support a friend whose relative is being treated. It's a more probable explanation and less of a mistruth. Yet I don't.

Not this time.

This is Mason. The reason he's asking is because he knows something's up. So because he's truly as kind as he appears, and cares as much as he does, I shove the lies aside and speak the truth. "I'm visiting my mother," I answer, wishing my voice didn't crack the way it does.

My tears release almost immediately, so even if I wanted to, it's too late to make up another stupid excuse like she works here in the kitchen— or insist that she's never assaulted me or mistaken me for her dead sister—that she's fine, and healthy, and-and everything I wish she could be.

Mason doesn't say anything. I can't even be sure he's looking at me. By now, I'm so embarrassed by my response, and so wrapped up in my long repressed despair; I can't bring myself to turn his way. The only thing that I'm aware of is that he's doing the "therapist pause", that brief moment of silence that permits the patient to divulge something else, regain his or her composure, or maybe cry a little more.

I take door number two for the win and force myself to calm. Some therapist I'll make.

"I've wondered who it was," he answers simply.

I look up. "What?" I ask, sounding nasal from how hard I wept.

He offers a sympathetic smile, one that assures me he's listening and reveals a trace of his concern. "Those who choose to work in the mental health field, be it as counselors or medical professionals, often do so to self-diagnose and treat themselves, or further understand those who have hurt them."

Oh. Well, I knew that. Really I did. But I'm not sure I need reminding. Not when I've failed this epically.

He continues when it's obvious that I can't. "Your passion suggested someone close to you was inflicted with mental illness," he explains. "So did your desire to know more, and your commitment to taking your clients to a healthier place." He tilts his head. "If your mother is here, I take it she's not in that healthy place you wish her to be?"

"No. But I'm trying to get her there."

He doesn't respond, but in his features I feel that he's pushing for more of an explanation. "I've been coming every day to speak with her." Like a dumbass, I point to the bag at my feet. "I even brought pictures that may help reorient her. It's something I've been doing for years."

"And has it worked?"

I straighten a little. "Not yet . . . she hasn't, I mean, she didn't have a good day. The doctors are trying to get the right meds for her, and adjust the doses . . ." My voice fades the longer I look at him.

"I meant have your efforts ever worked?" he asks me gently.

Mason is a trained therapist, with years of living and breathing in the crazy. His features never give anything away. But they do then. He thinks I'm spinning my wheels.

I want to point out the flickers of hope she's given me, and explain how there are moments she seems to remember who I am, and all that we've shared. I want to find words or examples that my work with her is paying off, and that it's only because I've done what I've done that she's not as far gone as she could be, and that there's still hope.

Yet there's something about his soft and knowing stare, the kindness in his voice, and the experience that comes with his title that makes me take a long hard look at these past few years in a way no one ever has. My mother, Flor Marieles—the woman who went from talking to us, to talking to those who aren't there, who went from taking care of those she loved, to being the one completely cared for, the woman who once called me her beautiful little girl in her soft voice, who now screams obscenities at me, believing I'm her deceased sister—is no longer my mother. That woman is gone, and she isn't coming back.

So when I answer, I can't tell him what *I* want to hear, and what for far too long *I've* needed to believe.

"No," I respond.

"Her mental health has deteriorated?"

His voice remains quiet, nonjudgmental. Yet it's because of what he's forced me to see in our brief exchange—in the two point five seconds I've sat next to him— that more tears come. The truth can be so painful, especially when I've been the one blinding myself from it.

"Yes," I admit, my voice once more breaking.

He nods, turning his head away from me briefly. "Do you want to know the toughest lessons I've learned in my field?" At my nod he explains. "That you can't help everyone. That there are no magic pills for those far beyond our reach. That love isn't always enough. And that sometimes you have to let go. For your own well-being, your happiness, you *have* to let go, Sol."

This time when I cry, it's that awful cry that force women to cover their faces, the one you feel down to your soul. And Mason lets me, let's me feel it, but most of all lets me own it. Because knowing your sick mother, the one you love with your whole heart, will never be well has to be one of the shittiest feelings in the fucking world.

It takes me a long time to calm down, and when I do, it's not because I feel that much better. It's because I know I can't continue sitting there. "Thank you," I say, wiping my tears.

He pats my shoulder and rises slowly. "This is a difficult time for you," he says. "If you want to talk, my office door is always open." He smiles a little then. "Now, if you'll excuse me, I'd like to visit with my father."

He ignores my slacking jaw, smiling politely before walking into the building and closing the door behind him.

CHAPTER 28

Finn

Diego "The Python" Lopez. Like me he's 12 and 2. And like me, he's been gunning for the belt for the last eighteen months. We're so evenly matched in height and weight, the odds are almost evenly split. He's a brown belt in Brazilian Jujitsu, an old school wrestler, and a brawler on his feet exactly like me.

The difference is, he's still that laid back kid he always has been. Me . . . I don't know what the fuck I am anymore.

Bam, bam, bam. I throw punches, dipping my head so my spinning back kick catches Angus's gloved hand as he lurches away.

"Finn, *enough*," Killian yells, over Angus's swears.

I back off, not because I'm done warming up, but because I catch the fear in Sofia's eyes, again. Hell, everyone here is looking at me like I've lost what's left of my sanity.

Maybe because I have. I shake it off, reasoning this rage is exactly what will get the job done tonight.

"He's not ready," Curran mumbles to Killian. They're standing beside each other, both with their arms crossed. "Is it too late to call it off?" he asks.

I point to Killian. "You're not calling shit off." He stiffens, realizing I'm seconds from losing it. "What?" I ask. "I'm standing right here. It's not like I can't fucking hear you."

"Finn, please," Sofia says, stepping toward me.

She wraps her arms around mine, and leads me away. Unlike the other changing areas we're usually assigned to, those that are smaller and limited in space, tonight we're in one of the newly constructed locker rooms. An hour ago it was packed with fighters warming up. Most are new, trying to make a name for themselves and dreaming of that main card lineup I'm a part of.

They're gone now, either hanging in the lounge watching the remaining fights, or getting stitched up as a result of all the hits they took.

Sofia squeezes my arm. "Finn, I don't want to tell you that you shouldn't fight tonight."

"Then don't," I answer. "Sofe, you're seriously the only one I can still talk to. Don't let me down by making me think I can't."

"I'm always here for you, Finn, and I'll always listen. "She lowers her hands, tilting her head to the side. "That doesn't mean I'll stay silent when I think you're making a mistake. Right now, you're not focused. I'm worried you're going to get hurt."

"Or hurt the other guy so bad he won't get back up?" I question. Yeah. I've thought about that, too.

It's what Killian did to his opponent following his breakup with Sofia all those years ago. He was so angry and lost without her, he made hamburger out of the champ's face, earning him the win twenty-eight seconds into the first round.

I want to say that Sol—with all this anger she unleashed when she dumped me—maybe did me a favor and gave me the advantage I need. I want to say that thanks to her, I possess the power and wrath to wipe the mat with Lopez and earn my title match. Except if I do, I'd be lying to myself even more than I have been.

I'm just as lost, just as angry, and just as vicious as Killian was. I didn't understand what he was going through when it happened—couldn't grasp how one woman could wreck him so bad and inflict so much pain. But now, I'm living and breathing that shit.

Ire is what I feel. But it's not enough to win a match. It

makes you sloppy, makes you take risks, so impatient you screw up. Can it make your swings harder? Yeah. If they connect. Yet as much as I know this, and that I need to get past it, I'm so far deep into that rage, there's no coming back. Not anymore. So I take a breath and say a silent prayer that when I do unleash tonight, the ref will be smart and quick enough to save Lopez in time.

"Finn . . ." she says, shaking her head like she wishes she could somehow ease all the agony slapping me around.

Yet she can't, and because I'm not feeling shitty enough, I ask something I shouldn't. "How is she?" I huff when she just looks at me. "Just tell me."

I expect her to lie, or at least water down the truth. But she doesn't, laying it all out there. "She's not well because she's not with you."

Killian and Curran march forward as I square my shoulders. Even though I'm the one who asked, I'm shocked by Sofia's brutal honesty. But if she's telling me this, it's because she's worried about Sol and probably scared for her, too.

Sofia knows my brothers are behind her, but continues, speaking quietly like she's already regretting what she has to say. "She needs you, Finn. And I think you need her, too."

"Finn, time to go," Killian says, trying to talk over her.

Sofia speaks fast, albeit in that gentle way of hers. "But she needs you to be healthy, and that's something you're not right now."

Killian places his hands on Sofia's shoulders, trying to silence her, but she continues, rushing to finish. "Finn, you have to keep it together out there—"

I stomp past her. "Tell her I love her."

"What?" she calls, hurrying behind me.

I whip around. "Tell her I love her . . . and that I need her, too."

It's like her heart breaks right in front of me, but I don't wait for a response. I yank on the T-shirt Wren tosses me and head out, not waiting to see if anyone will follow.

My girl is hurting. Maybe not in the same way I am, but in

a way that still counts and matters to me. Sofia wouldn't be telling me as much if it wasn't true. But me getting better like she needs me, too . . . Christ, I have no idea how to do that or what it's going to take to get me there.

The cameraman backs away as I storm forward. I don't know what he sees in my face, but it's enough to keep him further back than usual. Killian and Curran rush to reach me, flanking my sides and joining my camp. The rest of my family must be scrambling to get to their seats, but for now all I see is the entrance to the arena.

Killian starts muttering instructions over the blast of the Eminem song I picked, the roar from the crowd and the music making it hard to hear him. But all that noise doesn't compare to the steady pound of my pulse beating in my ears as my rage surges and takes on a life of its own.

Sofia said what she did because she wants me to stay in control and focus. But how do you control a bloodthirsty beast who can't be satisfied—who's so crazed, so mindless, so fucking angry?

I tug off my shirt when I reach the cut man and pass it blindly to Curran, I think. Shit, I'm so irate I can't keep still. I remember to open my mouth for my check, but with my skin feeling like it's crawling away from my bones, I barely remember to lift my hands for inspection.

Maybe Lopez will get in a punch or two. But with everything I'm feeling, he won't get much more than that.

"Finnie—*Finnie*," someone yells.

The voice behind me is familiar. But I don't care enough to look.

"*Fuck*, get him out of here," Killian says, his odd tone cutting through the mayhem and forcing me to turn in that direction.

The hollers from the crowd, those that steadily build the moment I stepped out of the locker room and that vibrate the floor at my feet disappear. Like the flick of a switch, everyone is suddenly gone, everyone but Killian and old man Kessler . . . the father of the man who raped me.

As loud as thunder, the noise from arena returns in a

deafening crash. My body trembles, my muscles twitching from the urge to start pulverizing. But despite the need, I don't lurch forward. I stand there, frozen as all the hate and anger of my past collides with the agony of my present.

Killian shoves his face in old man Kessler's, crazed that he's here. Curran while clearly pissed to see him, hauls Killian away from where Kessler is leaning over the railing. I feel hands smack against my chest—telling me to keep it together, to keep going. But by now, I'm breathing so damn fast, I'm hyperventilating.

Old man Kessler scowls as if confused, yelling at the top of his lungs in his thick Philly accent, "I just wanted to wish Finnie well—tell him I wish my boy could've turned out like him—that he could've made something of himself."

It's what he claims. What he doesn't know is everything his son took from me, everything he *did* to me! More officials arrive, the press shoving their way forward. But I barely sense them, blindly slipping away and into the octagon.

I don't feel my feet strike against the metal steps nor pass along the smooth surface of the mat as I make my way to my corner. I'm just suddenly there.

Killian is on the other side of the fence, yelling to me, "Finnie, Finnie. It's okay, Finn. It's okay."

Curran is saying something, too, but his words are jumbled like he's speaking another language.

I think I should raise my hand when my name is called, but I don't. It's only when the ref calls us over that the fog I'm in begins to lift. This is bad. Real bad. I know it then. Yet it's when my opponent and I touch gloves that I realize my living hell has only just begun.

I stagger back and simply stand there, failing to notice Lopez charge. All I see is Norman, the guy all the little boys in the neighborhood knew we should stay away from, but no one knew exactly why.

You're Little Finnie O'Brien, aren't you? his tenor voice asks.

I'm not aware my hands are down until Lopez nails me with a right hook that sends me flying against the cage. I bounce off, shaking as I fall onto my side. Lopez lands on top of me, nailing me repeatedly in the face.

It's only from the hours and years of training that I respond. I roll away from the cage, going into defense mode before the ref can pull him off me and declare a knock-out.

My hand snatches Lopez's wrist, grasping it tight before he locks me into a choke. Except as much as my body knows what to do, my head isn't cooperating. It panics, just like I did that day.

Instead of positioning myself in full guard, I try to escape. He catches me with an elbow. The blow unlocking the next memory.

You like Legos, right? Killian says the ones from Star Wars are your favorite.

You know my brother? I asked him.

I know all of them. Especially Killian. He laughed again. *Didn't they tell you we're friends? Jeeze, you look just like them.*

I scramble to my feet and out of Lopez's way. But instead of nailing him with a kick or a strike of my own, I back away like I'm fleeing for my life.

You like toys don't you?

I have plenty of toys to play with.

Aw. Don't hurt my feelings, little dude.

Come on, just come in for a little while . . .

The door slamming shut and locking behind me made me jump. I knew I was in trouble, just like I am now.

Lopez catches me with a kick that sends the air shooting through my lungs in a pained rush. More blows, more kicks, pain pouring out of me, just like it did that day.

Lopez is on me again. He's not letting go.

And neither did Norman.

Something in me snaps. It's not rage. It's not misery. It's not fear. It's vengeance.

And I take it all out on Lopez.

CHAPTER 29

Sol

I hurry into my dark house, flicking on the light in the hall, my hands shaking with nervousness. Tonight is Finn's fight. And, against my better judgment, I'm going to watch. I'm only hoping that the late hour doesn't mean I already missed it.

The keys make a little clinking sound as I drop them on the tiny end table. I'm glad my father is at work. If he was here, the match would be that much harder to watch.

It's not that Papi hates Finn, actually that couldn't be further from the truth. It's more like I'd be proving to him how much I miss Finn.

Papi . . . he's been asking a lot about Finn lately. But it's what he told me yesterday morning that really touched my heart. "You lost your smile when you lost that boy," he said.

I can't deny that's true. That doesn't mean I shouldn't keep my distance. God, I'm so messed up. In accepting that my mother will never recover, I tore open wounds bred from guilt, sadness, and everything I managed to suppress all those years I lived in denial.

"You're mourning the loss of your mother," Mason explained to me during this afternoon's therapy session (after I admitted there are days I can't seem to stop crying). "You know she's gone, and that she's not coming back . . ."

No, she's not.

I shrug out of my coat and hang it in our tiny closet, trying not to think about the tears that hard truth brought, or how difficult it was to function in the hours that followed. Acceptance is supposed to be a path toward healing, but that's not where it feels I'm headed. Everything hurts so much more: my mother's rapid decline, watching my father say goodbye to the woman he loves, and every ounce of pain I've felt being without Finn.

The epiphany Mason helped me realize triggered so much more than just my mother's loss. It triggered the sense of loss I felt when I walked away from Finn, the man I'm still crazy in love with.

I find the remote beside an old photo of my mother, set to the right of our T.V.. I slump onto our old couch and flick on the tiny flat screen, trying to find Fox Sports One, and not focus too much on the picture of my mother. This is Finn's moment, so for the time being, I want to keep my mind on him.

I'm sure I'm being masochistic, but I can't *not* watch tonight. This match will determine who'll meet the reigning Lightweight champion and Finn has worked so hard to get here. I know what this can mean for him. Watching is my small way of sharing this moment with him.

My body gives a little bounce when I find the right channel. I don't see much, just an overhead shot of the octagon before the program cuts to commercial break. My heart sinks a little. I didn't even get a small glance at Finn. It's pathetic, I know, but I miss his face.

My phone beeps in my purse, announcing that I have a text. I rummage through it, hoping Finn is performing well. I know he's not attending counseling, even though Sofia told me his family has urged him to return. That doesn't stop me from hoping he'll change his mind, especially now that I'm interning at the center again.

Based on my past work performance, Mason convinced his partners to make it a paid internship. That was generous, especially since it's the only way I'm making money. Come fall, I'll need every dollar I can spare to pay for the costs of grad school not covered by my grants and scholarship. Mason, being the awesome boss he is, sweetened the opportunity by providing me with pro bono therapy sessions once a week.

I can't say these sessions are easy. But I also can't deny I need them.

I scroll through my messages. One is from Tía, telling me she made *tamales* and that they're in the fridge. Three are from my girlfriends, begging me to go out with them tomorrow night, and a few are from Sofia.

It's the ones from Sofia that hold me in place.

If you're there please call me.

Are you there? Are you watching?

Call me. Please call me now.

My throat goes strangely dry. I don't know what's happened. I only know it's happened to Finn. I tap the screen to call Sofia when the television cuts back to the fight and I catch my first look at him.

Every inch of his face is swollen and blood is pouring from a gash above his eye. But it's his stare that makes him unrecognizable. There's no familiar intensity, no warmth I've known so well. He's angry. Yet there's something there that goes beyond rage, and Jesus Christ in heaven, the fear it stirs threatens to stop my heart.

"Unbelievable," the announcer barks as the camera zips to the stupid ring girl lifting the Round 2 card above her head. "Finn O'Brien went from *The Walking Dead* to the *Terminator*."

"Something is definitely up with O'Brien," the other announcer agrees. "I thought the ref was going to stop the fight within the first few shots Lopez got in—"

"But then it was the bell that saved Lopez at the end of the round!" the other announcer interrupts, like he can't believe what he saw.

My jaw slacks open when the camera zooms in on Lopez. His eyes aren't even visible, and . . . holy shit, are his teeth *bleeding*?

I don't realize I'm on my feet until the bell starts the next round and Finn attacks.

"Oh!" the crowd yells. Finn strikes Lopez with a roundhouse kick that connects with Lopez's head and sends him soaring backwards.

Finn rushes him, jumping on top of him and nailing him with a hailstorm of hammer fists and elbows. I should be out of my mind excited. But this isn't a fight, it's a punishment. Finn is *punishing* Lopez.

I clasp my hand over my mouth. Finn is no longer there. He's succumbed to that dark place where he relives his trauma and where he's finally able to fight back.

My hands shake. I fall back onto to the couch when the ref rips Finn off Lopez. Finn staggers backward, his bruised eyes scanning the octagon like he's not sure why he's there or how he arrived. Killian races in, so does Curran. But instead of leading him toward the announcer, they lead him out, *fast*. The cameras follow, despite how Finn's camp surrounds him, trying to shield him and keep the reporters away.

Finn appears to be hyperventilating, shoving his brothers away when they crowd him. He's not well. My God, something is horribly wrong with him.

My phone buzzes in my hand, startling me. It's another text from Sofia, one that causes my eyes to sting.

Without thinking, my focus travels to the photo of my mother, taken in a time when I was still her little girl and she could still love me. I have all this education, experience, and drive to help those in need. But it wasn't enough to help *her*. I can't shine a light in her dark place, I can't pull her back into reality, and I can't help her see what is actually there. And if I could have, I'm already too late.

Tears drip down to splash against my phone as I read Sofia's text again.

Finn is in trouble. He needs you.

No. I can't help my mother. But I can still help someone else that I love.

I drive so fast, it's a wonder I'm not pulled over. The Wells

Fargo Center isn't far, only about twenty minutes from my house. But tonight, it feels like an eternity.

Sofia knows I'm coming. Except now that the fights are over, people are looking to leave, and it's making it harder to park. I pull into a spot I think is close, but the size of the arena is so huge, I'm still far from the entrance.

My fingers dig into my purse, trying to find my phone as I run toward the building. I curse when something sharp pokes me, but manage to snag my phone and tap my screen to redial Sofia. She answers on the first ring. "Hello?"

Like a maniac, I weave through the crowd of people making their way out, speaking fast. "Sofia, I'm here. But I'm not sure where to go. I'm almost to the entrance. But I don't have a ticket or-or—"

She hears the panic in my voice and tries to calm me. "It's okay, honey. We'll help you. Hold on." Her voice becomes muffled as she speaks to someone else. "Sol is here. She's almost to the entrance . . . Okay, where? . . . Okay . . . Okay. . . Sol? Seamus is coming for you. When you reach the entrance don't go in. Walk toward the left and stay along the edge of the sidewalk. He'll find you, okay? He's coming for you."

"All right, all right," I repeat. For as gentle as she keeps her voice, I can tell she's scared, too. I reach the front and cut a hard left. "How is he?" I ask.

The time it takes her to answer speaks volumes, but the way her voice trembles reflects the extent of her fear and almost makes me lose it. "He's not good," she answers.

My knees give a little. I don't know what condition I'll find Finn in, and I'm not positive my presence won't trigger more trauma. I can't even be sure I'm who he needs.

What I do know is that I'm not beaten and I'm not broken.

And neither is Finn.

I lurch forward, refusing to give up on him.

The crowd engulfs me, swallowing me whole. I'm not sure how Seamus will find me, or how I'll be able to see him. But suddenly he arrives, riding inside a golf cart.

The guard driving punches the horn, parting the large

cluster of people.

"Seamus!" I yell, waving and desperate to get his attention.

He sees me, instructing the guard to stop. He gets out long enough to help me into the back and slide in beside me. Seamus looks the most like Curran with the exception of his dark hair and leaner build. He always greets me with a big smile, and an even bigger hug. That's not the case tonight.

He sits in silence, keeping his attention ahead. Maybe he doesn't want to say anything the security guard might hear, or maybe the situation is just that serious. Whatever his reasons accelerate my anxiety, making me want to claw at my skin.

The golf cart zips down the lot, stopping at a side entrance where the press and a few reps are gathered. The reporters are speaking into their mics, their cameramen poised directly in front of them. Behind them, a wall of fighters stand with their arms crossed, evidently refusing to let anyone through.

"God damn leeches," Seamus mutters.

By the way a reporter lunges our way, I know he's not talking about the fighters. Seamus reaches for my hand, tucking me against him and shielding me as more press scrambles forward.

"Here with us is one of Finn 'the Fury' O'Brien's brothers . . ." one reporter begins.

"Mr. O'Brien, is it true your bother is suffering some kind of emotional breakdown . . ."

I don't know Seamus as well as the other O'Briens. But as his body grows rigid against me, I know it's taking everything he has not to yank one of the cameras being rammed in our faces and smash it over someone's skull.

"Let us in," Seamus yells when we reach the concrete steps.

The fighters part just enough to allow me and Seamus to squeeze through, sealing their makeshift fortress of bodies the second we pass. As soon as the heavy door slams behind us, Seamus takes my hand and drags me down the hall running. I clutch my purse to keep it from smacking against my hip as we sprint past more fighters leaning against the white cinderblock walls.

As we round the corner, I see Declan, Finn's older brother and acting District Attorney, standing beside Curran. Their expressions tighten as they speak to a swarm of security guards and officials gathered outside the locker room.

Declan straightens when he sees me, a flicker of what I interpret is relief flashing across his features. "I assure you he's fine, and that we'll be leaving the premises shortly," he tells the crowd.

My eyes round at his words, and at the way Curran's jaw squares when he spots me. They're counting on me to get Finn out of here—to talk to him, calm him, or something. But their expression are so aggrieved, I'm not certain I'll be enough. I only know, I have to try.

Despite my determination, I don't think I'm prepared for what I see next. My steps feel heavy as Seamus leads me into the locker room. Curran and Declan follow, or at least I think it's them. I don't see them as much as sense them behind me.

My focus stays ahead, toward the people gathered along the open area. Wren waits beside Angus. Both glance over their shoulders as I near, and Seamus releases my hand. Wren smiles softly when she sees me, the fear riddling her beautiful face easing slightly. Angus is eerily quiet, the sadness darkening his round face making him resemble a man further into his years, and one who's used to hardship.

I want to hug them both. But I'm not here for them, not now. So I inch closer, a chill finding its way down my spine when I see Killian.

On the surface, anger appears to dominate his physique. Tack on his large and imposing size and I should only sense his menace. Yet all I feel is a helplessness so heavy, it cloaks his aura like a winter blanket.

Sofia stands loyally beside him, offering her strength and comfort despite the tears looming in her eyes. She lifts her hand, beckoning me closer. I reach out to her, clasping it hard when my stare travels ahead.

Finn is standing with his head pressed against his arm, leaning heavily against the wall. Pieces of broken wood and protective gear litter the tile floor. His hands are soaked with blood, and the skin over his knuckles shredded down to the bone. But it's his profound breaths and slumped shoulders that give me a glimpse of the pain within.

And it's awful.

And heartbreaking.

And everything he doesn't deserve to feel.

"Finn," Sofia says, leading me forward. "Sol is here."

The overwhelming emotion claiming the air is fear: fear that Finn is somewhere he can't recover from, and that they've lost the brother they so adore. But as much as I'm scared, too, I know he's not gone. He's strong, and brave, and capable. He always has been . . .

So as I approach, there's no hesitation. All that remains is the love I feel for him. My hand finds his shoulder. "Hi, baby," I whisper.

My tone is so soft, I'm not quite sure he hears me until he lifts his head. "Are you really here?" he asks, his tone as ragged as his breathing.

"Yes, I'm here with you," I answer, my voice breaking.

His face, swollen from his fight scrunches tight. "I'm fucked up," he says, his deep timbre pained. "I'm really fucked up."

"Maybe," I say. "But that doesn't mean you can't get better." I swallow the aching lump that builds. "Nor does it keep me from loving you." When he doesn't respond, I inch closer, losing the space that remains between us. "Let me help you, okay? Let me love you like you need me to." He doesn't move, his still form ravishing what remains of my hope. "Finn . . . please let me."

Again, his face scrunches, revealing the depths of his torment. He lowers himself to his knees, circling my waist and pulling me to him. I curl around him, clutching his head as he releases his anguish, and allowing myself to release my own.

"I'm sorry," he chokes. "I'm so damn sorry . . ."

CHAPTER 30

Finn

Ever have a psychological breakdown? If you haven't let me be the first to tell you they suck. A lot of what happened when I made it back to the changing area is still blocked from my mind. I remember some things: my hands swelling and the skin tearing open as I bust shit up. And lashing out like a crazed beast when anyone neared me.

The voices of my brothers were muffled, like I was somehow being held underwater. It was Sofia's voice that kept me from becoming fully submerged yet it was Sol's presence that dragged me from the water. She lifted me out of that hell filled with hate and misery.

I hate Norman Kessler. I hate what he did to me and every kid he got his hands on, every little boy who was afraid to tell on him and who was too small and weak to fight back.

He tore me up. He broke me down. But no way will I let him keep me there. Not anymore.

Sol stays glued to my side as we make our way out of the arena. My family surrounds us, but they're not alone. Fighters from varying weight classes—some who faced off—but more who just came to watch, gather around us, creating a wall and blocking reporters that dare to edge close.

I hear the questions, all of them. They don't know much, but they know and saw enough. I ignore them and so does my family. The voices fade in and out as my mind struggles to put one foot in front of the other.

With how I'm feeling, it should take forever to reach Kill's car. But before I know it, we're suddenly there. As the door shuts tight behind me, I robotically reach for my seatbelt and snap it in place.

Sol settles against me, resting her head on my shoulder as my arm curls around her.

"Seamus has your car," Sofia tells her from the front. "Where would you like him to drop it off?"

She's asking Sol where she's spending the night, asking her to make a choice. I keep my gaze ahead as I wait for her to answer, working to keep my hold around her loose. I don't want to force her to stay with me. I mean, I want her with me, but only if she wants to be.

She lifts her head only long enough to answer. "At Finn's," she responds. "I'm staying with him tonight."

Kill nods his head as if relieved. I almost expect Sofia to ask her if she's sure, but like Kill, the tension along her shoulders seems to lessen at Sol's reply.

And they're not alone.

I keep quiet the whole way back to my place, even as me and Sol follow Wren into the house. All my brothers are there. I can feel them watching me, but I can't look at them. The rage has lifted, but it left a shit ton of shame behind.

Tonight should have been one of the best of my life. I had the chance to earn my title bout and I got the job done. But from the moment I saw old man Kessler, the experience became something out of a nightmare, one that followed me long after I left the octagon.

Except now with Sol here, I want this night to be what it was supposed to be: A great one. And I want these steps we're taking to be among the first that gets me to a better place.

My family mumbles their goodnights and goodbyes around me. I'm sure they're speaking to me. But shame is that wicked thing that keeps me quiet. They keep their distance except for Wren. Once she locks the door behind us she hauls me to her, hugging me close the way big sisters do when they're scared and they want you to know they love you.

I hug her back because I love her too, keeping my free arm around Sol. "I'll be upstairs if you need me," Wren says, hurrying away when it seems like she's ready to lose it.

Sol leans heavily against me as we make our way to the rear of the house. I'm beat up, and pretty damn bloody. She knows as much so we keep straight, passing my bedroom and heading straight to the bathroom.

I kick the door shut and strip out of my clothes when she starts the water in the shower. Maybe it's too much too soon—standing there naked in front of her—especially after all our time apart. But there's nothing there she hasn't seen, touched, or tasted. I drag my hand through my hair when that familiar twinge warns me I'm seconds from getting hard.

I pull back the clear curtain and step into the claw foot tub, letting the warm stream hit my face. Swirls of pink flow down the drain as the blood coating my body dissolves and washes away. But as I look up and turn so that the water can hit my back, I freeze.

Through the clear curtain, my eyes latch onto Sol's almost naked body. Her jeans, top, boots, and socks are gone, and as I watch, her bra falls to the floor. I'm already stiff when she tugs off her panties, but when she parts the curtain and steps inside, my erection lifts parallel to my stomach.

She bites down on her bottom lip when she notices, her eyes returning to mine and pegging me with a gaze I've seriously missed and have only recently seen in my fantasies. "I'm going to wash your hair, okay?" she says.

I nod, guessing she wants to take care of me and edging closer when she pours shampoo into her palm. She shudders when my thick length pokes against her belly. But I don't touch her, not yet. Instead I bend forward, allowing her to wash my hair.

As she rinses my hair, I lean in closer and tilt my chin. I don't know if I kiss her first, or if she meets me somewhere in between. But her fingers leave my hair to thread around my shoulders, pulling me tighter.

Our kiss is slow at first, playful, like it's our first time kissing. But as it deepens, I'm reminded that this isn't our first time doing what we're about to do. I don't ask her if she's still on the pill, or question if we should use something. I just lift her onto my hips, and ease my way inside. Her head falls back against the tile wall when I'm all the way in, exposing a throat I can't wait to nibble.

My tongue flicks the drops of water speckling her skin as my hands adjust her legs against my waist. She releases a groan, encouraging me to withdraw slowly. I want to start thrusting, my body crazy with need. But I wait for her head to loll forward, for her eyes so heavy with lust to fix on mine before I start. Our foreheads meet, her heady stare intensifying with the steady pound of my hips and her ankles fastening securely around my back, driving me into her deeper and faster.

Giving how much my body has missed hers, and how tight she feels, I don't expect to last. But I do, sucking on her erect nipples as she repeatedly comes. When I finally release, it hits me harder than I ever felt, tensing every muscle in my body. But as my hips slow and I fill her, that's when I feel the full impact of her with me.

Sol is here. Her slick body pressed against mine. Her sweet face staring back at me, and her embrace begging me never to let her go.

I shut off the water and lift us out, stopping to kiss her when my feet hit the bath mat.

"Are we back?" I ask her, trailing a strand of wet hair away from her face. I'm hoping like hell we are because I've never needed anyone like I need Sol.

She smiles softly, causing the drops of water to slide against her cheeks. Even though it appears like she's crying, I swear to Christ, I don't think I've ever met anyone more beautiful.

She shifts her hands behind me, adjusting her hold around my neck. "We're back," she whispers.

I kiss her again like I need to, smiling against her mouth when I pull away. "Let's get dry," she says, taking my bottom lip with her teeth and giving it a pull. "And then let's get to bed."

She turns, snagging a towel from the rack. We both laugh as she does her best to dry us off. Still, I don't let her go, and she doesn't try to get down.

I keep her with me, carrying her naked down the hall and to my room. We flop on the bed, and spend the rest of the night making up for lost time.

"I love you," she tells me sometime around dawn.

My fingers smooth against her cheek, trailing down her throat and to that spot between her breasts where I press a kiss. I adjust my position against her. "I love you, too," I say, my eyes searching her face. "And I swear to God, if you let me, I promise to love you forever . . ."

A knock on the door wakes me a few hours later. I pull the sheet at our waists up, draping it around Sol. I don't expect someone to barge in, that doesn't mean I'm taking a chance on anyone seeing my girl naked. "Yeah?" I ask, once she's covered.

"Do you want lunch?" Wren calls from behind the door.

"You're cooking?" I ask. Shit, I must be worse off than I thought.

"No, dumbass. I'm ordering from Angelo's," she fires back. "You want something or not?"

It's not until Sol laughs against me that I realize she's awake. "You hungry?" I ask her.

"Starved," she says, groaning a little. "Thirsty, too, but I'll just have water from the fridge."

"Four steaks, some cheese fries, and a calzone," I yell toward the door. "Sound good?" I ask Sol, lowering my voice.

"Mmm. Real good," she answers, snuggling against me.

"There're a few bills in the kitchen drawer—"

"It's okay, Finnie. I got you," Wren interrupts.

I don't miss the relief in her voice. She knows I'm okay. At least for the moment. I can't deny last night was messed up.

I didn't have a drink. I didn't take any shit I shouldn't have. What I had was an emotional breakdown, one that was probably years in the making. It messed me up, clouded my judgment, and made me take out my pain on those who didn't deserve it. I'm sorry for everything I did.

Those things I remember, anyway.

The night is still fuzzy. That numbness that had become more friend than opponent latched onto my throat like a whip the minute I saw old man Kessler. It choked me to the point that I swear I couldn't breathe, or think. And when it snapped, it released all my rage and misery, blinding me with flashbacks.

Did Sol's absence contribute to my downward spiral? And did her mother's suicide attempt trigger a lot of shit I'd buried deep? Yes, on all counts. But I don't blame her, or her mother. I don't even blame old man Kessler— despite that he gave life to a fucking monster. I'll admit, his presence did a real number on me. But even if he hadn't shown, eventually something, or someone else, would have pushed me over the edge.

I know that now.

Sol shifts her body, resting her head against her palm. "What are you thinking?" she asks.

I knead her hip, welcoming the feel of her skin against mine. "That I'm glad you're here."

"I'm glad I'm here, too," she says, playing with the stubble along my jaw. "But what are you really thinking?"

Yeah, my girl knows me. "That I'm really messed up, and that I have a lot of shit to work through."

Her eyes grow sad. "I know," she agrees. "Me, too."

"So let's be messed up together, and maybe help each other through it."

"It won't be easy," she says quietly. "For either of us."

"No," I agree. "But it'll be impossible alone."

Her eyes brim with tears, but she manages to smile. "You're right. I can't do this without you." She pauses and sniffs, her eyes travelling over my face. "I really need you, Finn."

I know what she means. Seeing how I need her, too.

CHAPTER 31

Finn

The next UFC match is huge. I can't skip the first press conference of the promotional launch, despite that it's only been a week since I completely lost my shit. I take my seat between the other two challengers, at the opposite end of the long table, and away from the three champs on the other side.

This line up will break records, sell-out more seats than any of the previous, and have sponsors nut-punching each other so their ads run in the right places, and at the right times. Already hotels are selling out around the arena. Sydney, Australia. That's where it's at. So who gets the first question from the sea of reporters taking up every square inch of space? Not the president. Not any of the current champs. Not when scandal sells seats and I'm currently the reigning king.

Cameras click and flash as the first reporter flings his question my way. "Hey, Fury. Is it true you suffered an emotional collapse following your fight with Lopez?"

"Yup," I answer.

There's a brief pause when the reporter just looks at me. He's probably shocked I answered him point blank. But he's also expecting me to say more. I don't, prompting the president to motion to a reporter with red hair. "Next question," he says.

"Fury," the reporter calls out, not that it shocks me. "Was the pressure to win a shot at the title too much for you?"

"No," I respond.

She waits for more. But when I don't respond, she quickly asks her next question before she's cut off. "I find that hard to believe, seeing how your head seemed elsewhere during the fight."

"That's because Lopez was trying to knock it from my shoulders," I offer, earning me a few laughs.

She frowns. She doesn't want to let it go. And neither does the next reporter who follows. "Then what was the cause of your meltdown?" he challenges. "Tough guys don't easily break down, but you did that night."

He didn't flat-out call me a pussy, but eluded enough that I can't let his comment slide, even when the president prompts another reporter. I speak over him, answering the idiot who claims I'm not as tough as I appear. "I've been dealing with a lot lately. And it all came crashing down the other night."

"What sort of things have you been dealing with?" some other guy questions at the same time someone else asks, "How do you expect to win your title match if you're this emotionally unstable?"

The Philly boy in me wants to respond with a, "Fuck you and your mother."

The fighter in me wants to come out swinging.

Yet it's the man in me—the one who's tired of hiding, of slapping on a grin and acting like it's all good—who's tired of pretending that he wasn't lured into a house as a little kid and assaulted—who looks out into the audience where his family and his woman are watching.

I have to make a choice. This isn't the best arena. I know it's not. But from deep in my gut I know I *have* to make this choice: Keep acting, pretending, and hiding, or move forward and be who I'm going to be, damaged but living and maybe finally happy.

My family . . . my woman. Hell, all of them could have walked away and not looked back. They could have screamed and hollered, and sometimes they did—sometimes they were the ones who came out swinging. But no matter how angry they sometimes got, how many times they couldn't find the right words, how many nights I kept them up, they hung in there. If that's not love, I swear to Christ I'll never know what love is.

My stare falls on Killian, the one who first knew, and to his woman Sofia, who's known her own share of pain. It then travels down the row to each of my brothers, and Wren, too, before it stops on Sol. I don't meet their eyes for long, but it's long enough that they realize what I'm about to do.

Like I mentioned, I don't blame old man Kessler. But as I shift in my seat in front of the press, between Amarato who's next in line for the super heavy weight belt, and Griffith who's going to come out swinging for the welter-weight title, I own what I did, and finally put the blame where it belongs.

"I was assaulted as a kid," I say. I shrug like I'm past it even though the silence overtaking the room affirms that everyone here knows what I know: that I'm not past it, and that the memory still eats me alive.

I'm greeted with dead silence. At first. Then the murmurs begin, slowly building until it seems everyone with a mic is asking questions at the same time. I respond to the heavyset reporter closest to me, the loudest guy there who asks, "When you say you were assaulted, do you mean sexually?"

I wait then answer, "Yes."

More lights flashing, more cameramen pushing their way forward, and yeah, a lot more questions. "It was a neighbor, someone who lived near me who I mistakenly trusted," I explain to the reporter who asked me who it was.

"How old were you?" a female reporter yells.

"Was the pedophile a man or a woman?" the guy in the back shouts.

I start speaking, but it isn't to anyone in particular, not anymore. I'm telling myself, staring out to the screen on the opposite side of the room where my face is being broadcast bigger than life. If I'd been given the choice, or maybe thought about it ahead of time, I wouldn't want to look at me then. But right now, I see it as blessing despite all the sins from my past. That image shows me that I'm still me, despite the words I say next. "I was ten, and he was a man." The clicks lessen with everyone's growing shock, so do the murmurs making their way along the crowd.

Again, the silence returns, swallowing the room whole and cementing everyone in place. Including me.

"What do you want people to take away from your experience?" a deep voice asks me.

The voice is so loud, and appears so suddenly, it cuts through the quiet like the voice of God talking down to me. But it's not God. Not even close. It's the president of the UFC, standing at the podium waiting for an answer.

He smiles like I've seen him do when a fighter makes him proud. He's known me for a while because of Killian, and we've spoken a few times following some highly publicized matches and at parties. But I never expected him to look at me with this level of respect. I hoped it would eventually come with a belt win, but not for something like this.

"What?" I ask. I heard his question, but there's more to what he's asking.

He realizes as much and rephrases his statement. "There are millions of people watching you right now, Finn," he says. "Lots of them are kids who have probably been through what you've been through. What would you like them to know?"

I glance down at my folded hands resting on the table, taking a moment to absorb everything he said. There are millions watching, and because of it, chances are there are several thousand who've been hurt like me, watching, too.

I think I should say something smart and articulate like Declan would, or answer in that crowd-pleasing way Killian always manages. But I'm not them so I say what I feel, and what I wished I would have believed long before now. "That it's not their fault," I say, once more catching sight of my face on that giant screen. "That there are a lot of bad people they'll encounter in life. But that doesn't mean life can't be good, or that you can't be happy no matter what happens to you."

"Are you happy, Finn?" a female reporter asks.

It's weird for someone in this circle to call me by my first name. "I'm working on it," I answer, grinning because I mean what I say. "Because I want to be, and because I think it's something everyone deserves."

There are a few smiles and approving nods my way before the conference resumes full swing. But it's what happens at the end that I don't expect. It starts with Amarato clapping my back as we stand to leave, then Griffith telling me I did a good job. But when our opponents on the opposite end walk over to shake my hand, I'll admit, it gives me one hell of a pause.

It's not a pity thing—at least, that's not how I take it—especially with how pissed some of them appear, and how more than one seems to understand where I'm coming from, and maybe where I've been. We start to pile out. I'm not saying what I did wasn't hard. In fact, my chest is tightening in anticipation of the inevitable shit storm that's coming—from social media—everyone who knows me, and from the haters who are going to be assholes just to be assholes. Most of all I'm dreading those questions I may not be ready to answer. Yet it's my family, and how they look, that halts all thoughts of anyone but them.

Sofia is teary, Tess, Curran's wife, is too, but they're sweet like that. Sol, she's my girl. I knew what I had to say would make her cry. That doesn't stop her from throwing her arms around me when she sees me and meeting me with a kiss.

I smile against her lips as I lower her to the floor, happy she's with me, and out of my mind that she plans to stay. My smile leaves town as the rest of my family makes their way forward. Wren . . . no matter what she says, and how hard she's been denying it, I know she's had it rough lately and that something is going on with her. So when I see her wiping her eyes, I'm not completely shocked that she's crying. But to see Angus break down, to watch Seamus and Declan drag their hands down their reddening faces, and for big bad Curran to pinch the bridge of his nose like it's going to somehow plug those leaky tear ducts, I'll confess, it's hard to watch.

Yet it's Killian—my closest brother, the guy who did what he could to make things right—that I swear to Christ almost makes me crack. Almost.

I meet his face as the first of his grief releases. "I should have been there," he tells me.

He should have been there to protect me he means. I frown, keeping Sol glued to my side. "You've always been there for me," I tell him truthfully. My eyes scan each member of my family. "All of you."

I mean what I say, trying to make them understand that like Sol, they're everything to me, and that I appreciate all they've done and sacrificed for *me*—their youngest brother who never kept quiet and always found trouble. Instead I make them release more of their pain, and some of their pride too. But that's my family. And that's why I love them.

The thing is, now it's time to get better, to show them I love me, too. Hell, I owe them that much.

Mostly though, I owe it to myself.

EPILOGUE

Finn

Ever ride the crazy train and wonder how you're going to get off? Let's say me spilling my soul on national television was the ticket on and I got promoted to conductor. Like I thought, social media exploded. Yeah, yeah, there were trolls saying shit I didn't need to hear or want to know. But what shocked me to hell and back was all the love that came from it.

That's right, God damn love.

I had kids—some little, some big—calling me their hero. I had emails pouring in from all over the world where fans called me an inspiration and a true champ. But it was hearing from people who told me I gave them courage and hope that really hit home.

The head of Victim Services from the D.A.'s office, someone I'm pretty damn sure Declan is hot for, arranged for me to speak at schools, shelters, and conferences, once it became clear no one was letting the news of my past go. At first, I didn't want to do it until I saw the impact. A kid came up to me following the first school I visited, telling me he was being hurt at home. He lives with his aunt now. It's been a hard adjustment. But the last time I talked to him (yeah, we keep in touch) he told me for the first time in his life, he's not afraid to close his eyes at night.

I always considered myself a fighter, but I never thought I'd actually have a cause—not one like this. Not one that matters so much. It's good. Who am I kidding? It's pretty damn awesome. I'm still working on me. Still seeing Mason. Are the bad moments still there? Sometimes. But they aren't as bad, and the good times . . . yeah, they've never been so sweet.

Curran opens the door and pokes his head in from the hall, causing the roar of the distant crowd to fill the locker room. "Finnie, it's time," he says.

Jesus, he looks nervous. I tug on my Reebok sponsored T-shirt as Killian's eyes cut to me.

"You ready?" he asks.

"Yup," I answer, shaking out my arms, but doing little to shake off the energy bouncing me in place.

"I'm serious," he says.

"So am I," I tell him.

His stern demeanor vanishes at the sight of my grin, flashing me one of his own. "Yeah, you are, aren't you?"

I snag Sol as she hurries up to me, meeting her with a kiss. Hell, I'm not going into my championship bout without a kiss from the best woman I know, and the only one who'll hold my heart, forever.

"Love you," she whispers against my ear as she clutches me.

"Cool," I respond because it damn well is, and because one day soon, I'm going to give her a ring.

She laughs, before racing ahead with my family to find their seats. I march out, Curran and Killian flanking me. A camera is shoved in my face. I keep my head down the entire length of the hall until I step into the arena and the capacity crowd loses their shit.

That's when I raise my chin, focusing on the octagon and thanking God Almighty that my time has come.

The cage door slams shut behind me as I jog into the octagon minutes later. Killian asked me if I was ready. I told him I was because it's true. In standing up to fears, taking back my life, and grasping the happiness that for too long has dodged out of my reach, I've already won the fight of my life.

But as I look out and face the champ as he enters across

from me, and I hear Sol scream, "Go, baby!" from the stands, I have to say, I can't stop my grin despite the seriousness of this moment.

Yeah. I already won the fight of my life. Now, it's time to win the next . . .

This book contains excerpts from *Feel Me* and *Crave Me* the forthcoming books in the O'Brien Family novels by Cecy Robson in addition to *Inseverable,* the first book in her Carolina Beach novels. The excerpts have been set for this edition only and may not reflect the final content of the forthcoming novels

READ ON FOR AN EXCERPT FROM

Feel Me

An O'Brien Family Novel

by Cecy Robson

CHAPTER 1

Melissa

I stare at the nameplate perched on my father's desk: *District Attorney Miles Fenske*. It proclaims his position, allowing those who read it a glimpse of what he's accomplished. Yet it's only a glimpse. It's not a true representation of all he is, or all he means to me. The nameplate is cheap, unlike the generous soul who stares back at me with the same loving expression he's held since the first moment I saw him.

What are you thinking, Melissa? He signs to me, moving his hands in beautifully fluid motions.

We're alone in his office. He doesn't need to sign to keep our conversation private. He could whisper, and I would still be able to read his lips. But he knows I'm more comfortable communicating with my hands, probably because American Sign Language is one of the many things we learned together. As a child I considered it our very own secret language, something he and I could share away from the hearing world.

That you're making a mistake, I sign back.

My comment earns me a smile, but I can see his concern, despite the crinkles around his eyes that deepen when he grins. "You're going to have to trust me," he says aloud.

I let out a breath. He knows I trust him. How could I not?

I was brought to the Lehigh Valley District Attorney's office when I was about six years old, after my biological mother had attempted to sell me in exchange for drugs. My mother probably thought it was a brilliant plan. Being born with profound hearing loss, I couldn't speak, couldn't communicate, and couldn't understand. Which meant, I couldn't tell anyone what was about to take place.

My primal instincts ordered me to run, that I was in danger, so I did—thank God I did. I kicked and fought, dodging the hands trying to grab me, and scurrying out of my window.

To this day, I remember the way the cold metal grating of the fire escape felt against my bare feet, and the way my mouth struggled to form what I thought were words as I banged on my elderly neighbor's window. Miss Lena, the lady with too many cats and twice as many grandchildren, yanked me into her apartment when she saw me. She called the police, but by the time they arrived, my mother was gone. I never saw her again.

Not that I regret it.

I was placed in foster care, confused and frightened about what was happening and certain I'd eventually return "home". Instead, I was brought before the young Assistant D.A Miles Fenske. He was supposed to handle my case, dispose of it, and move on. He was never supposed to welcome me into his heart. Yet that's exactly what he did.

"Melissa," he says. His words aren't clear—not as clear as they can be, my hearing aids can only do so much, but I hear enough to sense the emotion in the way he speaks my name. "Why are you so sad?"

I raise my chin. "Declan O'Brien will never be the man you are. He's not the right D.A. for this position." I shake my head. "He belongs in the Trial Unit, Arson, Fugitive, anywhere else but where you've placed him."

"I know you don't like him . . ."

I raise my brows.

".. . and that your first encounter wasn't a positive one . . ."

"That's because he was an asshole," I mumble.

He chuckles. "I assure you he deeply regrets what he said. But Declan is smart, quick, and kind."

I don't agree. Not completely. Is Declan intelligent? Brilliantly so, and absurdly astute in court. With short wavy blond hair and a dashing grin that lights his blue eyes, he's also gorgeous, and he knows it. But is he kind? I'm not so sure that he is. "He'll never be the man you are," I repeat.

"I'm not asking him to be. I simply want the best person for the job, someone who will help the victims who need him most."

"That's what you claim. But he doesn't have experience

handling delicate cases where offenders often inflict irreparable trauma.”

“No, but as the head of Victim Services, you do,” he offers with a knowing gleam.

My nails dig into the wooden armrests. “If you’re trying to hook us up, I’m going to be seriously mad at you.”

The edges of his mouth curve. “I’m only asking you to help Declan as he transitions into his new role. This new assignment won’t be easy on him.”

“Because he doesn’t want it. He wants to be the head of Homicide.” I stand with my hands out, pleading. “Daddy, please reassign him. The Sexual Assault and Child Abuse Unit is not where someone who seeks glory belongs.”

My voice trails as I catch a glimmer of his pain. “Daddy?”

At once, his face scrunches, flushing red only to grow alarmingly pale. I race around his desk, clutching his shoulders to keep him upright as he grips his side and beads of sweat gather along his receding hairline.

It’s only because he lifts his bowed head and a healthier shade of pink returns to his cheeks that I’m not screaming for help and dialing 911. “Daddy?”

He offers me a weak smile and pats my arm. “I’m all right,” he says, leaning back in his chair.

“No, you’re not,” I say, my eyes stinging. His light blue dress shirt clings with sweat along his arms and plump midsection. He’s not well. My father is . . . *sick.* “What aren’t you telling me?”

His hand slowly eases away from his side. For a moment his eyes search my face, as they’ve done a thousand times throughout my life. “The doctors discovered new tumors along my colon,” he finally says. “They’re planning to resection my bowel and dispose of the affected area with the hope of avoiding chemo this time around.”

Very carefully, I straighten, despite that my heart has all but stopped beating. My father was diagnosed with colon cancer years ago and barely survived the aggressive treatment. If it’s returned, now that he’s older, and not as healthy . . .

“When were you going to tell me?” I ask, struggling to

keep my voice clear as it shakes, my fear likely worsening my speech impediment.

He sighs. "Friday, over dinner."

To give me the weekend to absorb it, no doubt. "And your surgery? When is that?"

"A few weeks." He frowns as if debating what to say. "I'll be out of commission for a while. In my absence, Declan will lead the office as acting District Attorney." He looks at me then. "And I ask that you help him, regardless of your feelings toward him."

Declan

"This isn't where I fucking belong." I'm beyond pissed, and started typing my resignation letter at least six times today only to delete it. Yet for as much as I don't want to head the Sexual Assault and Child Abuse Unit, I'm not a quitter. "Fuck," I mumble, dragging my hand along my face. "*Fuck.*"

My brother Curran crosses his arms over his chest, not caring how it creases the shirt of his Philly PD uniform. But then Curran doesn't care about shit like that. "It's still a promotion, Deck," he says. "You got this D.A. spot straight out of law school and have made more of a name for yourself than most douche-bag attorneys ever will." He holds out a hand. "No offense to the douche-bag attorneys of the world."

"That's my point. After all I've accomplished, I should be the one leading the Homicide unit."

I shove away from my desk and pace. When Miles gave me these new digs, I thought it was just the start of all the good things coming my way. When he assigned me a county car and a personal secretary, it only reinforced that my hard work had paid off. I was on my way …until I wasn't.

"I spent months dismantling a mafia empire, Curran."

"I know," he says. "I was there."

"I brought down a major crime boss—and his second in command, and his third."

"Yup. Saw that, too," he agrees.

"I received international attention—the trial of the century, the media called it—and for what? To be shoved someplace I don't belong."

"Why don't you think you belong there?"

Out of all my five brothers, Curran is probably one of the biggest ball busters. But he's not messing with me now. He's being serious.

"Do you want to hear about babies and women being hurt? Day in and day out?" I ask. "These are the cases I'm going to be dealing with."

"Someone has to do it, Deck. It's the right thing."

"I'm not saying it isn't. I'm only saying I may not be the man for the job. This shit's disgusting, what these low-life assholes are capable of."

"Is this about Finnie?" He huffs when I straighten and don't answer. "Christ," he mutters.

As easy as that, my brother nails it on the head. For all he sometimes pisses me off, my brother isn't stupid. "Finnie didn't deserve what happened to him," I say, feeling my anger burn down to my gut.

"Of course he didn't," Curran snaps. "No one does. But as his brother, you owe it to him to put monsters like the guy who hurt him away."

I sit back in my chair and rub my jaw. "I don't know if I can."

Our youngest brother was sexually assaulted by a neighbor when he was ten. It screwed with his mind. What he doesn't realize is we've all suffered, too—not like he has—of course, not like he has. That doesn't mean we don't hurt for him or haven't spent sleepless nights worried about him.

Nothing bad was supposed to happen to Finnie. He was the baby. The one who counted on us. The one we were all supposed to keep safe.

With this new assignment—hearing stories like Finnie's on a regular basis?—God *damn* it. "I don't think I can do this," I say yet again.

"Deck, you have to, man."

A knock on the door interrupts us. I know who it is before I even ask. "Come in," I say, assuming my attorney pose because for now, I have to. For now, I'm a professional. Even though all the Philly boy in me wants to do is rage.

My boss, Miles Fenske walks in, followed by his daughter Melissa. Miles smiles warmly, nodding my way.

Mel? What can I say? She's the one person who's never been taken by my charm. Today's no different. Unlike the other females who work here, from interns to attorneys, she doesn't meet me with a grin, doesn't flash me a little leg, doesn't pretend to flirt. Brown hair, brown eyes, creamy skin, with a steel-hard exterior, she walks in with her hips swinging, her bright red dress hugging her hourglass figure, her full lips pressed into a firm line, and her unyielding stare meeting mine.

She doesn't like me. Not that I blame her. Too bad this is the one woman I can't seem to get out of my damn mind . . .

READ ON FOR AN EXCERPT FROM

Crave Me

An O'Brien Family Novel

by Cecy Robson

CHAPTER 1

Wren

I drop the keys in Mr. Esposito's hand and smile. He stares at them in his open palm like a precious gift, because to someone like him who's worked hard his entire life, it very much is. "Thank you, Wren," he says, meeting my smile. "I never thought I'd own a new car. Let alone be able to give one to my son as a gift."

"You deserve it, Mr. Esposito," I tell him, shaking his hand. "And so does your son for getting into Drexel. Tell Antonio, hi for me—Oh, and be sure to have someone take his picture when you hand him the keys." I motion to my office behind me. "I want to add it to my memory wall."

"I will." He presses his lips tight as if considering what to say. "Your father would be proud of you," he tells me. His soft brown eyes take in the massive dealership, fixing on the sales board displaying my current rank at number one. "Very proud."

I hold onto my smile as he walks toward the brand new candy apple red F-150 hugging the curb, ignoring the brutal January wind that sweeps in when the doors to the lot zip open. Mr. Esposito pauses when he opens the driver's side door. I had the boys in the back place a bow on dash like I do for all my customers. I think it's a nice touch, and a way to thank them for their business. Apparently, Mr. Esposito agrees. He tosses me a grin over his shoulder, hollering his thanks as he slips inside and pulls away.

The moment he disappears so does my smile. "Your father would be proud of you," he said. He meant it as a compliment. Mr. Esposito has always been nice like that. But instead of filling me with a sense of pride, his comment sparks a twinge of pain. Some things never change. And some people you never forget.

My heels click against the bleached white tile as I cross the showroom. It's been a nasty winter with all the snow we've had, but I can't say it's been bad for business. My eyes narrow when they fix on Oscar looming over Penny. Penny is sweet, smart, and an overall good kid. She hasn't been here long and she's trying. Too bad Oscar is stomping on her success, luring customers away from her every chance he gets.

"You snooze, you lose," he tells her, pegging her with one of his more sleazy grins.

Penny was making headway with the guy who walked in, until Oscar shoved his way between them and baited him away, making Penny look like she didn't know what she was talking about. If I hadn't been busy with my own customer, I would have stepped in. Nothing gets to me more than men who target those weaker than them.

"Wren!" Suze calls, waving from behind the finance counter. "You have a call."

"Okay. Send it through," I yell, hurrying across the floor, but not before I make sure Oscar steps far away from Penny.

The phone rings one, twice, before I slam the door behind me with my foot and reach across my desk. "Erin O'Brien," I say.

There's a brief pause before I hear, "Hi, Wren."

Shit. My stomach twists the way it always does when I hear his voice. "What do you want, Bryant?" I ask, digging out my cell phone from my desk drawer.

"I miss you," he says.

"Do you miss hitting me, too?" I fire back.

I'm talking tough. It's what I do. Too bad I don't feel so tough. Not when it comes to Bryant. That familiar sense of fear sends a chill down my spine, reminding me what happened the last time I pissed him off. I hit the record icon on my cell phone, hoping to catch him saying something I can use against him. But the damn thing beeps and for all Bryant is an asshole he's not stupid.

"Are you recording me, pretty girl?" He laughs when I don't answer. "Now, why would you do a thing like that?"

"Because I don't trust you, because you hit me—oh, and because you're an asshole."

"I don't know what you're talking about," he says, keeping his voice easy. "I'm just returning your call. You keep calling me so—"

"That's a lie," I say, my face heating with anger. Since he knows I'm recording him, he's trying to switch things around. "Don't call me again. I want nothing to do with you."

I hang up the phone then. It's been two months since I last saw him. Two months since he last put his hands on me. I could call the police. The problem is, he is the police . . .

Evan

My Jaguar skids, again, and again, and again, fighting to keep pace with the other drivers insane enough to travel the Blue Route in this weather. Chunks of wet snow pelt my windshield. My wipers squeak against the glass as they race to keep my line of sight clear when yet another vehicle cuts me off, pelting my windshield with more melting ice. My current struggle with life and death does not, of course, discourage Maxine from barking messages over my Blue Tooth. "Yodel called again, they want you to reconsider."

"No," I answer, cutting my steering wheel toward the left when my car veers right. "We're representing Mellon, their biggest competitor. It's a conflict of interests to supply both companies with the same technology."

I mutter a curse, when the minivan in front of me slams on the brakes and I just miss ramming into her bumper. And because we're in Philadelphia, the City of Brotherly love, the woman rolls down the window—allowing snow into her vehicle just to wave an irate middle finger at me. "Rich Bitch loser," she cries out.

I rub my face. Why am I here again? Before I can finish the thought, Maxine reminds me.

"Evan, I don't think your stepfather will agree with your decision. The company needs the revenue."

"Not at the expense of our ethics." The company is at risk,

yes, but it's mostly due to poor business practices such as the ones Maxine is suggesting I entertain. I understand she learned these tactics by my predecessor, but he was conniving snake—which is why he's currently serving time for embezzling the company's money and I was recruited from our London branch to save the enterprise from financial collapse.

"What about your eleven a.m. with the V.P. of County General?"

"Have Ann and Clifton begin if I'm not on time. I emailed them the presentation last night—"

"Do you really think they're qualified?" she interrupts.

I open my mouth to argue and insist that they are—and to remind her I'm her superior, not the other way around. But Ann and Clifton are still fairly new. They're not at the level I need them to be. However, they're learning fast under my tutelage and the only ones from the original staff that I currently trust.

"Evan?" she presses.

"Maxine, Ann and Clifton will handle it. That's my final word." I disconnect then, swearing as I take the ramp and practically glide down sideways.

"Get a real car, fucker," another proud Pennsylvanian hollers.

I rub my face again, both because I'm tired and equally frustrated. Three in the morning. That's the hour I arrived home earlier today. It wouldn't have taken me as long had I been driving a vehicle capable of enduring this ridiculous weather.

I glance up, releasing a tense breath when the sign from the Ford dealership I researched this morning comes into view. Saving iCronos will take me time. Time I can't spare driving a Jaguar on roads better maneuvered via dogsled.

My car slows to a stop in front of the massive dealership. The combination of the vehicle I'm driving along with the expensive suit I'm wearing beneath my long wool coat commands attention. The moment I step inside, a young woman with short dark spiky hair hurries over. "Good morning, sir. Are you interested in acquiring a new vehicle?" she asks.

She seems young, but eager, a respectable attribute. Yet no sooner does she finish speaking than a man about my age steps in front of her, adjusting the jacket of his gray suit. "I got this, P," he tells her. "Get us some coffee, will you?" He holds out his hand. "Hello. I'm Oscar Nelson. Welcome to Ford Nation."

My frown bounces from his hand to the young woman whose face is now bright red with anger, humiliation, and possibly more. "Are you his secretary?" I ask her.

"No," she answers. "I'm a car sales representative for Ford Nation—"

Oscar begins to talk over her, but it's the stomping sound of quickly approaching footsteps that lures my focus. A woman with a pinstripe jacket and matching skirt storms forward, the quick motions of her long toned legs causing the edge of her skirt to brush above her knees and swing her hips seductively. Long hair flutters like a black silk sail behind her, revealing a face better suited for my wildest dreams. Sapphire blue eyes shimmer behind a thick layer of dark lashes, lighting her creamy white skin and full pink lips.

I spent the first two years following my completion of my masters in either a lab or boardroom packed with men in alternating stages of balding, and these last three months working eighteen hour days trying to rebuild an empire. I haven't had the opportunity let alone the time to meet women. But if I knew women like her existed, I would have spared a moment.

Good . . . *Lord.*

I don't realize I'm gaping until she stops directly in front of us and juts out her chin. "Problem?" she asks Oscar.

Oscar stiffens his posture. "No. I was just showing Mr. . ." He motions to me. "My apologies, what's your name, sir?"

"Jonah," I say, returning my full attention to the stunning young woman. I offer her my hand. "Evan Jonah."

A smile eases along her face, revealing a set of perfect white and drawing more attention to her delicate features.

"I'm Erin O'Brien, but I go by Wren," she says, shaking my hand with a firm grip before releasing me and easing the smaller woman forward. "How can Penny and I help you today, sir?"

"I was looking for either an SUV or a truck than can handle this winter," I answer, doing all I can to keep my eyes from trailing down her body.

"Then you've come to the right place. Penny, will you show Mr. Jonah—"

"Evan," I interrupt, mentally kicking myself for morphing into a fourteen year old boy the moment my eyes locked on this woman.

"Okay, Evan," she says. "Penny, please show Evan our latest members of the Ford family to get an idea what may fit his needs."

"Of course, this way, sir," Penny answers with a smile.

I reluctantly follow behind Penny. Only because it's now obvious I can't rip my eyes away from Wren. But as we reach a black Explorer my attention trails back to her and Oscar. They've moved away from the main showroom and closer to the rear offices. Yet that doesn't stop me from hearing their exchange.

"What the fuck was that?" Oscar snaps.

My spine stiffens. I storm forward, ready to demand he apologize for using such foul language in front of a lady.

"You being a raging asshole," Wren replies.

I'll admit, her response gives me pause. And she doesn't stop there. "Look, I know you have to compensate for your less than average-sized dick. But that doesn't give you the right to mistreat Penny or pounce on every client she approaches. That's bullshit and you know it."

"Um, perhaps a truck will be more to your needs," Penny says, motioning to the far section of the dealership and away from the heated conversation.

I'm not typically a voyeur. I also don't typically interact with women who speak this way. But it's not just Wren's use of language that captivates me, it's her strength, and her desire to protect her small friend.

"Where the fuck did you hear that?" Oscar responds. "I don't have a small dick."

Of all his possible retorts, *this* is the one he chooses.

"Suze," Wren calls over her shoulder in the direction of the finance counter. "What was it you said about that night you went out with Oscar?"

The woman behind the counter scowls and holds up her pinky. Wren smirks. "Looks to me like you should have called her back." She pats his shoulder. "My condolences to your man parts."

She starts to walk away, pausing when she realizes I witnessed their interaction. She must know I heard her, but instead of making a quick escape or attempting pretend as if I didn't, she marches toward me, keeping her head up. "I apologize, Mr. Jonah—"

"Evan," I clarify as she reaches me. Good heavens, and there's that smile again, stirring one of my own.

"Evan," she repeats. Her eyes skip to her friend. "I see Penny is taking good care of you."

"Actually, I thought perhaps you can take over," Penny says. Her stare bounces between Wren and I, likely recognizing how entranced I am by her.

Wren tilts her head. "I don't want to intrude on your sales pitch," she says.

"You're not," she responds, carefully edging away. "I'll take the next one. Honest."

She watches her walk away, before placing her attention back on me. She considers me a moment, as if trying to figure me out, but then motions back to the Explorer. "This is the latest model in Ford luxury, capable of keeping you safe, meeting your needs, and packed with plenty of toys," she begins.

I follow her as she leads me around the vehicle. The ease in her speech and her relaxed posture reveal a woman who knows her products and her job well. I question her about the vehicle's most basic facts first: mileage, warranty, and safety features, before testing her intelligence further. She doesn't disappoint, explaining the vehicle's functions in great detail down to the engine's construction, adding to my growing attraction to her.

"Would you like to take her for a ride?" she asks. She punches my arm affectionately, drawing my attention briefly away from me face. "This way you can see how smoothly she handles the road and then you can then say, 'Wren, how did I ever survive without a Ford.'"

"I'd like that," I answer, keeping my smile. This woman who appears more elite model than sales rep knows exactly what she's doing. "Very much."

"Good," she says, pointing at me. "You'll wonder how you ever got along without her."

As I watch her walk away, I start to wonder that myself.

READ ON FOR AN EXCERPT FROM

INSEVERABLE

A Carolina Beach Novel

by Cecy Robson

Prologue

Callahan

Three days.

That's all I have left until this shit ends.

Three days shouldn't feel like forever, not compared to the eight years I've bled for the Army. Thing is, good men have been killed in less time. In as quick as a blink, a squeeze of a trigger, or a small breath right before a grenade blows is all it takes to shove someone right out of life and well into death.

That's what makes three days as long as it is. Three days is plenty of time to die.

My eyes tear when the wind picks up and shoots grime through the small hole of my lookout point. This damn blown out piece of cinderblock is only big enough to allow me a view of the street below, but not so small I don't get smacked in the face with more filth. The tarp flaps above me as I spit out another coat of the dirt-sand mix spackling my teeth. Christ Almighty, I need a swig of the water resting near my elbow. But my thirst, like everything else has to wait.

I have a job to do.

I adjust my hips against the cracked cement of my bed, bathroom, and home all rolled into one, thankful that the agonizing ache stretching over the lower half of my body has settled into a now familiar numbness.

Out of all the points I'd scouted, and all the accumulated years spent in this position, I should be used to it. And in a strange way, it should almost be home. Yet nothing ever has been.

But in three days, maybe something finally will be . . .

I shove my pussy thoughts away and breathe as my fellow

Rangers stalk along the street. It's then I see them, a mother and daughter walking straight toward my team. Less than one city block separates them from the men counting on me to keep them alive.

The hell? How did they get past the other sniper unreported? Rogers was new on watch. But the duos' quicker than normal pace alone should have told him something was up. I train my scope on their faces; their expressions are blank, unreadable. 'Cept that's not what keeps my attention.

The little girl can't be more than five. So why the fuck isn't her mother holding her hand? I lift my radio and bark a warning, dropping it beside me as I lock my scope dead center on the woman's head.

The radio crackles and Modreski chimes in, yelling at his team to hold their positions. He asks me what my plan is, 'cause he knows if something's caused the short-hairs on my neck to rise, then he and the boys damn well need to listen. But I don't hear him, with a breath and a squeeze of the trigger, I leave a kid without a mother.

Just beneath the sleeve of her *abayah*—the damn dress that hides more than their skin—I see it, a detonator that would trigger the explosives likely strapped to her chest. A few Rangers I know—Simons and Boreman, rush forward. I start to mutter a curse, pissed at her for making me shoot her in front of her kid. But the curse lodges in my throat when I see the kid isn't looking at her mother lying next to her dead.

She's watching my advancing team as she lifts the detonator clasped tight in her hand.

Photo by Kate Gledhill of Kate Gledhill Photography

CECY ROBSON is a new adult and contemporary author of the Shattered Past series, the O'Brien Family novels and upcoming Carolina Beach novels, as well as the award-winning author of the Weird Girls urban fantasy romance series. A 2016 double nominated RITA® finalist for Once Pure and Once Kissed, Cecy is a recovering Jersey girl living in the South who enjoys carbs way too much, and exercise way too little. Gifted and cursed with an overactive imagination, you can typically find her on her laptop silencing the yappy characters in her head by telling their stories.

www.cecyrobson.com

Facebook.com/Cecy.Robson.Author

instagram.com/cecyrobsonauthor

twitter.com/cecyrobson

www.goodreads.com/goodreadscomCecyRobsonAuthor